This Book Might Be About Zinnia

ALSO BY BRITTNEY MORRIS

SLAY

The Cost of Knowing

Marvel's Spider-Man: Miles Morales – Wings of Fury

The Jump

Life is Strange: Heatwaves

This Book Might Be About Zinnia

SIMON & SCHUSTER BFYR

New York   Amsterdam/Antwerp   London
Toronto   Sydney/Melbourne   New Delhi

An imprint of Simon & Schuster Children's Publishing Division
1230 Avenue of the Americas, New York, New York 10020
For more than 100 years, Simon & Schuster has championed authors and the stories they create. By respecting the copyright of an author's intellectual property, you enable Simon & Schuster and the author to continue publishing exceptional books for years to come. We thank you for supporting the author's copyright by purchasing an authorized edition of this book. No amount of this book may be reproduced or stored in any format, nor may it be uploaded to any website, database, language-learning model, or other repository, retrieval, or artificial intelligence system without express permission. All rights reserved. Inquiries may be directed to Simon & Schuster, 1230 Avenue of the Americas, New York, NY 10020 or permissions@simonandschuster.com.
This book is a work of fiction. Any references to historical events, real people, or real places are used fictitiously. Other names, characters, places, and events are products of the author's imagination, and any resemblance to actual events or places or persons, living or dead, is entirely coincidental.
Text © 2025 by Brittney Morris
Jacket illustration © 2025 by Rachel M. Silva
Jacket design by Laura Eckes
All rights reserved, including the right of reproduction in whole or in part in any form. SIMON & SCHUSTER BOOKS FOR YOUNG READERS and related marks are trademarks of Simon & Schuster, LLC.
For information about special discounts for bulk purchases, please contact Simon & Schuster Special Sales at 1-866-506-1949 or business@simonandschuster.com.
Simon & Schuster strongly believes in freedom of expression and stands against censorship in all its forms. For more information, visit BooksBelong.com.
The Simon & Schuster Speakers Bureau can bring authors to your live event. For more information or to book an event, contact the Simon & Schuster Speakers Bureau at 1-866-248-3049 or visit our website at www.simonspeakers.com.
Also available in a SIMON & SCHUSTER BFYR paperback edition
Interior design by Laura Eckes
The text for this book was set in Acta.
Manufactured in the United States of America
First Edition
2 4 6 8 10 9 7 5 3 1
Library of Congress Cataloging-in-Publication Data
Names: Morris, Brittney, author. | Title: This book might be about Zinnia / Brittney Morris. | Description: First edition. | New York : Simon & Schuster BFYR, 2025. | Audience term: Teenagers Audience: Ages 12 up. | Audience: Grades 7–9. | Summary: "Spanning two timelines, one teen searches for her biological mother and the other copes with giving up her baby for adoption"– Provided by publisher.) | Identifiers: LCCN 2024057024 (print) | LCCN 2024057025 (ebook) | ISBN 9781665904018 (hardcover) | ISBN 9781665904032 (ebook) | Subjects: CYAC: Adoption–Fiction. Birthmothers–Fiction. | Teenage pregnancy–Fiction. | LCGFT: Novels.) | Classification: LCC PZ7.1.M6727 Th 2025 (print) | LCC PZ7.1.M6727 (ebook) | DDC [Fic]–dc23) | LC record available at https://lccn.loc.gov/2024057024 | LC ebook record available at https://lccn.loc.gov/2024057025

*To everyone who's gone no-contact with
someone who didn't deserve you.*

*Thank you for honoring your boundaries,
even when it's hard.*

CHAPTER 1

Zinnia

2024

THE HAZMAT TEAM LOVES ME.

I always skip the "we had an incident" pleasantries. They know there was an incident. Nobody calls hazmat while they're having a picnic. I tell them *exactly* what they'll find in the bathroom.

"Needles," I say as I pull the steam lever, blasting this soy milk into foam with a hiss. "Blood and glass all over the floor."

A heavy sigh comes through the receiver.

"Still don't have a sharps container?" he asks.

"If you've got a free one lying around, Milo, I'll install it myself."

Oh yeah, the hazmat team also loves me because my best friend since Water Babies is among them.

Another, heavier sigh comes through the phone.

"Couldn't you put up a sign?" he asks.

"What is it with you non-food service people thinking a sign will solve everything?" I grin at his logic. "Ever seen a 'Please do not partake in illicit drugs on the premises' sign? Think it would do any good?"

A third sigh.

We've known each other so long that I can read the different subtleties in them. This one says, begrudgingly, *Fine* and *I'll be over in a minute.*

"You're the best," I return.

"And you're going to be late."

It takes me a second to realize what he's talking about. I roll my eyes and glance at my watch.

"I've got four hours."

"Two left in your shift."

"*Plenty* of time."

Hair. Makeup. Dress. Shoes. How long could that possibly take? It's homecoming, not my wedding day. Besides, the real fun happens *after* homecoming.

No, not that.

I've registered for Harvard's application and sent my guidance counselor a rough draft of my essay, and tonight I'm registering for the rest of them. *All* of them.

"Shouldn't *you* be worried?" I ask. "You have a biohazard to clean, a shower to take, *and* a gift to get me."

THIS BOOK MIGHT BE ABOUT ZINNIA 3

There's a pause, just long enough to confirm that he forgot that last detail. We agreed weeks ago that we, the two singlest people in the whole school—me, the allo, too preoccupied with life to give a shit about romance, and Milo, the ace, uninterested in anything but books and boba tea—would get each other a homecoming gift. A token of our friendship. And in true Milo fashion, he hasn't gotten mine yet.

Four hours out.

"How do you know I don't have your gift?" he asks, clearing his throat.

"Because it's you," I say with love.

"There's a good reason this time."

"There's always a good reason," I say, and trill my voice along the chorus of Hoobastank's most famous song, "'And the reason is youuuuuuuuu.'"

"Stop," he mutters through the receiver. "You're making me want to take up vaping again."

It's such an outlandish suggestion that I know to write it off.

Besides, I should be more embarrassed than he is right now. He's presumably at home, just him and his mom, and I'm standing in the middle of the Bean Rock Café belting out a song older than Facebook.

"Gotta go, my customers need me," I whisper to him. "Love you, see you soon!"

Click!

I belt louder along with the music playing faintly overhead. I nod at Harlow, the girl at the register with curly red hair voluptuous enough to match mine in volume and double it in length.

She reaches into her pocket for her phone, and the music grows louder. Heads turn. The couple in the corner, Tam and Sam—who *always* sit in the same spot every Tuesday because it's the only day they both have off work—look up at me. Sam lowers his head and pretends not to hear us, but Tam starts bobbing her head, nostalgia lighting up in her eyes.

"Let me guess. Oldies?" she asks. I nod. She shakes her head, exchanging a knowing glance with Sam.

Tam mouths along as Harlow and I lean in together and serenade everyone in here.

I hear more voices behind us now, and as the music swells, and I realize everyone is watching us, I grab the metal foam spoon, which makes a great mic in a pinch, and time it perfectly with the start of the chorus.

"'I just want you to knoooooow.'" *Hisssssss* goes the steam wand. Now we're all singing—everyone behind the counter—and I can't think of a better pregame concert before my big night.

I twirl away from Harlow and flip the steam wand back off so we can all hear one another. We belt out the chorus, and I carefully scoop some grounds into the filter basket, tamp, click into place, and pull a couple of ristretto shots for the older lady swinging the door open now. Ruthie always prefers the ristretto, but she always forgets.

THIS BOOK MIGHT BE ABOUT ZINNIA

I don't.

Mr. Lawry, dressed in another one of his wool herringbone suits, swipes his latte from the bar. He's always in around this time, frowning, muttering, waiting for his twelve-ounce, nonfat, no-foam triple latte after ordering with a single word: "Latte."

"Where's the vanilla?" whispers Marybeth, the tiny girl to my right, stocking shelves even though it's her second day. She's probably never seen this kind of chaos behind the counter of a coffee shop, but at the Bean Rock Café, everything's chaos, all the time. Just the way I like it.

I use the break between verses to whisper quickly, "Back cabinet, bottom shelf, oldest in the front," and then sail smoothly back into the final next verse.

Harlow sings faithfully along with me, as most of the customers have gathered at the counters to join in the verse at the end. My heart soars as we all belt it out. Sure, I like this song. But these people—most of them a decade or two older than me—sing it like it stirs up memories from a loooong time ago. Well, maybe not *that* long ago, that isn't exactly fair.

Since before I came around, at least. When did this song come out—'02, '03? *Way* before I was born.

Wherever I was born.

"'A side of me you didn't knoooooow.'"

Anyway, I don't really need to know.

"'A reason for all that I doooooo.'"

I have this coffee shop, where I have a perfect attendance record and know exactly where to find everything. I have my best friend, Milo, and I have my mom and dad, who have been with me through everything since the day they got me.

Three hours later, while I'm brushing lavender eye shadow over my upper lid, I hum the last line in my head: *And the reason is youuuuu.*

I observe my makeup in the mirror. Simple enough. Lavender eye shadow, black liner on top, white liner on bottom, and no foundation. No need to cover up my mark.

I run my fingers along it—the birthmark by the edge of my hairline. Some say it's shaped like a fish. Others say it's a heart. Me? I don't really care. Whatever it is, it's me-shaped.

"Happy homecoming," says Milo. From the edge of my vision, I can see he's holding out a colorful box. When I look and see the bright yellow ribbon piled high on top, I smile.

"A professional wrapping job? You shouldn't have."

He shrugs. "Just open it. Promise what's inside will make up for the wrapping."

"Nah-uh," I say, scrambling for my secret drawer that's not so secret to Milo. Just gossipy love notes and tampons in there. Nothing he hasn't seen before. "Not till you have yours in hand first." I pull out a box, lovingly wrapped in a hand-sewn cherry blossom furoshiki cloth.

"Show-off," he says.

"Just taking care of the planet."

THIS BOOK MIGHT BE ABOUT ZINNIA

"Making up for all those glittery plastic pieces in that eye shadow, huh?"

"Fuck off and open it," I say, unable to hide the laughs bubbling up. I know his smiles, too. This one says, *Ha, I win.* But he opens the box anyway, and I watch, confident in my book-selecting skills.

He unties the cloth and crumples it up in his free hand, unaware that I took the time to iron it this morning. Definitely ironed it for me. I could've wrapped the book in a paper bag and Milo wouldn't have cared, but if I give a gift and it doesn't look *perfect*, I'm gonna have a problem.

"What's it about?" he asks, still staring at the cover. But I can tell by the way his fingers run along the front that it's a hit.

"Open it and see!"

"*The Well*," he reads. "Sounds like a mystery. Maybe about a guy and a well?"

"Just read the back already," I say, eager to open my gift. I weigh it in my hand. It's *huge.* Pretty heavy, too. My shoulders are starting to sag from the weight of it.

"'Follow third-year medical resident Avery Weinstein as she journeys through the underground catacombs of Savannah, uncovering medical mysteries long forgotten in the era of the antebellum South.'"

"So . . . ? What do you think?"

He looks up at me after a long pause and shrugs. "Why's it called *The Well*?"

"You'll have to find out!" I say. He's asking questions already. We're off to a great start.

"Interesting."

Even better.

"My turn!" I say, unable to hide my excitement any longer. I wedge my finger under the tape keeping the paper together, but my elbow-length white glove sticks to it. I yank the wrapping paper off so fast, Milo takes a step back to give me space to rip into my prey.

"Jesus Christ," he says.

The minute the paper is off the front, my jaw drops.

I can't breathe.

"Jodelle Rae West?" I ask. "She has a new book out? When were you going to tell me?"

"Right now," he says.

I flip the book over, and my eyes fly faster than my brain can follow. I read the back out loud in what sounds like a single sentence—or maybe even a single word.

"'Jodelle Rae West makes her striking return to the blank page with *Little Heart*, spinning an enchanted tale of love, loss, and a father's never-ending quest to find what's truly important.'"

Sounds . . . *cliché*.

But I can't say that.

"Sounds . . . ," I start.

"Cliché?" he finishes.

THIS BOOK MIGHT BE ABOUT ZINNIA

Damn to hell my revealing face.

"I mean, not entirely—"

"Knew you'd think that. I know how you are about genre fiction. But read the first paragraph."

I resist the temptation to roll my eyes and pull back the cover. I clear my throat, beginning my dramatic reading of whatever magic these pages are about to reveal.

"'It all started with a heart-shaped birthma—'"

I stop reading and raise an eyebrow at him.

"Milo . . . ?"

"Keep going," he says.

I steel myself. Purely coincidence that this character has exactly the same birthmark as I do. But still, dope!

"'It all started with a heart-shaped birthmark. That's what I remember most about her. Not her beating heart, for I hadn't known it long. Not her heart of hearts, for I hadn't known it at all.'"

I pause before reading the next line.

"'I lost her far too soon.'"

CHAPTER 2

Tuesday
2006

MY HANDS WON'T STOP SHAKING.

I can feel my pulse in my ears. And my chest. Everywhere, actually.

"Tuesday Walker," declares Dario, holding my résumé *right* up to his face, even though his monstrous glasses are at least a quarter inch thick and magnify his eyes to the size of golf balls. He leans forward on the creaky dining room chair, and I adjust in mine, just as creaky.

Does every chair in this place creak so bad? How old is Café Alba, anyway?

Hissss goes the steam wand from behind the bar across the room. A boy my age adjusts his stance, focuses on the pitcher in his hand as the steam dissipates and the wand goes to work heating the milk. His hair is a mop, playful golden curls dancing around his ears. Between that and his puka shell necklace, he looks like he stepped right out of the ocean, surfboard in hand.

Without warning, his eyes rise to meet mine, and I tear mine away.

Oh God, did he see me staring at him?

I curl my toes in my shoes and try to focus on what Dario's saying, but there's something stuck in his teeth, and every time he says a word that forces his lips together, it moves just a little and—

"Tuesday, did you hear me?" he asks.

"Huh?"

I snap out of my thoughts and blink him into focus.

"I *asked*," he continues with a sigh, "why do you want to work at a café when you have no experience? You don't have any experience, do you?"

"Oh, right, um," I start, pressing my hand to my thick headband to make sure it's still containing my baby hairs. The hair around my temples is just *barely* hanging on lately, so I can't spare a single one to this snowy Philadelphia winter.

"I . . . ," I begin, knowing I can't lie. "I don't have any."

His eyes dim. His eyebrows go flat. His face goes blank at that answer. I try to clean it up.

"But I really want this job. And I—"

The steam wand clips into sharp silence.

"Did she say she doesn't have any experience?" comes a voice from the bar. I look back up at the surfer boy as he steps out from behind the espresso machine, drying his hands on a dishrag before flinging it over his shoulder.

His burgundy apron is splotched with marks, some light, some dark, and I lock in that it gets messy back there. I can handle that. I'm used to mess.

"Relax, Justin," comes Dario's voice.

Golden hair, electric blue eyes, shoulders like Hercules, shares a name with Justin Timberlake himself, and he's *looking at me.*

Here I am trying, to slow my heart rate, and here he is, not helping.

"I thought you worked at Blockbuster," he says.

"Justin," Dario interjects, "when you wear the black apron, you can do the interviews."

Justin swipes a broom from against the wall and starts sweeping nothing into a pile of nothing.

"I'm not interviewing, I'm cleaning while we're down," he says, and nods toward the door with his chin. "Like you told me to do. Anyway, Blockbuster totally counts. It's not too different from what we do here, just with DVDs instead of drinks and merchandise."

Dario resigns to let Justin do what Justin does, like this happens all the time, and turns his attention back to my résumé.

"Says you worked there for six months. What happened?"

THIS BOOK MIGHT BE ABOUT ZINNIA

"I had a medical incident," I recite, exactly what Mom told me to say.

Dario raises an eyebrow at me, and I explain further without really explaining.

"It won't happen again."

Justin sweeps his pile of nothing right up to our table. He's looking at me, I can feel it, but I refuse to meet his gaze as he asks me another question.

"You good with food?" he asks.

I nod.

"We're right by the train station, so we get a lot of, uh . . . questionable folks. You good with that, too?"

I nod again, concentrating so hard on sliding my thumbs against each other before my nerves completely melt out of my body.

I need this job.

"What's your favorite coffee drink?" he asks further.

"I don't really drink coffee," I admit, glancing up at him. "Sorry."

"Yeah, me neither," he says, and smiles.

What?

A barista who doesn't like coffee? I thought I was the only one! I look up at him again.

"Really?"

"Nah, coffee's never really been my thing. More of a hot chocolate guy myself," he says, grabbing a chair from a nearby table and sliding onto it backward, joining us as the third wheel at this one-on-one interview. His legs straddle the back of the seat, and I *refuse* to let my eyes wander. But as he folds his arms over the top and rests his chin on his wrists, I can't help it.

He's got muscle. Serious muscle. Sporty type. Jock, even. But at least he's nice.

I remind myself they always are—the cruel ones, anyway—before they turn back into all the rest, and it cuts even deeper because you dared to believe they would ever like you.

I swallow, feeling my eyes burn with tears. I choke them down, *will* them back into my body.

"Can I ask something else?" Justin asks.

"Pfft," says Dario, motioning openhandedly to me, "be my guest."

That conjures a smile out of me. It's clear they've known each other for a long time. Like a big brother–little brother type of thing. Justin looks at me again, studies my face this time.

His eyes are warm, inviting, calm yet electric. I want to keep looking at them. I wish he'd say something so it's less weird that I want to keep looking at them while he stares at me in total silence.

"If I asked you to burn a CD for me," he starts, "what would you put on it?"

My neck warms, and I glance at Dario, wondering if he's

hearing what I'm hearing. Burning a CD is . . . a big deal. It's what you do when you like someone. *Like* like them. I've never . . .

I don't know if I would ever . . .

I didn't even burn one for Ezra.

I clear my throat. "Like, what songs?" I ask, adjusting in my seat.

"Yeah," he says. "Guess what I like. Read into me."

"Uh," I begin, ignoring the intimacy of that last sentence.

What do I even say? I've only just met him! Everything in me screams this is an unfair question. But then I wonder what he does when he gets home from a place like this, with steam wands and angry customers, and apron splotches, and creaking chairs, and beeping coffee machines, and I wonder if he would put on his headphones and play a CD full of more noise or something softer.

His eyes, everything about them, invite me in, and I find my answer.

"You look like you listen to Blink-182," I say. A smile plays at the corner of his mouth. "Maybe Linkin Park? Green Day? Good Charlotte? But I feel like those might be the CDs you play in your car when someone in the passenger seat would laugh at what you actually want to play."

He straightens, looks me up and down, intrigued.

"Sounds like you know what that's like?" he asks.

I smile because I absolutely do. Mom doesn't know I know

who *any* of those "basic white-boy bands" are—"secular music," as she calls it. But I love them. I love them all.

"I feel like you listen to softer stuff," I venture. "So if I had to burn a CD for you, I would add 'She Will Be Loved' by Maroon 5, 'Perfect' by Simple Plan, and 'How to Save a Life' by the Fray."

His grin tells me I'm on the right track.

"I'd love that," he says, resting his chin on his wrists again. I can't stop smiling. I feel like my face might be stuck smiling forever.

Then I remember what this is. He's *way* too cute for me. This has to be a trick. A trap. I don't know what his angle is, but I won't be a pawn in whatever scheme this must be. Maybe he even has a thing for Black girls. An unhealthy one.

There has to be a catch.

I turn back to Dario and clear my throat. He looks between me and Justin and raises his eyebrows.

"Well, is that the whole interview then, Justin? Are you done?"

It yanks Justin back to reality.

"Yeah," he says casually. "We're hiring her, right?"

My heart skips. *Are they?*

His words carried the tone of a kid picking out a puppy and asking his father, *Can we keep her?* I smile and look to Dario for an answer as he pushes himself up from his chair.

"We'll call you," he says firmly.

Justin meanders back to the counter, broom in hand, then leans it against the wall.

"Can we call her with a yes?" he asks.

"*Justin*," spits Dario. I stifle a laugh.

Six weeks in and I still have no idea what I'm doing.

I sling the wand so fast between drinks, I accidentally flip the lever while the wand is pointed up, sending hot steam spewing into my face. I yelp in surprise, not because it actually hurt. But Justin still reacts like it might've.

"*Tuesday!*" he exclaims, rushing to my side. He flips the lever off and the wand back, then looks me up and down, his eyes huge with concern. I step back from the bar, the three empty cups I was working on lining the counter. Every eye in the café is trained on me, maybe a dozen customers staring me down in total silence. I feel my eyes well with tears; damn these hormones.

Justin nods toward the break room door.

"Why don't you take a fiver, huh? I've got things out here for a bit."

A *fiver*? Dario doesn't do *fivers*. He's a nice boss, but he also doesn't play. Fivers, freebies, and favors don't fly.

Anyway, what if I take this break and Dario sees me sitting in the break room while I'm on the clock and fires me on the spot, and I have to go back home to Mom and explain why I got fired only six weeks into a minimum-wage job, and I can't be trusted to do anything, and I should just work at the church every week where I can be kept out of trouble and . . .

Justin is still staring at me while my brain does laps around a track littered with what-ifs, and as if he can read my mind:

"Go," he insists warmly. "I'll talk to Dario."

He says it so firmly and confidently that I believe him.

The break room air is cold and sharp against my skin, and the minute I step through the door, I'm diving for my backpack with my two favorite things in the world inside: my Walkman, currently spinning Hoobastank's CD, and my journal.

I pull both out and set them on the table, along with my pen, then put on my headphones, hit play on track eight— "The Reason," my favorite—and curl up in the cozy little chair in the corner. The soreness has faded just like the nurses said it would, enough that I can sit like this without much pain, but it's still enough to remind me why I write.

I flip open to the next empty page, click my pen open, and pour my heart out as those first few piano and guitar notes blend and marry in my ears.

I'm not a perfect pers—

The break room door swings open so hard, it slams into the wall, startling me out of whatever groove I was about to get into. I look up to see Justin frantically grabbing for the door

THIS BOOK MIGHT BE ABOUT ZINNIA

and swinging it shut softly, apologetically, before looking to me again.

"You okay?" he asks, flipping his golden bangs away from his eyes. The hair underneath glistens just a bit with sweat and sticks to his forehead, and I notice his face is a tinge redder than usual.

"You didn't have to do that," I offer, shutting the journal and resting the pen neatly on top.

"I did," he says, sliding into the chair next to me. "You were dangerous out there."

Embarrassment floods my face, hot and unwelcome. "I'm trying," I say.

"Oh, I didn't mean . . . ," he starts. "We all get like that, where you work too hard, take on too much stuff, and overdo it until you can't really think."

Now that I think about it, I don't really know what it's like *not* to think. I've had so many thoughts every second of every minute of every day of the last year, and when I overflow with too many thoughts, when it feels like I might explode with them, I put them all in my journal.

As if reading my mind, Justin glances at it, purple swirls all over the front with a Paul Frank monkey sticker in the bottom right corner.

"You keep a diary?" he asks.

"Journal," I say. Diaries are for kids.

"You an author?" he asks, his voice all curious, no ridicule.

"Writer." I smile. "Authors are published. And talented."

"Not all of 'em."

I lean back in my chair, arms folded over my stomach, and smile at him again, studying his face as he eyes the journal, like he's trying to read it right through the cover. I decide I feel comfortable enough to play with him a bit.

"You don't seem like the type to fail English class," I say.

"Aw, don't tell me I look preppy," he says. "Please, anything but that."

"You've got a whole surfer vibe going," I say. "That's pretty California prep to me."

"Is it the necklace?" he asks, reaching up behind his neck to unfasten it. I note the muscles in his arms on full display now, and I swallow, and I try to move on with the conversation like I won't be thinking about them later. But just before I can, he continues.

"Maybe you should have it," he says.

"What?" I practically choke. "Why?"

"Borrow it?" he asks, setting it on the table next to my journal. "Looks better on you anyway."

If my skin tone were just a few shades lighter, he'd be able to tell how flushed I am. I *just* wrapped up a heartbreak, and here I am getting flustered over this goofball—what the hell is wrong with me?

"I should get back to the floor, huh?" I ask, looking for an out. *Any* out.

THIS BOOK MIGHT BE ABOUT ZINNIA

"Probably," he says. "But, uh, you should know, I think you'd make a great author."

"You haven't even read my writing."

"Well, I would," he offers, "if you let me."

I stare at him for a long moment, *too* long. So long that he breaks the silence between us.

"I'm sorry, that was probably too personal," he says, rising from the chair and clasping his hands. "You, uh, you enjoy your writing, and if you ever change your mind, I'll be there. Here. Around. You know. At work. I'm gonna go."

I suppress a laugh, poorly. Justin steps back through the door to the floor of the coffee shop.

I put my Walkman back into my backpack and hang the bag on the coat hook, journal still in hand. Justin's green backpack hangs next to mine, and I freeze for a moment, staring, imagining sharing what I've written. It's all been coded cryptically enough that no one would be able to figure out what it actually means.

Right?

CHAPTER 3

Zinnia

2024

I STARE AT MY FINAL HOMECOMING LOOK IN THE mirror. The lavender eye shadow makes my brown eyes pop. My dark hair looks black, slicked back except for a tendril hanging down to my nose in the front. And then there's that medium-brown birthmark at the top of my forehead and slightly to the right, the one I dodge whenever I put foundation on. If the rest of me is middle-of-the-bread-colored, the birthmark is crust-colored. I could cover it easily enough. But why would I? It's what makes me Zinnia Davis.

"You good?" asks Milo from behind me. He emerges from my bathroom, straightening his black bow tie. I gasp as I see him in the mirror, then turn fully to get a good look. His shoulders are sharp and angular, defined even under his

THIS BOOK MIGHT BE ABOUT ZINNIA

jacket, dark purple shirt tucked into his black slacks, shoes glistening like a freshly waxed sports car.

"Okay, Mr. Bond," I say with a grin as I stand and look him up and down. "Give us a walk."

He can't hide his smile or blushing cheeks, not even when he looks at the floor, but he turns and walks back to the window, and I can't resist hyping him up.

"Yaaaas, *yaaaas*, girl, *WERK*."

"Stop," he says, and I do, but with a giggle.

"I can't help it, you look great!"

He freezes, staring at me with huge eyes. "I was supposed to bring a corsage, wasn't I?"

He should know I generally hate any phrase that starts with "supposed to," especially if it's followed by a gender-based societal expectation.

"Pfft," I scoff. "So I can scratch at my wrist all night from the itchy floral tape? No thanks. Besides, you don't have a boutonniere, either. Sorry 'bout it."

I turn to look at us both in the mirror again. Damn, do we look good. Like, break-the-internet good. I can't help it. I pick up my phone and snap a picture of us.

"Mind if I post this?" I ask.

"Sure, whatever," he says with a shrug, then reaches to pick up his bag. "But maybe we should wait till we're king and queen."

He can't be serious.

"You really think we're going to win homecoming tonight?" I ask. "It's based on votes, you know. And we're assholes."

"If we're assholes, then Kendra Wilkins is Satan herself."

He's got a point. She checks all the boxes for it. Softball star. Attitude enough for the rest of the team. And a nepo baby. Got into Stanford after her dad donated the Wilkins Softball Stadium. Can't stand her. *But* if it's based on votes, then maybe it's a good thing she's insufferable.

"Nobody likes her, you know," he says. "They're all just afraid of her."

"Sometimes fear is what earns votes. Rather be feared than loved, right?"

"I'll take love any day," he says, unable to hide his grin. He's staring at his shoes, lost in thought as he says it, and I roll my eyes.

"Sap," I say. "Is that the real reason you got me such a romantic book?"

"Uh, it's not a romance," he says, shaking his head.

"It's literally called *Little Heart*. And it's *purple*."

I spot it on the vanity and study the cover again.

Little Heart.

I pick it up, open it to the first page, and plop down in the beanbag in the corner.

"What are you doing?" asks Milo.

"We still have, like, an hour till homecoming," I explain,

THIS BOOK MIGHT BE ABOUT ZINNIA

25

patting the beanbag next to me. "Get your book and cozy up! We don't have many more nights like this before graduation, remember?"

Something in his eyes sinks.

"Yeah."

A single word, but it says everything.

"Milo, I'm sorry. I know you hate when I bring up graduation, but . . . I just . . . want you to know how grateful I am to have you in my life."

He sinks into the beanbag next to me, cradling *The Well*, eyes glued to the floor.

I rest *Little Heart* in my lap. This is important. He looks up at me as I take his hands in my gloved ones and squeeze his fingers, staring directly into his big brown eyes.

"Whatever happens once we're out of this academic hellscape? We're friends forever."

He cracks a grin, still not looking at me.

"Even if you get into Harvard?" he asks in a tone that suggests he already has suspicions.

"Obviously," I say with an eye roll. "And I told you it's a guarantee. Both my parents went, remember? I'm a shoo-in."

It's true. I swear to God my parents have been talking about Harvard since the day they got me. Even took an extra year to *really* decide if they should have me repeat kindergarten in case it affected my college prospects. Softball? Sure! Harvard loves a well-rounded prospect who can do books *and* sports. Chess club? Absolutely! Shows strategic maneuvering and deductive reasoning. Harvard *loves* that shit. Piano lessons, swim team, summer camps, AP *everything*. All of this for the sole purpose of earning me a spot in Harvard College's class of 2029.

"And it won't change us. We'll still have FaceTime, remember? And we still follow each other on . . . actually, literally everything."

"Yeah," he says quietly, and for the first time in months, he's impossible to read. He lets go of my hands and opens *The Well*.

So I dive back into *Little Heart*.

> I lost her far too soon.
> Actually, that's not true. How can you say you've lost someone when you're the one who gave her away?

Ouch.

That stings, the thought of being given away, like some prized possession and not a person. My parents have been my parents since before I can remember. I was only hours old, apparently. Zero record of my birth parents, and I think they must've wanted it that way. According to Mom, the state of Pennsylvania offers birth moms a chance to request visitation, among other privileges, and my birth mom wanted none of them. She really handed me off to Oak Park Adoption Agency reps at the hospital and fuckin' *left*.

THIS BOOK MIGHT BE ABOUT ZINNIA

Maybe she thought it'd be easier that way.

... Or maybe she hated me that much.

I shake off the feeling and read on.

> Her father, the king, would never understand. I haven't spoken to him since . . . well . . .
>
> Since the day he was crowned.
>
> But I never forgot my Little Heart.
>
> Even when I was sure I'd never see her again, I always left her breadcrumbs.
>
> I hoped that maybe, just maybe, one day, she'd find her way back from the Wise Old Oak.
>
> Back to me.

The Wise Old Oak?

... Oak Park Adoption Agency?

And that heart-shaped birthmark?

That's an interesting coincidence.

I turn to the jacket flap with the author profile, where I see a black-and-white photo of Jodelle Rae West staring back at me, arms folded over each other, lips pursed in a knowing smile, eyes clearly blue or green even though the photo's in gray scale. Her blond hair falls over her shoulders in wisps, her long, slender nose matching its curve.

"You good?" asks Milo, jolting me back into reality.

"Yeah," I say too fast. "Uh, I'm good. Great."

"Totally believe that."

"It's just . . . this book sounds a little . . . detailed?"

The altitude on this boy's left eyebrow when he looks at me.

"It's a *novel*," he says, and smirks. "No one writes a hundred thousand words without some detail."

"Look, all I'm saying is you really did your research. There's a Wise Old Oak in it. And you know I was adopted from an agency called Oak Park. The heart-shaped birthmark?"

"Okay?" he asks. "Where is this going?"

"Just thanks for feeding my ego," I say with a grin.

"Oh, because everything is about you, O Queen of the Universe." He smiles.

"Listen, I've been told I *radiate* protagonist energy, and all I'm saying is maybe Jodelle Rae West got a tip from the universe that I belong in a book."

Right on cue, Mom appears in my bedroom doorway. Enter antagonist.

"Is that what you're wearing tonight?" she asks. Maybe she hopes that smile of hers will soften the implications of her question. It doesn't.

Milo stands and nods at her respectfully before turning to offer his hand to help me stand. Sometimes he's an expectation-bending gender rebel, and sometimes he's a gentleman, and I love him for it.

THIS BOOK MIGHT BE ABOUT ZINNIA

I take his hand with a smile and stand, still holding the book close.

"Huh?" I ask, genuinely confused at what's bothering her now. Platform heels? Sweetheart neckline? Elbow-length sparkly white gloves? What could be more retro about this look?

Her eyes flutter from my face to the book, and I hurry to shut *Little Heart* and tuck it away behind a stack of more books on the vanity before she can see it. But I'm not fast enough.

"What's that?" she asks.

"A book."

Wrong answer.

"I can see that." She smiles, her eyes narrowing so slightly that most people would miss it. I don't. "A book about what?"

"It's Jodelle Rae West's newest," I admit, hoping that's enough for her. "Milo got it for me."

"She got me this one," he offers, holding out *The Well* as a welcome distraction. "She says it's nothing like the movie *The Ring*, but I'm not convinced."

Thank God for him. It works. Mom's distracted. I spot an opening.

"Isn't this outfit exactly what y'all wore in the nineties?" I ask as I give this lavender dress another twirl.

"Well," she says, leaning against the doorframe, studying me, "it just . . . seems like it's missing something. It's less . . . ball gownish than it looked on the rack."

I rest my sparkly white-gloved hands on my hips and look down.

"It's the corset, isn't it?" I ask. Even with the sweetheart neckline—classic—it's totally sheer. Very updated. Very *now.*

"And the midriff."

"It's not midriff, it's sheer. *Vogue.* Chanel. Ariana Grande. Olivia Rodrigo." Let me see, who would she know from her era? "Audrey Hepburn."

She snorts. "If Audrey Hepburn stood on a corner for a living."

Oh. Sex-work jokes. Fantastic.

"Look, the good news is," I say, hiking up the bottom and stepping past her, "you're not the one wearing the dress."

She stops me with a gentle hand on my shoulder.

"Darling, don't be like that, okay? You look beautiful."

She smiles at me—we're the same height while I'm in these platform shoes. She reaches for the curl hanging down in front of my eyes to fix it.

"Aht," I say, dodging. "It's part of the look."

The rest of my hair is pinned back with huge sparkly banana clips. *Exactly* like they wore in the '90s.

"I have to go," I say. "Don't want to be late. Come on, Milo."

I step past her, but she gently catches my wrist.

"Where's your corsage?" she asks. My face is blank, I'm sure, as I look for words. And then my mom looks to Milo and

THIS BOOK MIGHT BE ABOUT ZINNIA

cocks her head. His face turns into a strawberry instantly, and I dive in to save him.

"I told Milo I didn't want one."

After he told me he didn't bring one, but she can live without that part.

"Really?" she asks. I nod. "All right, well, I . . . guess that's all right. You don't want a purple rose or two to liven things up? I could drive you to Wegmans and—"

"Thanks, Mom, but I'll be okay. It's just homecoming."

She releases my wrist and lets me make my way to the kitchen, where I have my sparkly silver clutch waiting for me, but not without peppering me with questions.

"You have your keys?" she asks. I hold them up and jingle them. Then I step onto the linoleum with a *click-click-click* of my platforms.

"You have your insoles in?"

"Yes, Mom."

"Great, we don't want your arches to fall. Oh! Did you pack snacks?"

"They're serving dinner, Mom."

"Take snacks anyway in case it's served late. And a water bottle! You can't be dehydrated on the dance floor."

I take a water bottle from the pack in the pantry.

"It'd be easier to stay hydrated if you'd let me get a refillable one. The environment would thank you too."

"So you can accumulate bacteria in it all day? No thank

you. You know, I saw a video on YouTube once where they cut into a children's bath toy and found *black . . . mold.*"

"Okay, so I'll find a water bottle that's not a bath toy."

"Zinnia."

I sigh and hope to God she finally lets me go. But she gets that Mom face again and steps forward to cup my cheek.

"You look so beautiful," she says. But before I have time to thank her for the compliment, she glances at Milo, then lowers her voice and leans in and says, "Did you pack protection?"

"*Mom!*" I exclaim. What, does she think Milo and I are . . .

"I'm just asking!" she says, hands in the air innocently. "If this was the *real* nineties, you wouldn't even know what protection *is*. When I was a kid, they didn't teach sex ed until you were four centimeters dilated."

"Oh my God, Mom, *yes*, I have protection," I say, pointing to my forearm, where the birth control stick lies implanted.

"Oh, that's new," she says, gearing up for another debate. "Fine. But take some condoms with you anyway. Birth control doesn't protect you from STDs."

I sigh because, dammit, she's right. She holds out a couple of condoms wrapped in gold foil.

"Did you buy these just for me?" I ask, taking them in my hands, and then *her* cheeks go strawberry red and she clears her throat.

"Don't worry about it."

THIS BOOK MIGHT BE ABOUT ZINNIA

Oh my *God*, these are Mom and Dad's condoms. The minute I get there, I'm throwing them out. I get protection and all that, but there's absolutely no way.

"Okay, bye!" I declare, turning and bolting for the door. Milo scrambles behind me, and we make our way to my little blue Corolla.

"Drive safely!" calls Mom from the front stoop. "Remember, rolling stops will get you a ticket."

"Thanks, Mom!" I holler, slipping into the car and slamming the door. Milo slides into the passenger seat and shuts his door, cutting Mom off in the middle of her sentence.

"Zinnia, I love—"

Slam!

Sadness washes over me. I have to let her finish that one. I look past Milo and roll down the passenger window. She stands there cradling her arms around herself, and her voice breaks as she calls again, softer, "I love you, Zinnia."

She reaches up to wipe away under her eyes, careful not to smear her makeup, and sniffs. She dons a brave smile and nods to assure me I'm actually okay to go to this thing tonight. There's helicopter parenting, and then there's Apache attack helicopter parenting. My mom's the latter. And I guess with everything she and Dad went through to bring me home, all the paperwork, all the waiting, the *endless* waiting, I understand it.

Doesn't mean I like it, though.

"I love you, too, Mom," I reply.

I mean it.

But when I roll up the window and Milo and I look at each other, we let out twin sighs. Finally we can breathe again.

Mom goes back inside and shuts the door, but I'm sure she's going to watch us leave from one of the windows. I stare at the steering wheel for a moment, remembering the book.

I lost her far too soon.

I've lived my entire life until now not even thinking of her. Never really had a reason to. Is my life perfect? No. Is my mom perfect? Absolutely not. But have I ever once thought that maybe my life would've been happier if my birth mom had kept me? Not really. What else could I want?

Sure, there were times in the Target toy aisle when I was told the dreaded two-letter word every toddler hates, when I thought, *Hey, maybe if I'd been raised by my biological parents, I could've walked out of here with that toy today.*

And then I grew up and realized that given how much my parents make, and how much they've given me, including the fact that my college tuition was paid for by the time I was five years old, there's a *much* higher likelihood that my birth mom wouldn't have had Target money at all.

But for the first time in my life, I'm thinking about this differently.

What if my birth mom—whoever she is—is out there thinking of me? Who is she? Who *was* she, if she's not alive anymore? I've spent my entire life not knowing her name. What if every day of my life she's wondered what *my* name is?

How would Mom even react if I asked her? If I gave any inkling she's not *everything* I could possibly need or want in a mom?

I look back up at the house just as Milo asks, "What's up?"

I shake my head as I see Mom's face emerge between the upstairs curtains.

"I just don't think I can ask her," I say. "About my birth parents. Ever. She'd fall apart."

He reaches over, wraps his soft fingers around mine, and squeezes.

"What's got you thinking about that?" he asks.

He locks it in the moment I look at him.

"The book?"

"It's just got me thinking," I say. "About life, and how it might've gone differently if I'd been born to a completely different household. Who knows? I could've been raised in a palace in Delhi, or a rural village somewhere."

"Or an apartment in Detroit. Or a cardboard box in a public park," he says. "You could've experienced a million timelines by now, but you're in this one, where you could have *anything* you've ever wanted."

I take a deep breath and let his words sink in. Yeah, better to leave it alone. Be grateful for what I have. In a few weeks I'll have my acceptance letter from Harvard, and in a few months

I'll be moving out. I can at least give my mom the peace of knowing she's the only mom I need.

I turn the key and look at the clock on the dash. Ugh, we're still forty-five minutes early. And I left the book on the vanity.

"Shall we read in the parking lot to pass the time?" Milo asks, pulling both *The Well* and *Little Heart* from his black Doc Martens backpack.

I gasp and snatch up the purple glistening tome.

"You're the fucking best, you know that?"

"Yeah, I do," he says.

And off we go, to steal away forty-five minutes in the homecoming parking lot. Not to have sex. But to read together. Like we used to do during recess in elementary. Milo and I have *always* done this.

If only Mom knew me at all.

CHAPTER 4

Tuesday
2006

BY THE TIME I GET HOME, I CAN'T FEEL MY FINGERS. The knob on the storm door might be cold, but I'd never know. I turn it, jiggle it left and right until—*WHAM! RATTLE!*—it finally budges open.

"Mom?" I ask gingerly into the dark. I flip my phone open and check the time: 8:22 p.m. She might already be asleep in her chair. Blue light from the TV flickers on the wall from the living room around the corner.

I step inside, shutting the door gently behind me, then hang my backpack on the hook and kick out of my Vans.

"Tu-Tu, is that you?" she asks, her voice croaky and groggy. Yup, she was asleep.

I reach the living room and find a plate of half-eaten

chicken nuggets, an open bag of Doritos, and empty Tang pouches all over the table. Mom sits up in her recliner and cranes her neck to see me. Her hair isn't matted, but it hasn't been brushed lately either. She picks up a napkin and wipes the corners of her mouth.

"You're home early," she says with a smile, pushing herself up until she's sitting on the very edge of the chair.

"I told you I'd be off at eight," I say. I know I said that on our after-school phone call—the one I take every day after last period.

"You never said that," she insists, reaching her arms up into a stretch. Her lavender muumuu hangs on her like a tired sheet, and her matching bonnet has a hole in it that I haven't noticed before. "How am I supposed to keep you safe if I don't even know when you'll be home?"

I could press it, or I could nip this right now. I choose the latter.

"Sorry, Mom," I say, unbuckling my watch, which has left an imprint. God, I'll be so glad when this swelling goes down.

"After all," she says in a tone that I'm sure is supposed to be playful, "we don't want any more *accidents*."

It cuts right through my chest, the word "accidents."

"If you're looking for some dinner," she says, and sniffs, still assimilating to the waking world, "we should have Bagel Bites in the freezer."

Fine, I guess. Beats endless muffins and croissants from work, anyway.

THIS BOOK MIGHT BE ABOUT ZINNIA   39

In the kitchen I gently push aside a pile of recycling—an empty Capri Sun pouch and a Sunny D bottle rattle a bit.

"Hey!" she snaps from the living room. "We don't kick things in this house. Take care of what you have, Tuesday. I raised you better."

"I didn't—"

"You *did*. Don't tell me what I heard."

I hear her get up from the recliner and shuffle her house-shoed feet into the kitchen behind me as I manage to wedge the freezer door open and locate the pizza bites hidden among the stack of TV dinners and Lean Pockets. Now to find the baking sheet.

It's not in its usual spot—inside the oven.

"Mom, have you seen the baking . . ." And then I spot it in the sink. "Oh, you used it."

"I clean *every* dish I use, as I use it," she says. "You know that."

"Okay, then why is it in the—"

"You must have used it when you made dinner last night."

"I made potatoes au gratin, Mom. In the pie plate."

She lets out the most dramatic sigh I've ever heard.

"Ugh, Tuesday, I can't keep track of where every single dish in this house ends up, okay? I have enough to remember, working all day and taking care of you."

"Okay," I say, mainly to appease her away from the edge of the cliff she's been inching toward.

"Anyway," she sighs, scooping up some empty soda cans from the kitchen table, "how was school?"

"It was fine."

Please don't ask more about school. There's literally nothing I hate talking about more.

She walks the recycling to the big blue bin by the front door that's already piled high with cardboard and empty water bottles. "Just *fine*?" she asks.

Please, Mom.

"Yeah, it was fine," I repeat, knowing I have to give her more than that if I want to keep this conversation short. "In history class we learned about Mount Vesuvius."

"Oh," she practically sings, "history was my favorite. I loved learning about new cultures, you know? I always wanted to travel more when I was younger. I wish I had."

She comes up behind me and reaches up to my head, smoothing out my already slicked-back puff.

"Oh, this is so tight, dear. Make sure to give your scalp a break here and there so you don't end up with traction alopecia. So, Vesuvius."

What a whirlwind of a conversation.

"Yeah, Vesuvius," I say, trying to remember a single detail about it as I drip two drops of dish soap onto the pan and pick up the sponge. "It, uh . . . was a volcano that erupted without warning and wiped out Pompeii."

"Oh, there were warning signs," says Mom. "In the stars. The History Channel ran a special on it just last week."

"Cool," I say, which is easier than fighting her. I avoid eye

THIS BOOK MIGHT BE ABOUT ZINNIA

contact as I wipe away the crumbs from the pan—noting that potatoes au gratin don't even *leave* crumbs—and then I notice her staring.

Oh God.

She's got the grin. The *Mom* grin.

She reaches up. Smooths out my hair again.

"Why don't you go to prom with your friends next month, Tuesday?"

I resist the urge to wince at the word "friends," considering I have none, and instead catch myself grinding my teeth.

"I don't want to talk about it," I say, hoping for the love of all that's holy she'll leave it alone. But of course she doesn't.

"You realize you can't make friends without socializing, right?" she asks.

The last time I "socialized," I had an "accident." But I say nothing, hoping she drops it. She doesn't. She never drops anything.

As if on cue, my phone buzzes in my pocket. I slip it out, flip it open, and read the new message from an unknown number. It stops my heart cold.

Unknown: Hey. It's Justin. Hope you don't mind me texting. Got your number from Dario.

I try *so* hard not to let my face reveal that my stomach is doing flips.

I clear my throat and look up at my mom. A look of pity crosses her face as she smooths out one of my eyebrows and tucks some wayward baby hairs behind my ear. She doesn't suspect a thing.

"I just think you could be so much more feminine if you tried."

I can't help it. The rage bubbles forth, threatening to pour from my mouth like hot magma.

"I was feminine enough for Ezra," I mutter, forgetting for a moment that I'm saying it out loud.

"What did you say?" she hisses. I freeze. What can of worms have I just opened? "Little girl," she continues, her finger waving in my face, "God will deal with you. Do you hear me? I pray for your sins every single day because Lord knows you rack up enough for both of us. Disrespecting your mother. Sneaking off with boys at all hours. Letting up on your grades at the start of your *senior year*? I was trying to be understanding here and offer to drive you to prom so you can have some semblance of a normal school year after missing months of work, but clearly that was too generous for you."

"So you want me to go to prom, but you don't want me to have a life?" I demand.

"I wanted you to have one night to feel like a *girl*, Tuesday," she spits, "since this past year has forced you to become a *woman* before you should've had to."

"If my dad were here—"

"Well, he's *not*, is he?" she screams.

It shouldn't hurt this much. I never even knew him. He

THIS BOOK MIGHT BE ABOUT ZINNIA

died before I was born. But growing up with a monster for a mother has made me think of him as some kind of guardian angel. There's no way he isn't *somewhere* looking at everything happening in this house and scowling. I've heard that everyone has a strict parent and a fun parent. Unfortunately for me, I got stuck with the former.

There's no way he could've been as bad as her.

And I hope one day, whenever my mother and I both die and reach whatever forever is waiting for us, he gets the chance to look her in the eye and demand to know why she's been so horrible to their only daughter.

We stand there, locked in a stare-down, until she clears her throat and breaks the silence.

"Maybe you *do* need to stay home, where you can't get into any more trouble. In the meantime, I will pray for you, you hear me? I will pray for your soul. And until you return to your Lord and Savior, you will not utter *that boy's* name in this house."

The hum of the TV in the other room is all that cuts into the silence between us. We're the same height, so as we return to staring each other down, it's her intimidation versus my iron will. This time, at least, I have the power to walk away. I find an excuse.

"I'm not hungry," I say, dropping the pan into the sink and marching past her. Nothing is worth this conversation. Not even dinner. I hurry for the door, cradling my arms around myself. Sometimes I think I would've been better off with *anyone* else as a mom.

I'm almost to the hallway when—

"Tuesday!" Her voice explodes, broken, into the air behind me, stopping me in my tracks. I'm afraid to turn and look, but I do. Her hand is raised to her mouth, her face contorting into a pained wince. She lets out a sob. "I've been saving the dress that *I* wore to prom, for my only daughter. Consider it an early birthday present."

Guilt washes over me. She's been saving it for me all this time? And she *did* remember my birthday?

I don't know what to say.

"I hope you're happy," she snaps, foot tapping on the linoleum, arms crossed, eyebrows knit together in an angry bow.

I let a moment pass while I try to figure out what to say, but there's only one thing to say.

"I'm sorry."

She sighs, softening.

"Just try it on. If you decide you don't like it, well . . . I'll have done all I can. But before I die, I just want to see my only daughter in it."

She's really been waiting almost twenty years just to put me in this dress? My heart is pounding, the tears still threatening to come. How could I be so harsh? How could I say no?

I swallow. Nod.

"Where is it?" I ask.

THIS BOOK MIGHT BE ABOUT ZINNIA

"The attic," she says, her voice clearing up instantly. She pulls a pair of keys out of her muumuu pocket and tosses them to me. "Would you mind going up there for me? You know how my bad knee is."

I turn the keys over in my fingers for a moment, before she adds, "And, Tuesday . . ."

I look up at her.

"It's in a purple box at the far end of the room. Don't touch anything else up there. Understand?" she chides, stepping closer and leveling her eyes at me.

I nod.

My phone buzzes again.

Justin: This the right number?

I fire a text back as quickly as I can.

Me: Yeah! It's Tuesday. Hi.

Justin: About your writing. You ever thought about getting it published?

My throat forms a lump I can't swallow. *Published?* How? Why? I'd have to answer a million questions from people who read it and wanted an explanation. Like every single book we've had to read and dissect and tear apart and put back together in English class, inferring things from the text that I'm sure the author never even thought of.

Justin? Maybe one day.

The general public? No way.

I flip my phone closed without replying. Anyway, I have a dress to find.

The attic is *ridiculously* dusty. Fighting my way through a coughing fit, I pull my black turtleneck up over my nose as soon as I have both hands free from the ladder. It's dark and stuffy, and I can barely see, but I can make out half-open corrugated boxes lining the edges of the place, bursting with unfolded clothes and papers. I look hard, squinting in the dark, until my eyes adjust and I spot a slender purple box sitting precariously on a stack of . . . *stuff.*

All the way at the far end of the room.

Uneasiness settles into my stomach. I look down at the beam beneath my feet, only a few inches wide, like a balance beam, lined on either side by a sea of pink insulation.

There's no way Mom wanted me to walk across this thing, is there?

"Mom!" I call behind me. "Do I have to stay on the beam?"

"Oh yeah!" she calls back, clearly talking around a mouthful of food. "Stay off the pink stuff or you'll fall through the ceiling!"

I swallow, the pink ocean swaying just a bit as I fight off the dizziness. I study the box across the room, the only bright purple thing in this whole place. It must be the box with the dress. I extend my arms to either side and step forward.

THIS BOOK MIGHT BE ABOUT ZINNIA

Creeeeeak.

Goddammit, of course the beam creaks. Why wouldn't it? No one's been up here in years, clearly. Ezra's words echo in my head.

It's just us up here, Tuesday.

Remembering how he said my name sends a chill up my spine even now. I groan in spite of myself, shutting my eyes, wanting desperately to forget his face. The way his forehead grew dewy with exertion. I remember the way he breathed against me as his fingers traced my jaw, the way he looked at me as he said, "It's just you and me." The way I closed my eyes and gripped his shirt and drank him in.

"Ugh," I grunt, focusing my eyes instead on my feet, one after the other as I cross the beam. I'm halfway there when—

"Tuesday!" hollers Mom.

"What?" I snap.

"Excuse me?"

"Yes?" I try again.

"Did you find it?" she calls.

"I think so!"

Shut up and let me focus, I want to scream, *there's enough noise in my head!*

I'm making my way across the beam just fine, that purple box growing larger and larger as I approach, keeping in mind that a split-second distraction could career me off this thing and into the insulation sea. And then . . .

"It's a flat purple box, you can't miss it!"

Turns out an eye roll is enough of a split-second distraction to tip the first domino.

My feet stumble. I go flying forward. My hands find the beam, but my elbow finds the edge of a box stacked high with loose papers from magazines and newspapers. I watch, horrified and helpless, as it tumbles—"Mom, look out!"—into the pink, splintering the drywall below and sending an explosion of insulation fluff, paper dust, and blue TV light from the living room into the darkness up here.

"Mom!"

I'm frozen solid, coiled around the beam beneath me, as loose papers fall through the air around me. I can't stand up, and I can't see into the living room. But just when enough silence has passed that I start eyeing the window across the room as a means of escape so I can get to the landline and call 911 . . .

"Tuesday Christine Walker!"

The pitch of the screech is enough to make me wince, shutting my eyes against it. Ugh, can this day get *any* worse? I press the heels of my hands into my eyes. First Justin and work, then possibly going to prom, and now I've fucked up the ceiling, which we'll never be able to afford to fix.

I open my eyes again and sniff, the tears threatening to come, and find a piece of newspaper on the beam right in front of me. I stare at it, my vision blurring as I dissociate, but the

THIS BOOK MIGHT BE ABOUT ZINNIA

headline is so short, and so bolded, it catches my eye anyway.

ARRESTED

"Tuesday, are you all right?" comes my mom's voice.

"Yeah, I'm okay!"

But the curiosity already has me. Why is my mom saving this? I pick it up.

ARRESTED

Local businessman and entrepreneur Matteo Terreni was arrested on suspicion of money laundering but was released the very next morning. The Terreni family lawyer cited lack of evidence. "Everybody in law enforcement knows the Terrenis. I can't say much more, but I'm not surprised he's out already," said rookie cop Derek Foley Cooper in an interview.

I blink in total confusion, studying the picture of Matteo Terreni, with his dark curly hair and equally dark eyebrows, and his devilishly handsome smile, like a movie star's. The Terreni family. As in Ezra Terreni? My heart beats faster just hearing his name in my head. And this guy Matteo does look a little like an older version of Ezra.

The Terreni family declined comment in

> light of their preoccupation with the birth
> of Matteo's son, Ezra Michael.

Oh my God.

"Tuesday, keep talking to me so I know you're conscious!"

Irritation surges through me.

"I'm conscious, Mom!"

More conscious than she knows, reading this. I look closer. There's something sinister about his grin, the kind of smile you wear when you've cheated death.

Why would my mom have this? Was she researching Ezra's family? Why? Just because his family's trash doesn't mean he has to be, right?

. . . Right?

"Tuesday, can you get down?" she hollers from the living room. "I'm calling the fire department!"

"No, Mom, I'm okay!" I holler back, pulling at my shirt and stuffing the newspaper clipping into my bra. "I'm just, um . . . trying to find a way down!"

It's not a total lie. I do have to figure out how the hell I'm going to get down from here. I look around at the papers strewn all over the insulation, wondering what other secrets are up here. I *very* carefully press my hands against the beam and push myself up to my knees, when I spot another headline on a paper clipping just a few feet into the insulation zone. This one is also short.

DEAD

THIS BOOK MIGHT BE ABOUT ZINNIA

There's a portrait under this headline too, and my chest tightens.

I lean in closer, risking a fall through another section of insulation, to read more.

DEAD

Derek Foley Cooper, rookie recruit to the Philadelphia Police Department, was found dead in his home of an apparent self-inflicted gunshot wound. When asked for comment, police chief Eric Bryan said, "He was a good man who loved his family. It's a shame his life was cut so short." The loss comes just a week after Cooper took on the investigation into Matteo Terreni following his arrest. The Cooper family has asked for privacy at this time.

My heart is thundering as I link the two. Cop insinuates the Terrenis can evade the law. Cop is found dead a week after.

Coincidence?

My throat feels tight, and my hand finds my mouth as the questions surge.

Did Ezra . . . ?

Did the Terrenis . . . ?

Did they have him killed?

CHAPTER 5

Zinnia

2024

I CAN'T BELIEVE IT.

They call our names. "Zinnia Davis and Milo Reeves."

BOOM—lights, camera, confetti, applause!

We've won homecoming!

Milo and I shriek and pull each other into a hug faster than either of us can process it all, until multiple hands are ushering us onto the stage. We barely find our places in the middle under the blinding spotlights. I feel something heavy placed on my head, and I reach up and feel the crown. I know what it looks like from Brinley Harrison's crowning last year—it's *all* rhinestones, standing a good six inches off my head, with a huge zirconia crystal dangling in the middle. It fits *perfectly*, I can feel it. Milo presses his hand against my upper back and

THIS BOOK MIGHT BE ABOUT ZINNIA

holds up his scepter to the crowd with his other hand, his red-and-white kingly crown too big for his head, sliding down his sleek black hair.

The roaring applause swells as I wave to our classmates, who are masked under a dark haze past the glaring lights. I can hardly see any of them except a few faces in the front. Principal Keeley and the guidance counselor, Ms. One, stand among them, cheering us on. I wink at Ms. One.

She winks back at me and lets out a "whoop, whoop!"

Pretty sure I'm her favorite student. How could I not be? Shoo-in at Harvard? Straight As? Honor roll? Respectful? Pretty? Well, pretty enough. I clean up all right, and I know my way around a palette or two. I lift my gloved hand to my mouth and blow the crowd a thankful kiss. Our history teacher, Mr. Nostrum, walks the length of the stage and hands me a mic. His salt-and-pepper tweed suit does nothing for his warm skin tone, but his eyes are welcoming as he nods at me.

"Congratulations, Ms. Davis. Mr. Reeves."

Milo looks past me and nods his thanks at him.

"Thank you," I follow.

The applause simmers down to near total silence, and I raise the mic and clear my throat.

"Hello, Penn Valley High!" I grin amid another roar of applause. "Thank you all for crowning Milo and me your new homecoming king and queen."

And then I realize how formal and rigid and weird I sound. It's not me.

So I sweep my lavender gown to the side and work the stage.

"Wow, it's so weird to be up here. You know, if this had been a popularity contest, I don't know if we would've won. In fact, I was so convinced we *wouldn't* win, because we spend most of our time with our heads in books and so little time on the field."

I pause and survey the room, spotting a few smiles at the sentiment. I lean in.

"On *any* field, actually," I say with a sheepish glance back at Milo, who shrugs in agreement. A ripple of chuckles washes over the crowd. "Most of us here at Penn Valley have lived our whole lives in the tristate area. Long enough to tell the difference between a New York accent, a Jersey accent, and a Philly one. Long enough to know exactly how to use 'jawn' in a sentence and have no idea how to explain it to someone else."

More chuckles.

"But my world opened up," I continue, "when I started staying behind in the library at recess to read books. Shout-out to Mrs. Napp for cleaning up all the mini-candy wrappers I left behind as bookmarks. Sorry about that."

"I knew it!" calls a woman from the back of the room.

I grin, and I can feel my cheeks warm as the audience erupts in laughter.

"What I'm saying is, candy wrappers and all, reading

THIS BOOK MIGHT BE ABOUT ZINNIA

books—even fiction ones—showed me perspectives from all walks of life. Magical lore from ancient cultures in far-off lands, sure. But also, autistic kids my age. And nonbinary kids. Ace kids." I grin, glancing back at Milo, whose eyes warm. "Who are Black and white, like me. Who are adopted, like me. Who have and haven't been unwanted by people who share your blood, and wanted at any cost by people who signed papers before even meeting you."

The room is dead silent. All eyes are on me, faces serious. I smile to loosen everyone up.

"I've read about people who are different from me, which taught me to think outside the box I've grown up in. And I've read about people who are the same as me, which taught me I'm not alone. So if I can leave one message behind after graduation, it's this: Read more. Let kids read more. And fu—" I catch myself. "Screw censorship."

I give a half nod–bow thing to the crowd, who roars with applause, and I hold out the mic to Milo, since it's his turn. His eyes are *huge* and he backs away, cheeks bright red, forehead beading with sweat.

I know he's got some knowledge gems between those ears.

"Any wise words?" I whisper to him so quietly, the applauding crowd can't hear.

He gulps and takes the mic, offering me a final *I can't believe you're doing this to me* glare before lifting it to his face.

"Hi," he mutters, his low voice reverberating through the place, as smooth as a bass jazz singer. "Um . . . my piece of advice is . . . stop trying to keep up with social media. It's . . . designed to stay ahead of you."

Total silence.

I melt for him. My best friend. All the time he spends deathly silent, he spends thinking up stuff like this. He looks over at me. His *You understand, don't you?* look.

I'm all too happy to rescue him.

I pull the mic back over to me.

"Saying in twenty words what would take me two hundred." I chuckle. The audience joins me, grinning up at us as I sling my arm over his shoulder. "Milo Reeves, everybody."

A standing ovation.

More confetti.

Milo turns with his free arm outstretched to me, and I sink into his warm embrace. I'm not sure why, but I feel my eyes well with tears. It's like the whole room is cheering for *us*. For our fifteen-year friendship that's already withstood so much change. Now for the final hurdle.

College.

"Love you, Zinn," he whispers.

"I love you, too, Milo," I reply, burying my face in his shoulder. He holds me tighter.

"Promise we'll still talk when you get to Cambridge?"

My heart sinks.

When you get to Cambridge.

THIS BOOK MIGHT BE ABOUT ZINNIA

It makes it sound so much more *real*. I'm . . . really moving to Cambridge! Well, as soon as I get that acceptance letter, which is inevitable. So yes, I'm really moving to Cambridge! I'm leaving him. I'll be hundreds of miles away. Sure, we have X and Insta and TikTok, and even email, come the apocalypse. But it won't be the same.

"Come with me?" I say as a joke.

And he says nothing.

Because we both know that's not happening.

And later, when we're back at my house, and I'm dragging a makeup wipe across my eyes that comes away black, he lounges on the beanbag in the corner and pretends tonight won't end.

I look over my shoulder at him, his face just inches away from the book.

"Well?" I ask.

His eyes dart up to me, and then they roll.

"Ha," he says. "It's interesting. I'm learning a lot of . . . medical . . ."

Silence.

"Yes?" I ask, pulling another makeup wipe out of the pack.

"I'm learning . . . a lot of . . . medical, um . . ."

"You're doing it again," I say. Trying to read and talk at the same time. It's impossible for anybody, even the most brilliant mind I know. He sighs in resignation, setting the book on the edge of my bed and pushing himself to his feet. He stretches and yawns.

"I was getting stiff sitting that long anyway."

"Thought you were ace," I joke.

"You're the worst," he says.

"Love you too."

I check myself in the mirror, making sure I'm fresh-faced and ready for the best part of my nighttime routine. I reach behind me and unhook my strapless bra, hold the top of my dress close, and carefully slip the bra out the top, basking in the freedom of my most intimate skin breathing.

"Oh God," he says, turning away the minute he notices. "Warn me first."

"Sorry," I say, stepping behind the room divider turned makeshift dressing room in the corner, where I drop the rest of the dress to the floor. "If it helps, I promise I don't mind."

"Guarantee your mom does," he says, letting out a deep breath of relief.

"My mom minds *most* things," I say, unclipping the sparkly banana clips from each side of my head and resting them on the windowsill behind me. "Wait till she finds out we won homecoming not by being perfect, but by being ourselves."

"For real, though? Your speech was everything."

My heart lifts.

"Aw, you mean it?"

"Again, I don't say things I don't mean. And neither do you. So yeah, it was perfect. Just like you."

I catch that tone shift on "just like you." There was no lift

THIS BOOK MIGHT BE ABOUT ZINNIA 59

in his words. In fact, a darkness settled into the word "you."

"What does *that* mean?" I ask.

He sighs.

"I don't know, just . . . you have it all together."

"That's not true."

"Have you thought about how you're going to pay for college?" he asks, leveling his eyes at me.

Well, no. I haven't. But that's only because my parents have it covered. If they didn't, I'd be taking out student loans like everyone else. But I'd pay them off eventually, I know it.

I just stare at him, studying his face.

"I didn't think so," he says.

"Look, Milo, do you need money?" I ask. We've never fought over money before.

Ever.

Sometimes we'll walk around town near Franklin Square, where there's this *bomb*-ass dim sum place. I'll suggest lunch and then pay, because that's just what you do when it was your idea!

But I guess now, with the situation with his mom, maybe . . .

"No," he says. "I don't need money, Zinn. I just want you to understand how great your life is. I hope you realize that."

"Milo, where is this coming from?"

"I don't know," he says, eyeing *Little Heart.* "Your speech tonight was just so perfect, and mine was . . . I don't know."

"Yours was wonderful!" I exclaim. "It was concise, it was

well pondered, it was insightful. It was everything you could want in a homecoming speech. I'm the one who rambled. Besides, what if my life is perfect? Some wouldn't say so. I only have one friend—granted, the best friend anyone could ask for—*you*. For some people, friendship is a numbers game. Not me. Let me see, what else . . . *Oh*, my mom is a hovering—"

I catch myself talking too loudly and lower my voice.

"She watches my every move. You know this. I wouldn't be surprised if my room was bugged."

I'm not kidding. I look around the room for effect, but seriously, I wouldn't put it past her.

"Always watching," I whisper dramatically, before looking back up at Milo and realizing there are tears in his eyes. "Oh my God, Milo, what is it?" I ask.

"I've just been thinking . . . ," he says. "When you go to Harvard, you'll make more friends. More-perfect friends. You'll get bored calling me. You'll move on."

My heart is pounding in my chest. He can't be serious. Since the second grade it's been Milo and Zinnia. Zinnia and Milo. Does he think that's going to change just because I'm moving a few states away?

"Milo, I—"

The door clicks open.

Mom's face appears in the doorway.

"Zinnia, can I come in?"

I nod at her, wondering what is up with this change of tone.

THIS BOOK MIGHT BE ABOUT ZINNIA

She never asks before coming in. Because my room is "part of her house too."

She steps in, shutting the door gently behind her.

"I thought about giving this to you yesterday when it arrived, but . . . I thought after homecoming might be better. And I wanted to wait till your dad was home from work, but he had to stay late and . . ."

I spot the small white envelope in her hands, and my chest tightens. My heart stops. My whole body feels cold.

"Oh my God," says Milo. "Is that—"

"Harvard," I say. But this is all wrong. I just started my Early Action application last week. It's not even been submitted yet. They're not supposed to reply until December. *And* I'm supposed to get a big packet with welcome materials and lanyards and flyers about clubs on campus and everything. At least, that's how Mom and Dad got theirs.

I clasp my hands shut, as if maybe if I hold off picking up the envelope, this won't really be happening. This *can't* be happening.

But Mom's face is sullen. Ash. Her eyes are lightless behind her half smile as she holds the envelope out to me.

"Here," she croaks.

I stare at it and then at her.

Maybe they've changed how they do things. Maybe this is a letter telling me how much they're looking forward to getting my application.

. . . Or maybe not.

What could they possibly want?

I can't wait any longer, so I rip into the envelope and unfold the letter. My hands tremble so badly, I can hardly focus on the words as I read aloud:

> *Dear Ms. Davis,*
> *It's a pleasure to meet you. Before I begin, please understand that a decision has NOT yet been made as to your admission to Harvard College.*

All three of us let out a breath of relief, and I even chuckle at how much cortisol has been pumping through me for the last minute and a half. Milo smiles at me. Mom cups her hands over her nose and mouth and shuts her eyes to process all of this.

I read on.

> *I am the head administrator of the Harvard College Writing Center. Your guidance counselor, Ms. One, allowed me the privilege of taking an early look at your application essay to Harvard College, and she assured*

THIS BOOK MIGHT BE ABOUT ZINNIA

me that you hadn't yet submitted it. I am grateful for the opportunity, and I hope you receive my critiques with reciprocal gratitude. While your essay was decently written, and by all technical accounts "correct," I found it markedly calculated. It struck me as formulaic and expected. The story of your adoption is compelling—all personal stories are in their own way—but unoriginal. I have advised Ms. One to encourage you to rewrite your piece using a story that showcases what would make you a unique addition to the Harvard College class of 2029. Please consider this advice carefully. As you're aware, once you have submitted your application, resubmission will not be an option under any circumstances. I wish you luck in your endeavors.
Elena Valenzuela, PhD.

I stare at the letter for so long, my mom has to be the one to break the silence.

"This is *great* news, honey!" she squeals.

She can't be serious.

"What?" I ask.

"Don't you see what's happening? They *want* you there! They wouldn't send a letter like this to someone who didn't interest them."

Milo looks at me with just as much confusion as I'm feeling.

"They literally told me I'm unoriginal."

Basic. Ordinary. Boring. Stale. Mundane.

"They said your *essay* is unoriginal. But we can fix that! You still have until November first to revise it. Just think of something that makes you original, and you're in! It sounds like this essay is more of a formality than anything."

Resubmission will not be an option under any circumstances.

Doesn't sound like a formality to me.

"Zinnia," she urges, stepping forward and clamping her hands over my shoulders. I look into her eyes, just a few inches above mine now that I'm in my socks. Her hair, divided into a side part that she's tucked behind her ear, is looking a bit dry and sad, silver strands appearing here and there around her crown. I wonder if the stress of my college entry is wearing on her, too.

Her smile is there. Tired, but there.

"What's the most interesting thing you've done in the last year?"

Uh . . .

THIS BOOK MIGHT BE ABOUT ZINNIA

I think back. Chess club? Boring. Piano? Run-of-the-mill. Swim team? Heard it before. Summer camps? Practically mandatory these days. AP classes? Expected.

Shit, do I do *anything* interesting?

"I, uh," I think aloud, "I volunteered at that plant store in Fishtown last month. A hundred and fifty volunteer hours total?"

My mom lets go of me, pulls away, and exchanges a look with Milo that I can't read but don't really have to. Their silence says it all: my life is totally, perfectly *bland*.

"What, do they want me to do parkour or parasailing? Win the Nobel Prize or something? Jump on the next SpaceX shuttle?"

"No, Zinnia, stop being dramatic," says Mom. I know she did not just say that to me.

"I'm sorry." She breathes, pinching the bridge of her nose. "I shouldn't have invalidated your feelings like that. What I meant to say was no, Zinnia, I think you should go and think about what they're asking and come back to this when you've had some time. Okay?"

The urge to roll my eyes is otherworldly. Mom apologizes for invalidating my feelings only when someone else is in the room, when parenting becomes performance art.

"Yeah, okay," I say, racking my brain for *anything* interesting about me. I read a lot, I do a ton of different things, but they're all normal. All boring. I'm a biracial adoptee, taken in by two rich white parents who actually did their research on systemic racism, colorism, Black identity, and even hair care so they weren't clueless about what raising me would be like.

I can't even play the adversity card.

I stare into space toward my vanity, thinking. Maybe Milo's right. Maybe my life is *too* perfect.

The purple book sits there closed, the gold foil title gleaming in the vanity lights. *Little Heart.*

An idea lights up in my mind.

I look in the mirror, at the heart-shaped birthmark on my forehead, and I wonder if Harvard would find me more interesting if I wrote about what it was like to follow a bestselling novel to find my birth mom.

I look to Milo, who glances from me to the book to me, then cocks his head slightly enough to escape my mom's notice, but not mine. I can read his face like a book:

What did you just think of?

CHAPTER 6

Tuesday

2006

TWO MONTHS IN AND I'M ALREADY GOOD ENOUGH AT this to get annoyed by these goddamn people and their goddamn coffee needs.

At least I can swear in my head.

"What can I get for you?" I ask, tone even, eyes glued to my register screen. I don't even know what this customer looks like yet, but since it's below forty degrees outside, it's probably a hot drink, and since it's five forty-five in the morning, it's probably something efficient, made in seconds and not too pricey, so they can make it a habit.

One of those get-caffeine-into-my-veins-as-quickly-as-humanly-possible types. Businesspeople. College students. Gym sharks.

"Large coffee. Four shots."

Knew it. This person would buy an adrenaline shot to the chest if we sold them.

"Anything else?" I ask, my voice bubblier and more awake than I feel.

No answer, but he clicks a gleaming silver card down on the counter and asks the question I've heard a million times.

"Why's your name tag say 'Tuesday'?"

At least he didn't joke about me being—

"Born on a Tuesday?" He smirks.

I sigh.

A huge, warm hand rests in the center of my back, and my entire body goes stiff as I look over my shoulder and realize Justin is . . . touching me.

"A fifteen percent chance," he quips, leaning on the counter with a grin that's *way* too chipper for an opening shift—even if it's only three hours long—before we both go to class. "I heard a quad shot. Busy day?"

He takes a cup to the drip coffee dispenser, flips the lever, and lets the black liquid fill to the top in his hands—they're so nice. And warm. Probably.

Focus, Tuesday.

"We'll have that right out for you." I smile, the kindest way I've found to dismiss a customer to the delivery counter across the bar. He takes the hint, thank God, and I can breathe a sigh. So I turn to Justin, because I love hearing his voice.

"Fourteen," I say plainly, relishing the confused look he

THIS BOOK MIGHT BE ABOUT ZINNIA

gives me. "A one in seven chance is closer to fourteen percent than fifteen."

His mouth curves into a grin as he lids the coffee cup and slides it across the bar.

"A math whiz, huh?" he asks. "And you called *me* preppy. I bet you're on the honor roll too. Straight As? Cheer team?"

A laugh explodes from me. *Cheer team?*

"Now you're just flattering me."

"You look like you could be!" he insists. "Okay, glee club? You a theater kid?"

"Can't act for anything."

"I like that about you," he says, his voice suddenly soft as he folds his arms across his chest. "You're real."

I look up into those electric blue eyes and feel my heart race. What is it about this boy who's so refreshing and simple and unaffected by how awful the world is? Doesn't he realize how miserable life can be? How tortured humanity is? I wake up every day in pain, sometimes drenched in sweat, knowing I may have added to it. Made things worse. Or made things worse for someone who didn't ask for any of this.

Maybe being a good mother in 2006 means keeping kids far away from the world and all that's in it. Maybe forgoing motherhood in itself is a sacrifice of motherhood. Sometimes I wish my mom had been so selfless.

Just as I begin to sink comfortably into my darkest thoughts, Justin speaks again.

"Hey, you okay? You're kinda spacing out there. Wanna take your ten?"

It's a salve for my racing mind.

"Yeah," I say. "I'd actually really love that."

The back room is nice and cool. After I sink into my favorite chair in the corner, my screaming feet aren't screaming so loud anymore, and once my journal is open to where I left off in the story, my mind isn't screaming so loud anymore either.

I loved Land. I really did. Do. We coexisted once, I the sky and he the grounding force that guided me through life, less like a stone mountain and more like a winding stream.

Maybe preserving our flower in a tree was a frantic idea, half-baked and impulsive and borne of a primal fear of danger finding her. Was Land dangerous? Who's to say? If he was, he never let on. But a flower can't survive in the sky, either. She doesn't belong with me.

So I trusted her to the Wise Old Oak, not knowing what I would find inside.

Now I understand the mother of Moses.

THIS BOOK MIGHT BE ABOUT ZINNIA

I don't know Ezra's family. I've never met them. Don't know a thing about them—their names, where they live, or how they make a living. But I can't ignore what I found in the attic, and I can't stop wondering what the hell it has to do with my mom, and who Derek Foley Cooper is, or was, and why all of this was kept hidden from me.

Don't touch anything else up there. Understand?

What is she hiding?

Maybe I should ask her about my dad. Just once, again. Maybe now that I'm older, she'll be okay talking about it. What could've been so bad about him that she wants me knowing *nothing* about him?

Just because he's dead and gone doesn't mean he isn't still part of my story. And there's already so much I don't know about it.

Or Ezra's.

I pull out my phone, deciding this conversation would be better served via text. Then I can't hear her screaming at me in case this goes sideways.

Me: **Am I at all like my dad?**

A harmless conversation opener, I think. I hope.

Mom: **No. Why? Did something happen?**

My first inclination is to be honest, and I type, **I've lived my whole life not knowing half my story, and it's not fair that you're planning to keep it from me forever.**

But then I hit backspace until the whole thing is gone,

and I realize appealing to her emotions is the only way to get through—make her think I'm hurting over this, as a woman. As a young woman. No, an admittedly *lost* young woman. As a young mom who made a mistake.

Me: I feel lost.

Mom: You're not lost. You have me. I'm keeping his story from you for your own protection. Trust me, you don't want to know.

Me: Can you at least tell me what happened to him? His name?

Moments pass before I get a text back. Then another. Then another.

Mom: I can tell you I loved him.

Mom: That he loved you.

Mom: And that he wouldn't want you knowing anything about him.

That hurts me somewhere deep in my chest. Was he that much of a delinquent that he wouldn't want me knowing anything about him?

Me: Was he a criminal?

Mom: I said drop it, Tuesday.

That's exactly the confirmation I was looking for. If he weren't a criminal, she would've texted back a resounding no. But that was a yes. A vague, buried yet heavily implied yes.

So my dad was a criminal.

Wonder what his crime was.

THIS BOOK MIGHT BE ABOUT ZINNIA

The break room door swings open and Justin steps in, and my heart flutters. He spots me and smiles, stepping over and resting a hand on the chair across the table from me. I straighten in my chair, shut the journal, and pull it into my lap, where it's safe.

"This seat taken?" he asks warmly.

His apron is a mess, his hair overgelled and slightly sweaty at his forehead. He's his usual bubbly self but slightly dimmed today. Tired. Weary, even. I gesture for him to sit down, and he does.

"You okay?" I ask.

He lights up a bit at that and shakes his head.

"Just busy out there today. Maybe there's a convention happening in New York or something. Everybody seems to be taking the train today. There's a huge crowd waiting outside and—"

He catches himself midsentence and looks at me, glances at the journal.

"Well, don't let me weigh you down with work on your break. Whatcha writin'?"

"Oh," I reply, clutching the journal closer. "Just . . . more of the story."

"A story?" he asks, curiosity piqued and on full display. "You didn't tell me it was a story. You said it was a journal. Could I read it sometime? I'd . . . really like to."

I'd really like to.

But why?

"I, um . . . Maybe one day after I've edited it."

"Aw," he croons. "Well, if you write as well as you make coffee, you'll be famous in no time. Editor or not."

That's nothing like how it works. Even the greats have editors, and rightfully so. The writers know their craft, and the editor knows narrative structure and the publishing industry. It's a win-win for both parties. I've asked Jeeves some questions.

Not that I'll ever need to use the answers.

"I'd have to trust people enough to let them read it first," I say, and smile.

"You could start with me," he suggests.

The silence between us hangs thick and heavy as I blink in surprise and try to conjure words where there are none.

"I'm sorry," he says quickly. "You can trust me when you're ready."

"I trust you," I say too fast. His eyes flicker. I walk it back. "I mean, I think you're nice."

That's it? Come on, Tuesday, you can do better than that.

My inner monologue is starting to sound suspiciously like my mom.

"I mean, I think you're sweet."

"Sweet sounds good." He smiles.

Oh God, I'm giving him ideas.

"I mean, I don't . . . you know . . . I, uh . . . I don't . . . have feelings for anyone right now, if that's what you were thinking.

THIS BOOK MIGHT BE ABOUT ZINNIA

Not that you'd be thinking that, I just didn't want you to get the wrong idea."

I want to crawl into a hole somewhere and die of embarrassment.

"Wasn't implying anything," he says with a smirk, hands in the air in mock surrender. "Just that you can trust me not to bash whatever you've written. And that I really like how your mind works."

How my mind works?

He doesn't know the first thing about how my mind works, and that's probably for the best.

This journal, the one that's growing sweaty in my hands, is packed full of my most scrambled, disorganized thoughts. Sure, it's in story form, but it's nowhere near publishable. The bones are there, the story of the flower, and the land and the sky, and how they all develop and grow apart from one another, and how that's for the best.

But beyond that?

"Thanks," I say.

"You're welcome." He grins. "I won't bug you about it. But invitation's open. You can show me when you're ready, or not. Whatever."

He pats the back of the chair and stands with a smile and a sigh.

"Welp, gotta get back to the floor. Not on an official break. Just wanted to make sure you were okay."

My cheeks grow hot, however he meant it.

"Thanks," I say again, mustering a nod and what I hope is a warm smile.

Justin wanted to make sure I was okay?

He leaves back through the break room door to meet what I'm sure is a cacophony of coffee orders and customers in a hurry.

I glance at his backpack on the wall, the dark green Jan-Sport with the Spider-Man pin.

Could I, one day, trust him enough to send this home with him?

Bzzt. Bzzt.

Mom: **Make sure you're home on time today.**

CHAPTER 7

Zinnia
2024

But I never forgot my Little Heart.

Even when I was sure I'd never see her again, I always left her breadcrumbs.

I hoped that maybe, just maybe, one day, she'd find her way back from the Wise Old Oak.

Back to me.

"You're serious," says Milo the morning after prom, still in disbelief, shoving his hands into his pockets as he falls into step beside me.

"What could make for a more compelling college essay than embarking on a journey of self-discovery to find my birth mom, who I suspect is a bestselling author who wrote a book as a road map back to her? That's a *New York Times* bestselling pitch if I've ever heard one."

Milo wrinkles his nose at me.

"And *why* can't you just DM Jodelle and ask her if you're her long-lost daughter?"

"Because that would make for the world's shortest essay. And also because that's creepy as hell."

It's already weird DMing an author with personal questions, let alone something like *Hey, did you write this book about me?* Psychotic. I know how this works. Blocked immediately. Lawyers contacted immediately. Cease and desist immediately. Harvard acceptance gone immediately.

I can see in the way he stares sternly ahead that he's still not bought in here.

"Listen," I continue, "how hard can it be to make this book sound like Jodelle wrote it about me? Little Heart already has my birthmark, and she was taken away from her parents at birth. She *is* me."

"Did you forget the part where she becomes a feral ice princess lost to the forest of time?"

I blink at him. "I fail to see the inconsistency here."

He sighs and rakes his fingers through his hair.

"Let's just get this over with," he concedes, pulling out his phone. "Where should we start?"

My heart swells, realizing he's on board. What could be

THIS BOOK MIGHT BE ABOUT ZINNIA 79

more fun than looking for connections between two stories when there are none? Some people make a living out of it.

"Maybe start with the Wise Old Oak connection. Anything about Oak Park Adoption Agency that would suggest it's old? Or wise?"

"AirDrop incoming," says Milo, scrolling as we walk. "Looks like Oak Park was established in '71. Aaaand it burned down in '06."

My phone lights up with the AirDrop alert, and I accept, shoving my free hand into my peacoat pocket. This autumn weather is setting in earlier than it did last year. A screenshot of an article titled "Oak Park Agency Lost to Sudden Fire" pops up on my screen.

"Are you serious?" I ask. "That's a trope for the ages. Adoption agency burns down? A single hair on the shirt collar? She thought she was making love to her husband, but—*gasp*—he's actually been murdered and she's in bed with his twin."

"Why don't you put one of those twists in your essay?" he mutters.

I ignore him. But then the confusion sets in.

"Wait, that doesn't make sense," I say, frowning. "It burned down in 2006? Before or after I was born?"

"You were born January twenty-ninth. It burned down April fourteenth."

Almost three months later? That's . . . super weird. Why wouldn't my mom have mentioned they adopted me right before the whole place burned down? She would totally wear that like a badge. I can hear her voice now. *It's lucky we got you when we did—three months later and who knows how much more paperwork it would've taken!*

I wonder what's there now, where the agency was.

"Wait, what if, hypothetically, Jodelle wants me to look where Oak Park *was*?" I ask. "What's there now?"

It's not a completely unhinged thought, is it? If Jodelle supposedly left breadcrumbs for her princess, wouldn't she be smart to make the breadcrumbs something only the princess would recognize as breadcrumbs? I take to Google.

The spot where the building was is now . . . an empty lot.

Just a blank patch of concrete in Kensington.

"Never mind," I say.

We make our way down the sidewalk in Ardmore until we get to the sitting plaza. Sounds fancier than it is—an arrangement of outdoor couches and ottomans under a pergola. But at least they're cozy. And it's getting so cold that Milo and I are the only ones out here.

We sink into couches across from each other, eyes glued to our respective phones.

"Okay," he says. "So. Timeline here. You're adopted straight from Penn Montgomery Regional Hospital via Oak Park Adoption Agency. Eleven weeks later the agency burns down. Which is weird because your mom never mentioned the fire. Then what?"

"Uh, I grow up and live happily ever after."

THIS BOOK MIGHT BE ABOUT ZINNIA

But if this book is really supposed to be full of bread-crumbs, we can't get to the happily ever after yet. Not without some *drama* first. I read on.

> It started with the king.
> Born of royal blood, he looked down on his subjects from the highest tower in the castle, unaware of their worries. Iron-fisted and unkind.
> We were opposites from the start.
> I and King Land.

"King Land?" I ask myself.

"What?" asks Milo.

"The king's name in this book is Land. What the hell, that's such a weird name."

"That's gotta mean something."

"Well, it *has* to, for the purposes of this essay. And I'm sure it does for real in the book, but even with the context of opposites, it could mean anything. Land as opposed to sky? Land as opposed to sea? Land as opposed to take off?"

I flip to the author page again, where Jodelle Rae West's picture smiles up at me, and I wonder if I could contrive anything from her backstory.

"Milo, does she have an author bio on her website anywhere?"

"Way ahead of you," he says, then clears his throat to read aloud, "'Jodelle Rae West is the number one *New York Times* bestselling author of *Eastlake* and *Westlake*. *Little Heart* is her first adult novel. Jodelle was born and raised in Brooklyn, New York, where she lives with her two cats, Simon and Garfunkel.'"

Silence blooms between us, both of us thinking—and neither concluding anything.

"Should we dig up some Simon and Garfunkel lyrics for clues?" he mews.

"Hilarious."

It's time to read on.

> I couldn't tell him my intentions, the king.
> He wouldn't have understood.
> He certainly wouldn't have decided as
> I decided.
> What to do with her? She was perfect.
> Even her mark made her perfect.
> If he was Land, and I was Sky, and she
> was Heart . . .
> She was exactly as she was supposed
> to be.

I can't help but smile. Even if this book wasn't intended for me, it's nice to see another kid with a heart-shaped birthmark being complimented on it. Mom says when I was a toddler, I

THIS BOOK MIGHT BE ABOUT ZINNIA   83

asked about the birthmark. I would point to it and say "Heart!" all excited. And then school happened.

Other kids happened.

They tried to wipe it off my forehead. They pointed and laughed and called me the Queen of Hearts, not even in a badass way, but in the Disney's *Alice in Wonderland* way, and admittedly I could've been called worse, but it still hurt. It's not very big, either—the size of a dime—but it's *right on my forehead*, so it's the first thing most people notice. And Valentine's Day became a cruel joke. The number of times I had to hear "Zinnia doesn't even need to dress up" and "It's Valentine's Day every day for Zinnia!"

Bullies are so uncreative.

It's nice to see someone take something I've been teased for my entire life and depict it in a book as something beautiful.

"Any clues?" asks Milo.

I shake my head and look at Jodelle's picture again.

"What if . . . ," he begins softly, as if deciding how to arrange his next words. "Hear me out, and don't laugh."

"I'm totally gonna laugh," I say. He rolls his eyes but decides whatever he's thinking is worth the mockery.

"Well, if Jodelle Rae West is white. Like, *very* white. Blond hair for the sun, blue eyes for the sky, and white skin for the clouds—what if she's supposed to be the sky? And your birth dad, who would then have to be Black, is represented by the color of the land?"

My face must betray what I'm thinking, because then he says, "I know, it's problematic and borderline racist, but . . . do we know enough about Jodelle to label her not racist?"

"I mean, I've read *Eastlake* and *Westlake*, and they're actually pretty inclusive," I protest. "There's a Black family in there as secondary characters, and they're described pretty lovingly. No food descriptions for skin or anything, regular-ass human-hair descriptions . . . She does the bare minimum, at least."

I highly doubt she'd use dirt as an analogy for Black skin. *But* if it was a clue for me and only me, maybe I'd be the only one watching for the king to be Black.

"Maybe you're onto something," I realize. "If Jodelle is trying to tell me that my dad is Black, or to tell her broader audience that the king is Black, hoping I catch it, maybe she'd point to my dad as the first clue!"

Milo smiles proudly.

"Even if this whole thing leads nowhere, this is pretty fun," he says. "Hope you don't mind that we're kind of turning your hypothetical origin story into an Agatha Christie novel."

"Um, we're not?" I smile. "It's not a Christie novel unless someone gets murdered."

"Fine, Arthur Conan Doyle, then."

"I can get down with a good Sherlock story. So, Watson, since Jodelle is white, my birth dad is Black, so he's been nicknamed King Land. They're Sky and Land—opposites, another

THIS BOOK MIGHT BE ABOUT ZINNIA

vote for this to be a clue about his race. Oak Park is a tree in the book and an adoption agency in Kensington in real life. *Was* an adoption agency, before it burned down. What does this tell us?"

Milo is silent, staring down at his phone as I watch the wheels turn.

Nothing. It tells us absolutely nothing so far.

Time to read on, this time out loud:

> The king slept on the land, so in love with his family—the mountains, the rivers, the valleys—that he preferred the grasses and plains to his own royal bed.
>
> Our bed.
>
> He loved the earth more than he loved his own daughter.
>
> It would have helped if he had known she existed, but he could not see her.
>
> He could not see his own seed for the trees.

"So his family is . . . nature?" asks Milo. "So we're looking for a Black guy in his fifties who lives off the grid."

"She wouldn't be telling me to look for my dad in the Pennsylvania wilderness."

"Why not?"

"Because I'm not wandering around in the Pennsylvania wilderness."

"But what if he's just camping out in the Poconos waiting for you?" he chuckles, and then he goes dead silent. His eyes fly open, and he stares at me with mouth agape. "Zinn," he says. "Mountains, rivers, valleys? Mountainview River Valley Park?"

"Oh my God," I exclaim as a chill ripples up my spine. "That's a *great* connection! Believable, too!"

Puzzles have never really been my thing. Chess club was as close as I got to anything like that. I was asked to join Penn Valley High's cryptology club, but they were working on a puzzle that sounded . . . uh . . . shadier than usual, so I bailed until they figured out what the hell they were doing.

I dive back into my phone and type "Mountainview River Valley Park" into Maps.

"Uh, what are you doing?" asks Milo.

"Looking up directions," I reply, the implied *duh* heavy in my tone. "I know it's a few blocks from here, but I forget which direction exactly."

"Don't you have to work today?" he asks.

"Eh," I say, standing and slinging my leather satchel over my shoulder. "I've got two hours. How long can it take to walk through a park? Besides, if you think I'm going to pass up a chance to snap selfies to send in with my essay while we do this, you don't know me at all."

Mountainview River Valley Park is a nice-enough patch of greenery with all the expectations of a city park—play structures, an outdoor pool, tennis and basketball courts, trails that run all throughout the woods, gazebos, a couple of soccer fields, you know. Two little kids dart toward us, weaving around us as their apologetic parents give us a quick nod before jogging past to catch them. A mom walks by, pushing a stroller and talking loudly on the phone.

"I've just been worried he might have a speech delay, you know? How soon was Lynlee talking?" And then she pauses. "Ten months! See? Maybe I should get him into a program."

Ten months? I'm no parent, but that sounds *really* young. Are babies even walking at that point?

I make a mental note of reason 7,845 not to have kids. The sheer pressure of it all. I do not envy social media moms. Somehow they're always doing *everything*, and they're always doing everything *wrong*. My life is hard enough with just me in it.

The clouds have rolled in and completely covered the sky, but the brilliant orange glow of the sunset beams through most of them, turning the clouds a neon pink.

"Gorgeous," says Milo.

"Thank you," I joke.

"I meant the sky pollution."

"You think sunsets that vibrant are caused by pollution?"

"Yeah, you haven't heard? Generally, anything neon found in nature is poisonous—frogs, sea cucumbers, clouds."

"I guess that makes sense," I say with a smile. Milo walks beside me, his hand brushing against mine as we walk, and I look at him and wonder what life will really be like once I go to Cambridge. "So you haven't thought at *all* about what you want to do once we graduate? Sorry, it's just, you never talk about it."

"I, um . . . ," he begins, his voice shaky. "Well, you know the situation with my mom."

"Yeah."

I know exactly how she's feeling. It's why Milo never talks about her. She's glued to her TV chair these days, the TV doing most of the watching, since she's usually asleep. Steadily dropping weight, the number on the scale plunging as the number of daily medications climbs. She's wasting away, mummifying herself in her own pajamas. Milo brings her food and tries to focus on homework, while Natalie, the in-home nurse, dances around him to keep his mom comfortable.

I told him he can come over as often as he likes. He could literally move into my room at this point, and I wouldn't care. He's the brother I never had. I reach for him and squeeze his cold, slender fingers, and he looks at me.

"Never mind," I say. "How are *you* feeling?"

Cue the biggest sigh I've ever heard. A trio holding hands

THIS BOOK MIGHT BE ABOUT ZINNIA

89

walk past us, the woman in the middle making eye contact with me. Her short red hair sticks out from under a winter hat, and I realize, yeah, winter's coming *very* soon.

"I'm feeling a lot of things," he says, "but this is helping."

"What, following the book?"

"No," he says, "talking to you. I really appreciate your friendship, Zinn."

"Jesus, I'm not dead yet." I chuckle. "But I appreciate you, too, Milo."

We'll change after high school, but I know our friendship won't.

"Hey, you want to come over later and help me plan that super-early-graduation . . . *thing*?"

"You can call it a party without being a conformist."

"Yeah, but I never wanted a party. It's not that I don't do parties because they're conformist, I don't do parties because they *suck*. But my mom wants one. It might be her dying wish."

"Okay, so we won't have a regular-ass party, we'll have a Milo party! We'll get all recyclable-slash-compostable decorations, all of them black, with reusable plates and plant-based *everything*. Ooh, there's a viral recipe for vegan chicken with banana peels wrapped around barbecue skewers and roasted on a spit—have you seen it?"

"No," he says, the laughter bubbling just under the surface.

"Okay, it sounds unhinged, but it looks *delicious*."

"It sounds expensive."

"I've got it!" I grin. "I'll make some for the party with that vegan barbecue sauce you love."

"Most barbecue sauce is vegan," he says, and smiles. "But thanks, Zinn."

A warmth settles into my heart at the idea.

We walk down the main path, and I look around the park. The pathway was freshly paved, so it's smooth and still smells like asphalt. I smell something else, too, something sweet and salty—caramel corn, maybe? And I hear music—a guitar and a man's voice mixed among the tiny conversations around us. But I don't see him anywhere.

"So what exactly are we supposed to be looking for here?" Milo asks.

I don't know, but I take a deep breath of the evening air and can't shake the feeling of peace that washes over me, like turning in an assignment you *know* you aced. I think of all the ways I could make this essay *sing* if I really got into character.

What if Jodelle Rae West has been dreaming of me ever since she saw my heart-shaped birthmark at the hospital? What if when I read *Eastlake* and *Westlake*, I was reading my mom's words? That would mean I could pretend to have a mom who's super into reading like I am, if only while I'm writing this thing.

My heart skips as I wonder if my *real* birth mom is like that. What if we meet one day? What if we have the same taste in

THIS BOOK MIGHT BE ABOUT ZINNIA   91

books? What if she also can't get enough of a good whodunit?

Nothing against Mom—my adoptive mom—she'll always be my real mom. She grew me and pruned me like an unruly tree, so who cares who planted me? But . . . how cool would it be to have a second mom who was into the things I'm into? That's what moms and daughters are supposed to do, right? Find something they connect on—a hobby, an interest, a mutual understanding at least, a give-and-take while spending time with each other?

Otherwise, what else are moms and daughters meant to do together when both are grown?

A dark thought settles into my mind.

What are my mom and I meant to do together when we've done everything on the getting-into-Harvard list?

I waft that idea away and clear my throat.

"So," I say, "this is Mountainview River Valley Park."

I have no idea where to begin. We've already got so many pieces of fake clues on our hands. So many names. So many allegories. Mountains. Rivers. Valleys. Oak trees. Oak Park. Mountainview River Valley Park full of oak trees.

Time to read on.

"All right, Jodelle, we're here," I say, pulling out the book again and finding where I left off. I read aloud:

> I hid Little Heart away from him.
> Land was free. He was untamed. He

was an enigma, and I suppose that's why
I loved him.

"Huh," I say, zeroing in on that word "enigma." Milo does the same.

"So . . . he was behaviorally unregulated and emotionally unavailable?"

"Yup." I nod.

"Okay, cool, cool," he says, picking up the walking again, backward this time so he can talk to me as we meander. "So we're looking for an unregulated, emotionally constipated, midfifties Black hippie man who sleeps in a park for the love of the earth and not financial limitations?"

"We're getting nowhere." I have to chuckle. This whole excursion is quickly going off the rails.

"Yup."

"Let's just find something that could be the next bread-crumb, take a few selfies, and go."

I look back down at the passage I just read.

How is *any* of this information supposed to help my essay? Maybe I should get the *Little Heart* audiobook, fly through it, and write some contrived inner monologue about how I thought *really* hard about what it might mean for my origin story.

I stare down at the cover and let out a huge sigh, and Milo stops walking. He steps to me, takes my hand, and squeezes it.

"We don't have to figure this out today," he says.

THIS BOOK MIGHT BE ABOUT ZINNIA

"Yeah," I say, but even I don't believe my delivery. "You're right."

But I *really* want to. My application is due in two days.

A round of applause erupts for the guy with the guitar farther up the walking path as he takes a sip of water from his cup and coins clink into the case on the ground.

Even if we don't figure this out today, this cool air, the sherbet-colored sunset, this night with Milo—maybe one of the last we'll have before Cambridge—is too perfect to waste sulking about an essay.

"Come on," I urge, taking his hand and hurrying to the man with the guitar as he raises his hand to the crowd of about a dozen for silence.

"Thank ya, thank ya," he says, taking up his guitar by the neck again and glancing at me and Milo. His eyes are a deep brown. Kind. Warm. They crease at the corners like he's spent his whole thirty-some-year life smiling like that. Then he looks around at everyone else. "See if any of you young ones know this jawn."

I smirk at Milo, hoping he plays *anything* by Sinatra so Milo will know it. Or something from the '90s so it's all me. But as his fingers pluck the strings one by one, lingering slightly at the end of each run, I realize he's chosen neither. It's a pretty popular song, actually. Must have been released in the early '00s. But he's playing it *way* too slow as he starts in on the lyrics, turning it into a ballad.

"'I've got that word,'" he sings, his voice one of the most comforting I've ever heard. He reaches the end of the chorus, and before I realize what I'm doing, I hear my own voice join his.

"'Hummin' to myseeeelf.'"

Those warm brown eyes find me again, along with several other people around us, and while his guitar takes over the instrumental part between lines, he tips his chin, gesturing for me to . . . oh my God, he wants me to join him up there.

Do I know many more lyrics than that?

I look to Milo, whose eyebrows are raised sky-high, and I know what they're saying. *Girl, werk.*

And I guess if I want to write an interesting essay about following a bestselling novel . . . it had better lead somewhere interesting. So I guess it's time to werk!

I clasp my hands to keep them from shaking and step forward just as he reaches the next line.

"'I've got the place,'" he sings, eyes on me, and I don't fail him.

"'I've got the tiiime,'" I return. I'm no master vocalist by any means, but I can carry a tune at least. The small crowd we've amassed starts a clap, attracting more and more people from the walking path. A few people among them let out a whoop or two in my direction, and I feel the confidence swell. Milo is front and center, clapping along, watching me with that *You're killing it* look he always has at the ready.

What would I do without him in my life?

What *will* I do without him in my life?

THIS BOOK MIGHT BE ABOUT ZINNIA

The realization, all over again, that we're about to go our separate ways hits me square in the chest, and I have to swallow before we get to the chorus. I look to my left at the man with the guitar, and he nods back, reassuring me that he can carry us through the next part if I need him to.

I don't.

Together we belt out the rest of the chorus until his voice fades away on the last line, leaving just mine.

"'So I'm hummin', hummin' to myseeeelf.'" I solo as I hear the guitar slowing.

And he finishes the song with a flourishing series of explosive strums, complete with corny over-the-head arm spiral at the end. Applause rips through our little corner of the park.

"Thank you, everyone, that's my time," he announces, turning to me with a grin. "And please give it up for my impromptu vocalist here. What did you say your name was, darlin'?"

"Zinnia," I say, smiling, with a wave at the crowd.

"Zinnia, everyone!"

More claps as people start shuffling away, dropping bills and coins into the guitar case as they go.

"That was beautiful!" says the man, extending a hand to me. "Pleasure to meet you, Zinnia. I'm Ezzie. I'm here . . . most days, actually."

I shake his hand, and he bends to pack away his guitar in its case.

"Do you do this full-time?" I ask, slinging my bag more firmly over my shoulder and bundling my coat collar around my neck as a shiver creeps in. And then I notice his weirdly sparse outfit—a leather jacket over a T-shirt and jeans. "And aren't you freezing?"

He lets a puff of air out from between his teeth before standing again, case slung over his shoulder.

"You get used to the cold eventually," he says. "Gotta know where to sleep, though. Nighttime's when it gets real dicey. Shelters are mostly booked up, and open air's no good. Few folks get desperate enough to sleep under houses, but the ones with gas tanks are . . ." He pauses for a moment, something changing in his eyes. "Well, they can be dangerous. 'Lectric ones are fine, usually."

"Oh," I say. So he *does* do this full-time. He doesn't look it, given how clean his outfit seems, but he's apparently unhoused.

"Don't feel bad for me," he says. "I'm out here by choice."

My ears perk up at that. By *choice*? What if in my essay he were . . . but no, his skin is a subtle olive shade. Not nearly dark enough to cross Jodelle's shade and make mine.

"Couldn't really stay with my family, you know?"

"Yeah," I say, even though I very much *don't* know. I have two parents who would literally die for me, even if they have no idea what makes me tick. At least I'm safe at home with them. And I have the luxury of looking for my second set of parents—my birth parents—if I feel like it, or pretending a

THIS BOOK MIGHT BE ABOUT ZINNIA

bestselling novelist might be my birth mom for the sake of an essay, or not.

Milo steps up now and rests his hand on my shoulder.

"That was *great*, Zinn," he says, turning back to Ezzie. "I'm Milo, Zinnia's friend."

"Ah, great to meet you, Milo."

"Didn't know either of you were into the New Orleans Jazz Vipers like that," says Milo, grinning proudly.

Ezzie looks as confused as I do.

"Who?" we ask in unison. Milo's turn to look confused.

"Uh, 'Hummin' to Myself'? New Orleans Jazz Vipers, 2015-ish?"

Ezzie's smile turns warm and disbelieving at the same time.

"Son, 'Hummin' to Myself' is older'n that."

"Yeah," I chime in. "Like, '07 or something. And it's called 'I've Got That Tune.'"

Ezzie's eyes are on me now in total confusion.

"As in 1907? Little early."

What the hell is he talking about?

"Chinese Man released it in, like, mid-2000s. You know, with the music video with all the old cartoons in black and white?"

"Okay, whatever versions each of you found, they're both covers," chuckles Ezzie, index fingers in the air, assuming the professor position. "The original is by the Washboard Rhythm Kings. *Old*-school jazz."

"Sorry, man—if it's not on Spotify, I probably haven't heard it," says Milo. I nudge him. *Hard.*

"It's okay," says Ezzie. "At least y'all have heard *some* version."

"You could say, at least we've got the words. And the tune."

"Oh my God, Milo," I say, pinching the bridge of my nose.

"Keep this one," says Ezzie, pointing to Milo. "I like him."

He's hopped from the professor chair to the dad chair, but I don't hate it. Kinda suits him. But that reminds me.

"Hey, uh, weird question. Would you mind taking a selfie with us?"

He shrugs, smiles, and poses with an arm around each of us. I snap a few just in case they don't turn out or somebody blinks, and when I look at the photos, I realize just how perfect an idea this was. If I look closely, squint hard enough, my eyebrows *could* look like his, full and dark. And we both have big doe eyes, albeit different colors, with long eyelashes.

Essay's coming along great!

"Better get going, it's late," says Ezzie, turning to leave. "See you around, you two!"

"Oh my God," exclaims Milo. "Zinn, your shift!"

Shit.

I scramble for my phone.

Shit, shit, shit!

I'm already ten minutes late! Milo races to the park exit, and I'm right on his heels, knowing how Harlow gets when people

THIS BOOK MIGHT BE ABOUT ZINNIA

are late. And all because I got lost in the drama of following a good book. Understandable, sure, but *so* irresponsible. .

I glance over my shoulder at the last little clusters of people dispersing from the crowd, Ezzie among them, heading farther into the park, guitar case resting comfortably over his back as he walks. He shrugs his jacket more comfortably around his shoulders, and I can't imagine being him. Not knowing which house he's going to sleep under tonight.

And by *choice*.

My phone buzzes in my hand.

Harlow: **Ayo you okay?? Your never late.**

Normally, I'd shoot back with a text mocking her grammar. Something like *my never WHAT?*

But not while my heart is pounding at the thought of my perfect attendance record dissolving because I was on a *wild-goose chase* looking for my birth dad in a public park. I reach up and grip my hair, shutting my eyes hard against reality, before firing a text back while we wait for the train.

Me: **Yeah, sry! B there soon!**

Getting carried away looking for clues that aren't there instead of just, oh, I don't know, setting an alarm? I lost track of time. Made a mistake. Got lost in the story. Forgot who I was.

This isn't Zinnia Davis.

This isn't me.

CHAPTER 8

Tuesday
2006

THIS ISN'T ME.

I stare at the black velvet dress, which hugs me in all the right places. It cinches my waist and plunges between my boobs, showing a tasteful amount of cleavage, but *way* more than I'm comfortable with. I look like I should be sprawled on a chesterfield chaise with a Virginia Slim between my lips, short hair in finger waves with a single ringlet in front of my forehead.

But instead here I am, looking in the mirror at someone I don't recognize. I relax my shoulders, forcing them down from around my ears so I look a little less like Strong Mad.

It doesn't help.

Mom appears in the doorway behind me, and her face melts into the Mom face.

THIS BOOK MIGHT BE ABOUT ZINNIA

"Ohhhh," she coos. "Oh, look at my baby girl."

How can she still call me her baby girl when *I* have a baby girl?

Had a baby girl, I correct myself.

I shut my eyes and I see Ezra's face. My heart flutters, and I bring my hands together, hoping his memory will fade if I busy my hands, but I still remember his eyes as he looked me over. How they shut as he leaned in to kiss me. It wasn't love, I know. He didn't call me once while I was out of school. Didn't text. Didn't message me on Myspace. Or AOL. Or AIM.

Even if he really believed I was out sick from school for months and months with a random illness, to not even ask is unforgivable. I'm not sure what Mom told Principal Starr, actually—maybe a flesh-eating virus, or some niche disease that sounded so horrible, nobody would ask me to explain what it was.

I do not want to relive pregnancy any more than I have to.

Mom catches me staring into space and steps up to put her hands on my shoulders. I flinch back to reality.

"What's wrong, pumpkin?" she asks. "Don't you like it? You look beautiful." She studies me up and down again in awe.

"No, it's . . . fine." And then I fix that before I hurt her feelings. "The dress is beautiful."

She purses her lips to hold back the emotions I can tell are surging forth.

"My own mother would never let me wear something

so . . . I don't know . . . she would call it risqué—she thought I was wearing a mink shrug over it, but the minute I got to prom, I took it right off. But I think there's a time and place for a plunging neckline. And I think—I hope—after this year you've learned your lesson."

I feel my jaw clench involuntarily as rage bubbles up at the back of my throat.

Learned my lesson.

What was the lesson? Not to wear revealing clothing, or I might get pregnant? I was wearing a sweatshirt, bell-bottom jeans, and skater shoes, and Ezra slipped off each piece, one by one, just fine. Or maybe she means the lesson was not to flaunt myself and draw attention. Ezra approached *me* in the hallway. He invited me to *his* house that night. Or maybe she's hoping I've learned my lesson about trusting boys at all.

But I didn't trust boys. I didn't even trust Ezra. I just liked him.

I just wanted to run my fingers through his hair. I wanted to be close to him. I wanted to hear his secrets, what he thought of the world. Of his world. And I hoped he wanted me to be a part of it.

And unlucky for me, it turned out he wanted me to be his whole world for just one night.

And even more unlucky for me, it was on exactly the wrong day of the month.

So . . . I guess the lesson in all of this is not to be unlucky.

THIS BOOK MIGHT BE ABOUT ZINNIA

But then, what did it make my mom when she got pregnant young and ended up with me? Is luck, or lack thereof, genetic? Must be.

Final guess as to the lesson: Have good genes.

"Honey?"

"I'm fine."

I say it too fast. She doesn't believe me.

"What's wrong?"

I sigh. Might as well come out with it, or she'll start guessing.

"People will ask where I've been all this time."

She offers a half smile and steps in front of me, until I'm forced to look at her. She reaches up and cups my cheek, and her eyes widen slightly in realization.

"You need makeup. That's what we're missing."

How is that supposed to help me write an alibi?

"Mom," I say as she rummages through her drawers, pulling out brush after palette after lipstick. *"Mom."* That catches her attention, and now that I have it, I don't know what to do with it. "I, uh . . . I'm really nervous."

She smiles up at me in the mirror, unable to stop beaming at her daughter, who's finally dressing girly, just like she wants. She squeezes my bare shoulders.

"When I was your age, I was pregnant with you," she says. "I carried you, delivered you, nursed you, dropped out of school, and let go of any illusions of success I'd had before. And I promised myself that I'd give you a life that's better than what I had. That you would have more opportunities. I'm so *glad* you listened to me about putting this all behind you. Now, I want you to go tonight, and I want you to at least experience the last big hoorah of your senior year, like nothing ever happened. Hang on to your childhood for as long as you can, Tuesday. If you don't go tonight for you, then do it for me."

Like nothing ever happened.

Every hair on my body stands on end, and I feel my neck grow hot with rage.

She wasn't *nothing.*

My mom moves on before I can fully sink into the fury coursing through me.

"Just stay far away from that boy and you'll be fine."

"This isn't about Ezra," I say, even though I'm definitely *hoping* Ezra will be there so I can find out what the hell is going on with his family history. Ugh, what am I thinking? That's probably the *only* reason I'm going. "It's about everyone else."

Liar, I think.

"I just don't know if I can handle all their questions," I say.

"Darling," she says, dabbing the brush into the foundation, "that's just part of being a woman."

She taps my cheeks, then my chin, then my forehead as she continues.

"No matter where you go, or what you do, or who you grow up to be, people will *always* question your decisions. As a

THIS BOOK MIGHT BE ABOUT ZINNIA

career woman. As a wife. As a mother. You can stop to answer them, or you can keep it pushing."

I . . . guess she's right.

Whether I chose to keep the baby or not, somebody would've had something to say. *She shouldn't have gotten pregnant before she could handle a baby. She's the reason we have to pay so much in welfare taxes. Why is she applying for assistance when her clothes look newer than mine?*

And now that I've given her up, I'm afraid of different questions. *Why were you gone from school for so long? What condition did you have?* And, God, if anyone ever finds out where I really was, *Why did you carry a baby to term if you couldn't take care of it?*

"Just keep telling them you were out for a medical procedure and that it won't happen again. Because it won't."

Mom smiles up at me, pleased with her handiwork, before recapping the foundation and picking up a bright orange tube.

"Time for eyeliner," she says. "All the tweens are wearing it, so here we go."

By "all the tweens are wearing it," she means she saw a Nickelodeon special on the front of a *Covergirl* magazine that featured all the "hit makeup trends of '06," but she's probably right. To be honest, it's been hard to have anything on my mind but work, baby girl, Ezra . . . and now Justin.

God, why can't I stop thinking about him?

You can trust me.

I feel heat creep into my cheeks at the memory, at the thought of those hands slipping around my waist and pulling me close. Would he be gentle with them, or firm and commanding like Ezra?

That memory of the newspaper clipping I found slices my fantasy clean in two. The one that painted Ezra's family as a coalition of murderers-maybe-who-knows?

I look at my mom as she lifts the liner brush to my eye, and I wonder if she does.

Why did she have those clippings in the attic, after all?

I know I can never ask.

But maybe I can hint at it.

"Mom, I can't stop thinking about Ezra."

She freezes, brush inches from my eye.

"Don't tell me you're still infatuated with him."

"Infatuated" is the word she uses for me and any boy in my class. Anyone my age with feelings for someone else my age. "Love" is the word she uses for people her age with feelings for someone else her age. Grown-ups. People who have love all figured out, apparently.

"No," I say, giving her what she wants to hear, "of course not. But I keep wondering, maybe if I just *told* him he has a daughter out there. I don't know, don't you think he has a right to know?"

Her eyes narrow for a split second, but I catch it before she raises the eyeliner again. I shut my eyes and feel the soft brush line my lid in small strokes.

THIS BOOK MIGHT BE ABOUT ZINNIA 107

"If he wanted to know, he would have called you," she says bitterly. "He didn't even ask how you're doing. And don't think I didn't check the caller ID on the landline every time. I know his number from the school directory. His never came up. Not once."

"You think his family would care if they knew?" I ask.

"The Terrenis don't care about anyone," she hisses, with *way* too much venom to mean nothing.

"How do you know?" I ask.

They clearly care about their own, at least. Enough to have someone killed over it. Derek Foley Cooper was a big enough threat to their family that they took care of it out in the open. The way that article was written, *everyone* knew it was them.

She stops again and lets out the biggest sigh I've ever heard.

"I don't know, Tuesday, I'm tired, okay? Can't I do my daughter's makeup without talking about a boy, or are you that boy crazy even after all of this?"

That stings. Not just the term "boy crazy," which is the slightly more juvenile phrase for "slutty," but the notion that since I've been through "all of this"—i.e., birthing a child at eighteen—I should obviously be afraid to love again, or have sex again, or find someone of the opposite sex to spend time with again. Obviously, I should be hurt beyond repair, right? Embittered and broken, wary of boys, since I know from experience what they're capable of?

But it's not like Ezra learned about the baby and walked

out on me. He never even knew. He was never even given the chance.

From day one, after Mom and I both agreed abortion wasn't the route we wanted to take, Mom insisted that he never find out. It's not that I think abortion is wrong or anything, I'm still debating it, I guess—something she can *never* know—but I just didn't think giving baby girl away to a loving family would be worse. I keep hearing about all the families just waiting to adopt a child, and to be honest, I knew based on her skin color alone she'd go fast.

I look down at my chocolate arms, and I know wherever she is, she'll be halfway to Ezra's skin tone, so she'll have an easier time in this world. Hard facts to think about, but isn't that the job of a mom? Thinking about hard things to make sure your kid is okay?

"There," says Mom as she screws the cap back on to the liner and picks up the mascara.

"Do you think he's going?" I ask.

Her face, just beaming with approval at her cosmetic handiwork a moment ago, darkens like storm clouds foretelling a hurricane.

"You stay away from him, Tuesday." It's not a suggestion. "You gave up that girl so she would have a better life. And if you want to keep it that way, never let her father find out she exists."

My heart stops.

So Mom thinks Ezra is a threat somehow. That his family

is, even after she's several months into being raised by another family somewhere God only knows. That even after all this time, and the confidentiality of medical information and all that, the Terrenis could still find her. That they *will* find her.

And even though I'm not technically her mom anymore, what kind of birth mom would I be if I didn't find out exactly what she might be up against?

After a long pause, in which I realize I'm going to be alone in this, I nod down at my mom, giving her more of what she wants.

"Okay."

Her eyes linger on me for half a second too long, searching mine for a lie, looking for a crack in the foundation of my words. So I lay it on thick.

"You're right. I'll just . . . leave it alone."

After another half second her mouth curves, like she almost forgot to smile.

"That's my girl," she says, tapping my cheek before flinching, remembering I'm wearing makeup. Then she moves up to my hair and smooths my edges down. "You need some Vaseline. I'll go see if I have any in the cabinet," she says, turning to leave.

I watch her go, knowing she doesn't believe me.

As our Subaru rolls through the streets of Philadelphia, Mom lets out a huge breath.

"You excited?" she asks me for the millionth time.

"Yeah," I say, releasing my hands from the vise grip I didn't realize they had on each other. "Should be fun."

She's almost twelve weeks old already.

I can't tell Mom this, or we'll have a whole new conversation about *her* and how I should forget *her* and how *she's* gone and I gave *her* away so I could live my life without *her*. And then Ezra will come up, and Mom will realize that not only do I plan to talk to Ezra tonight, but I plan to talk to him about his family history and ask him what the hell it has to do with my mom. There's a reason those papers are in the attic, and I'm going to find out why.

If for nothing else, for baby girl.

Beep!

Mom slams on the brakes and leans on the horn as an SUV flies around the corner, turning left onto our street a couple of seconds into our green arrow.

"Shit," she mutters under her breath, and then apologizes to me, "Sorry. *Watch where the hell you're drivin'!*" The window's closed, though, so I guarantee he didn't hear that. "Philly drivers."

I don't mention that we're also Philly drivers, because Mom will say she's from Seattle, where people don't drive crazy like this.

THIS BOOK MIGHT BE ABOUT ZINNIA

As we turn, I realize how close we are to the school, and this dress is starting to feel a little breezy. I look down at the plunging neckline and tug it up a bit, feeling my shoulders bunch up around my ears again.

I wish I'd brought a jacket.

Even after all this time, the thought of seeing Ezra's face sends an electric pulse up my spine. I wipe away the thin film of cold sweat from my forehead.

"Oh, dear, at least leave your makeup alone until you get to the function."

I roll my eyes.

"Yes, Mom," I mutter, glancing at her, realizing she's wearing a black cardigan. "Uh, could I . . . maybe borrow that sweater? Just for the night?"

She smirks.

"Dear, then people won't be able to see the dress. Just work it, okay? Give it a chance."

No, then people won't be able to see me *in* the dress, which, the more I think about it, doesn't sound so bad. Why the hell did I agree to this?

Right. Do it for her.

"And dance a little, okay? For me."

It just gets worse and worse.

"Fine."

I'll agree to anything if it gets me the hell out of here.

We pull up to the school, and I can't hop out fast enough.

My platform sandals almost trip me up as I sling my tiny purse over my shoulder and shut the door.

"Hold on!" calls Mom from behind me over the sound of the window rolling down. "Let me look at you."

"*Mom*," I hiss as other kids shuffle across the sidewalk, milling around me and up the front stairs to the school. I catch one or two looking over at me, whispering, eyeing me like I'm some kind of ghost, an apparition haunting the school. *Look, there's Tuesday, back from the dead.*

I've been gone for only ten months. How does everyone else look so much older?

Jason, the tallest one on the South Philly basketball team, is somehow even taller now. Tyler from home economics is rocking a patchy mustache that he should definitely give up on. Chelsea and Courtney, the twins from American history, are wearing more makeup than I've seen either of them wear, ever. And they're wearing matching sparkly blue dresses that show off every curve they have, with high collars around their necks and cascading blond hair that falls in ringlets to their waists. Princesses. They smile at me as they walk past.

"Hey, Tuesday!" calls Chelsea. "Welcome back!"

I smile, some of the worry easing from my shoulders as I wave back at them.

"You gonna graduate with us?" asks Courtney. Chelsea elbows her. Tension's back.

"Uh, yeah," I offer. This seems to satisfy them, and they

THIS BOOK MIGHT BE ABOUT ZINNIA   113

smile and shuffle up the stairs into the building. I turn back to Mom. "I need to go."

"Tuesday," she says, and catches me, leaning over from the driver's seat so she can look at me again. I stop to listen, but I don't turn around. I already know what's coming. The same phrase I had to hear every day of school drop-off.

"Glorify the Lord in all that you do."

I clutch my bag and manage the words, "Yes, Mom."

Before I head up the stairs to find Ezra.

The music shakes the whole gymnasium with a new song—a deep bass beat that everyone in here knows by heart at this point. A few kids in the corner rap along with Timbaland.

I sing the next line in my head, and it calms me down a bit hearing music I've had to sneak to listen to through my boom box in my room on volume 1 so my mom wouldn't hear. If she ever found out I had "Promiscuous" by Nelly Furtado memorized, she'd kill me.

But she's not here anymore.

And Ezra is.

And then I spot him. Standing with Mike, Chris, and Josh next to the buffet table. My heart rate quickens at the sight of him through the dimly lit gymnasium with glowing pink and blue lights. The fog machine is working overtime, obscuring everything and everyone, so we're all dark shadows moving to the music. But I know Ezra's shape. Broad shoulders, and that sharp profile as he turns to look across the room. Is he taller now too? His hair looks darker than I remember, but maybe that's just the lighting. It's definitely longer now, curls falling just over his ears and halfway down his forehead.

I remember reaching up to touch that hair. How it smelled. How he smelled.

Whatever body spray he uses, I remember it.

I wonder if he still smells like that. . . .

Okay, Tuesday, keep it together. Remember what you're here for.

I clutch my bag and start walking before I convince myself this is a bad idea. It probably is. But I have to find out what exactly I'm up against with this—I don't even know what to call it—*Mafia* situation.

The music thumps so hard, I can't tell if I'm shaking or if it's just the rattling of the floor and walls.

You expect me to just let you hit it?

But will you still respect me if you get it?

I tug at my dress again, pulling it up, wishing I hadn't let Mom talk me into wearing it. The last thing I want is for Ezra to think I'm trying to flirt or be weird about this whole thing. I just want answers.

All I can do is try, gimme one chance.

What's the problem? I don't see no ring on
your hand.

I don't want any mess. I don't even want attention. I just want to know his family won't find out about baby girl, go

THIS BOOK MIGHT BE ABOUT ZINNIA   115

after her, and pull her into whatever they have going on.

I'll be the first to admit it.

I'm curious about you, you seem so innocent.

Mike notices me first, looks me up and down, does a horrible job at resisting a smile, and elbows Ezra. He turns to me, locks eyes on me, and suddenly I'm frozen where I stand. Even from ten feet away I can see his eyes flicker in the dim light. I could get lost in them. But I refuse to this time.

You wanna get in my world, get lost in it?

Boy, I'm tired of runnin', let's walk for a minute.

I steel myself. Clear my throat. Try to breathe as I step forward and the song descends into the chorus.

"Tuesday," he says, my own name honey in my ears.

Remember what you're here for.

"Hi, Ezra," I say, my voice sounding *anything* but casual. My hands are vise gripped around my bag strap as his eyes dip down for just a second before coming back up. He clears his throat and glances at Mike, Chris, and Josh, who get the message: *Give us a minute?*

And they leave, and then it's just Ezra and me. He closes the gap, and my forehead feels wet, and I feel wet somewhere else, too, and I hate myself for it. How does he still do this to me?

"I'm glad you're feeling all right," he says, *way* too close now. I glance around at the faces that have begun to notice us. People start whispering.

I take a healthy step back, and he stops, clearly blindsided.

"Uh, *so*," he continues, running his hand through the dark hair formerly hanging down over his forehead. Then he shakes it out and pushes it to the side. "What'd you, uh, have or whatever?"

My entire body goes cold. *What did you have?* As in . . . boy or girl?

Does he know about the baby?

"Ah, y'know what," he says, saving me from his own question, "that's personal. Forget I asked. I haven't been itching, so whatever you had is none of my business."

Oh my *God*. He thinks I was out for ten months with syphilis or something? I don't know, whatever Henry VIII had. Or was it Henry VI?

. . . Ivan IV?

The verses pick up again.

> *Roses are red, some diamonds are blue.*
>
> *Chivalry is dead, but you're still kinda cute.*

"Uh, anyway," he continues. "Did you . . . want to talk or—"

"Yes," I say, cutting him off way to sharply. I breathe, trying to relax. "Yes, uh, I just wanted to say . . . hello."

He softens and that grin returns, melting me.

"Hello."

I tear my eyes away, busying myself by playing with the little silver zipper on my bag.

"Nice dress, by the way," he says.

THIS BOOK MIGHT BE ABOUT ZINNIA

"Thanks." *Perfect in.* "It was my mom's."

I watch his eyes for clues. Any sign of hostility or apprehension at the mention of my mother. *What does his family have against her?*

If I'm ever going to get a chance to ask Ezra Terreni anything, it's now. So I summon every last ounce of bravery I can find and say, "I'm talking to you because my mom told me not to."

"Oh," he says. Now it's his turn to look around the room to see if we're being watched. My eyes follow his to Ashley and Ashley. Boy and girl. The emo couple with the fried bangs and matching snakebites. Eyeing us from their table, where they sit holding hands in total silence.

"You're here because she told you not to be here?" he asks with that half smile that says, *You're cute when you don't make sense,* and I try to focus.

"I want to know why she doesn't want us talking to each other," I explain badly.

He leans in close enough to whisper, even over the thumping music, and I can smell his body spray now and my heart stops. His voice is a gust of wind sweeping over gravel.

"Because she doesn't want us having fun."

"Ezra," I say, *fully* intending to sound sure and decided, but my own voice betrays how fast I'm falling apart under his gaze.

"Yeah?" His tone indicates he knows *exactly* how fast.

I hate that he makes me feel this way. But my mom's words pop up in my head. *Keep it pushing.*

"Does your family hate my mom?"

His eyebrows drop into the most confused face I've ever seen on anyone.

"Why would my family hate your mom?"

What? No way. He's bluffing. He's lying. But I'd be lying to myself if I said I believed that. Not with those soft eyes behind the words. Not with that earnest curiosity in his voice. He's genuinely confused.

"No reason, just, uh . . . wondering."

"Did she *tell* you my family hates her?"

I swallow. From the venom in my mom's voice, it sounded like she thinks his family hates everyone.

"Not directly," I say, not totally lying. "She just . . . said to stay away from them. And I thought maybe you might know why."

He clears his throat and glances away, regrouping and gathering his words before looking back at me. "My family has a lot of enemies, it's true. You don't become successful without making a few. But you're not one of them. In fact, I . . . thought about calling you. Several times. My mama wouldn't let me."

He did?

Focus, Tuesday.

Butterflies aside, that piques my interest. Does his mama have something against my family? Maybe just our moms are at odds?

"Why not?" I have to ask.

THIS BOOK MIGHT BE ABOUT ZINNIA

"She just said your family doesn't like people like us."

What the hell? Is this a race thing? My Black family doesn't vibe with his Italian family? Is that it?

"What do you mean, 'people like us'?" I ask, begging him to elaborate.

"I really have no idea," he says. "She didn't say any more. Told me not to ask questions. Told me to finish my dinner and go to bed. Both my parents work a lot, so I didn't question it."

Well, I certainly will.

"What did you say your parents do again?" I ask.

He clears his throat and says, "Manufacturing. My dad does a lot of business deals up and down the northeast quarter. It's . . . been a family business for decades. Speaking of family, what does *your* mom do?" he asks, his eyes narrowing just slightly.

"You know, my mom doesn't work," I say, folding my arms around myself reflexively. "She gets disability checks."

"Oh, disability checks," he says flatly with a nod, as if he doesn't believe me.

"You think I'm lying?" I ask.

"No, no!" he replies instantly. "You wouldn't lie, Tuesday, you don't have it in you."

The hell is *that* supposed to mean?

"But anyway," he continues before I can reply, "I'm glad you're here. I'm glad you're okay."

My heart melts at his smile. And for just a moment I

imagine him cradling her in his arms. Singing to her to quiet her in the middle of the night, standing by the big window in the living room, telling her a story about the moon and the stars that maybe his own mama told him when he was little.

I imagine him yawning and looking over his shoulder at me with weary, happy eyes, hair a total mess, and nodding at me, saying *It's going to be okay* in his own way.

I imagine him a father.

And the tears well.

"Thanks," I say, wondering if maybe in another life we could have been a little family. It hurts, wishing for something that can never be. My mom would kick me out, and it sounds like his would too.

We'd have to live in a motel, scraping together enough money to buy formula, while I tried to nurse and work at the coffee shop *and* finish senior year of high school.

I wipe away a quick tear before he can see, and I wonder what the hell I hoped to accomplish asking him about his family. Did I really think he would come right out with it and say, *Oh, yeah, my family's definitely murdered people in the past, and I'm so glad our magical night didn't get you pregnant, because then I'd be on the hunt for the baby, and how dare you give her away without telling me and—*

"Did you hear the news?" he asks, switching the subject with as much finesse as I have in this low-cut dress and sparkly

THIS BOOK MIGHT BE ABOUT ZINNIA

handbag. He steps aside and glances to the table behind him, where I see a huge silver crown studded with Swarovski crystals and a matching silver scepter with a softball-size glass gem at one end.

To the surprise of exactly no one at South Philly High, Ezra Terreni has been crowned prom king.

"Congratulations," I squeak out. Even though the whole concept of prom seems weirdly far away for me, even though I'm here in this gymnasium with all these people my age who probably don't think of babies any more often than they think about paying bills and working their fingers to the bone making coffee for people who don't give a damn how much money ends up in the tip jar.

But it's a status symbol, that crown. Ezra is adored here. Everyone loves him. Star student, kind, warm, caring. He said he wanted to call me. He said he's glad I'm okay.

He would be a *wonderful* dad.

. . . And he knows exactly where to put his hands.

Snap out of it, Tuesday, you can't have him.

"That's, uh," I continue, smoothing my hair against my head even though it's packed with enough Vaseline to stay put in a hurricane, "that's great, Ezra. I'm happy for you."

And then the natural question follows before I realize I don't actually want to know the answer.

"Who's prom queen?"

I catch his eyes waver before they drop to the floor.

"Uh, Amy Sullivan."

Predictable. She's also a star student, kind, warm, and caring. Once she loaned me her PE shorts when I forgot mine at home, taking the demerit for me so I wouldn't have to stay for detention and miss my shift at work. Amy deserves to win. And she's absolutely beautiful. Like, Jessica Alba beautiful. She could pass for her double if she were five or six years older.

"Ezra," comes that familiar voice behind me, and before I can look over my shoulder, in flies a whirlwind of energy from the one and only Amy Sullivan. She runs up to Ezra and flings her arms around him. "My king," she says, beaming. He looks at me over her shoulder with a face that's impossible to read. Is it confusion?

Amy finally loosens her grip and smiles up at him. Then, to my horror, she pushes herself up on her tiptoes in her Converse All-Stars, which are peeking out from under her sparkly baby-blue dress, and gives him the gentlest kiss, right on the lips. It's tasteful. Cute, even. Or it would be if I hadn't just been imagining him standing by my living room window holding our—

"Hey, Tuesday!" She smiles when she turns to look at me. "Glad you're back! Are you feeling okay after . . . well, actually, I didn't hear what you were sick with. You don't have to tell me, obviously, but people are wondering."

People are wondering.

She freezes like she's been struck by lightning.

THIS BOOK MIGHT BE ABOUT ZINNIA 123

"I mean—"

"What she means is," Ezra cuts in, stepping in front of her, "we're glad you're okay."

The look he gives her says, *Right?*

I look from him to her to him to her, and then at their hands, intertwined behind him, and a pang of anguish rips through me.

Ezra and Amy are *together.*

Amy looks on as I realize what the situation is. Not only is *the* Ezra Terreni not interested in me, Tuesday Walker, whose absence was barely acknowledged except as juicy gossip, but he's dating Amy Sullivan. *Perfect* Amy Sullivan, who's just inches shorter than him in platform heels, while I'm a good foot shorter. Amy's curvy and full in all the right places, while my pencil-skinny frame can barely hold up this dress.

The tears come again, and a dull ache trickles along my jaw as I hold them back. I want to run, hide, and die where I stand, all at the same time.

For ever thinking I could have something with Ezra, for picturing him holding our little girl, for imagining him telling me, *It's going to be okay.* I feel like an idiot. He's standing here before me, hands linked with his just-crowned prom queen, so as far as his life is concerned, it *is* going to be okay. He has his crown. He has his girl.

What more does he need?

The second the first tear falls, I turn and speed-walk as

inconspicuously as I can toward the double doors I came in through, shoulders high and squared, clenching my jaw, hoping it'll shut the floodgates. It doesn't. Two more fall.

"Tuesday!" comes his voice behind me. Now my name sounds bitter in my ears. I never want to hear it from his mouth again.

God, Ezra, at least spare me the humiliation. I clutch my bag and walk faster, sure there are eyes on me from all directions. I feel them closing in. My head hurts. The room spins. I haven't felt this sick since my first trimester.

I feel my face contorting into a grimace as I walk, and I realize all I want, more than anything else in the entire world, is to sit alone in a dark room and cry.

I slam into the crash bar, burst out into the open air, scurry down the stairs like a wounded rat, and bolt down the street in my sandals, which I'm not even sure were made for walking, let alone running.

Students here and there walk past, headed to the gym, all of them staring at me like I'm some kind of resurrected girl, returned to them from another realm. They'll all have stories about how they saw me running, and how they still don't know what I was out sick with, and they'll probably ask, *How was she sick enough to miss school but wasn't sick enough to sprint out of the gym like that?*

And right now I don't care.

In fact, I don't want to sit in just any dark room.

THIS BOOK MIGHT BE ABOUT ZINNIA

I want *my* room.

Once I'm well past all my classmates, and I turn the corner to the next block, I slow to a walk and scramble for my phone. I dial the only number I have memorized.

"Honey?" comes my mom's voice.

"I want to go home."

I will hear nothing else. I don't want to explain anything or even tell her why I'm done with prom already. I just want to lie down in my own familiar covers and forget about how Ezra's felt around me. Around us.

"I want to go home," I say again, my voice breaking.

She waits so long, my chest aches with anticipation. *Please, Mom, just this once, let it go.*

"Okay," she says. I don't believe it.

Really?

"Okay," she says again. "Just let me clean up a bit here and shower, and, uh, I'll pick you up in a couple of hours, okay?"

I hear giggling down the block and look to see a group of six kids my age walking in more formal wear, and before they can notice me, I turn and cross the street. I absolutely don't have time for her to shower and take her time and whatever else she wants to do before coming to get me in *two hours*.

I keep walking, hiking up the dress so it stops catching between my knees as I walk, looking around and realizing where I am. I walk deeper into Kensington, where the crumbling streets are even more crumbly, and the chain-link fences are falling apart, and it's impossible to tell the difference between a building with tenants and a condemned one.

The agency is just around the corner.

A thought strikes me.

If I can't get answers from Ezra about his family, maybe I can at least find out where she went. Maybe she was adopted by a family outside Pennsylvania. Who knows, she could be living with a rich family in the Hamptons or on vacation in Dubai. Nonexistent to the Terrenis entirely.

And as a mom—even a mom who will probably never see her again—shouldn't I at least make sure she did end up somewhere safe?

I swallow and shut my eyes, overcome with a welcome mix of relief and gratitude at a mission. A purpose. I have a reason to be out here.

"Tuesday?" comes my own mom's voice as she fails me, and I let her.

"Never mind," I say, my voice as even as I can manage. While my own mom chooses to leave me out here dealing with a crushing weight she doesn't even know about and probably never will, I resolve to do better.

Even though I'm out of the picture entirely, I won't fail my daughter. I will do better. I will *be* better.

"I'll see you in two hours."

"Okay," she says, and then as an afterthought, "I love you."

It's not a statement, it's a question. One that demands a response. Desperately begs for one.

"I love you, too," I manage.

Seeing me walk through Kensington in a prom dress, people probably assume I'm a Temple student. A few men stand outside a convenience store across the street, staring at me. I want to look away, but I'm afraid if I do, they'll do something ridiculous to get my attention. Like catcall.

So I stare instead, hoping it will trigger the opposite reaction. Being a girl is hard anywhere, but especially in public spaces. But then one of them—the one sitting on the stoop holding a cane, with a half ring of white hair around his head that's being eroded by pattern baldness—waves and smiles.

Not a hint of creep in his mannerisms. Just friendliness.

I smile and wave back, and the taller one in the white tank, muscular, with tattoos and sagging jeans, turns and spots me.

"Ay, sis, you straight?" he calls.

I nod, then realize maybe he can't see that from where he is.

"Yes," I say. "Thanks!"

Even in a gown with a plunging neckline, I must look under eighteen, because they're being kind and not trying to get at me. Either that or they're just genuinely kind and wondering what the hell a girl is doing walking through Kensington at twilight in a velvet gown.

In fact, now that they've been polite, I wonder if they would jump in to rescue me if something *did* happen to me out here.

I feel safe enough to retreat into my own mind.

I may not have the journal with me, but I can still write.

Land wasn't his family, but like the earth, he must have been forged in fire.

He said what he said so comfortably. *My family has a lot of enemies.*

And I believe him.

I don't want to meet his family, and I certainly don't want baby girl to meet his family, whether they accept her existence or not. If they want her gone, like they wanted that officer gone, she'll be gone.

The thought turns my stomach sour. I want to throw up.

And if they want her to be one of them, she will be one of them. And I don't want that happening either.

I picture her face, the glimpse I caught before they whisked her away, and that tiny little heart.

I want her to live a normal life. As normal as I can hope for. I don't want her inheriting my problems, and I certainly don't want her inheriting Ezra's.

A siren wails a block over, startling the life out of me. I clutch my bag and follow the flicker of lights across buildings as a fire truck turns the corner and whizzes right past

THIS BOOK MIGHT BE ABOUT ZINNIA

me down the street. Sirens are common everywhere in a big city. On the news every night, at least one person seems to pop up who's died of a gunshot wound or been stabbed in an armed robbery, or had a random medical incident not tied to systemic poverty or violent crime. So I don't think much of a fire truck flying past. Until I hear more sirens join in the chorus. At least four.

And then I turn the corner, the last one before my destination—the adoption agency.

The tower of black smoke reaches the sky.

The flames lick the side of the building, easy to see from the spot where I freeze, at the back of a scattering of onlookers, hands raised to their foreheads to shield their eyes from the blaze.

My heart races as I watch fire hoses unroll and blast sprays of water at the building with the sign at the bottom that reads OAK PARK ADOPTION AGENCY.

"Tuesday!" calls my mom's voice.

"Mom?" She flies up in our little hatchback with the window rolled down, gesturing for me to get in. What the hell is she doing here already? "I thought you were going to shower—"

"Thought better of it," she snaps, and I slide in and click my seat belt. She watches the growing crowd of gatherers as she slowly rolls the car into a U-turn on this narrow street, her eyes darting around like she's a rat trapped in a cage. I've never seen her so frantic.

"Are you . . . okay?" I have to ask.

"Of course," she insists. "I was just out running some errands. Are *you* okay? What the hell are you doing wandering around Kensington? Honestly, Tuesday, I can't even drop you off at school for prom without you straying into danger willy-nilly?"

She sighs and moves on before I can get a word in.

"Did you stay away from him?"

Oh God. What do I tell her? If I say no, it'll be a lie and she'll find out somehow. She *always* finds out. And if I say yes, she'll chew me out for hours and I'll never hear the end of it. But now it's been too long of a pause. I'm done for.

She lets out the most disappointed sigh I've heard since I told her I was pregnant.

"Tuesday Christine, you *talked* to him, didn't you?"

"He walked up to me!" I insist. *That's* a lie I might get away with. "What was I supposed to do?"

"Well, I hope you didn't mention you-know-who."

You-know-who. She's a baby, not Voldemort.

"Or our family," she adds.

I scramble, searching for the perfect answer, because I most definitely *did* ask him about our family *and* his family, and found out he's skeptical about my mom getting disability checks, for some reason. Once again I take too long.

"Tuesday!" she exclaims.

THIS BOOK MIGHT BE ABOUT ZINNIA

"Well, *you* weren't going to tell me," I hiss. "What was I supposed to do?"

"You were supposed to leave the whole situation alone! What are you thinking digging your grubby fingers into this? Leave it alone!"

"Why are you keeping so many secrets from me?" I demand. "I don't know a thing about the Terrenis or what they have to do with us, or why you hate them so much. I don't know about my own father, not even his name. How am I supposed to know why I need to keep my fingers out of it if I don't know what *it is*?"

"Because I said so!"

And I know that's the end of the discussion. She glances up to her rearview mirror again, and I turn and follow her eyes.

"It's nothing," she says, noticing my curiosity. "And by the way, this has *nothing* to do with your father. I want you to know that."

I remember Ezra's face, the doubt in his eyes. Ezra's a lot of things, but he's not a liar. He has tells. Everyone does. And in that moment he showed a glimpse of something I can't ignore.

And with her stressing that she wants me to know this has nothing to do with my father, it now makes me wonder if she wants me to *think* this has nothing to do with my father.

"What was his name?"

She clears her throat.

"I don't want to talk about him. Please, Tuesday, my back

is already hurting today—can you spare me *one* difficult conversation?"

She gets a better grip on the wheel as we roll onto the turnpike. "Just, listen, don't talk to him about it again, okay? You should know by now that you can't trust men—boys—with anything. You have to be careful how you talk to them, okay? It could emasculate them."

CHAPTER 9

Zinnia

2024

"HEY, FUCKFACE," I GREET MILO AS HE WALKS INTO the break room, backpack slung over his shoulder.

"I was right, wasn't I?" he asks without missing a beat, seeing past my cheerful tone.

"Yeah," I sigh, trying not to sound too dejected.

I was late to work. Too late. And got written up.

I guess it's not the end of the world. I'll have to leave this job anyway when I go to Cambridge. But that perfect track record was just so . . . perfect.

"So, what are you in for?" I ask, referring to his presence here as a representative of the hazmat team, and alluding to a prison sentence under the oppression of late-stage capitalism.

"Someone dumped a mattress out back that's covered in

some kind of corrosive. I think they were trying to dissolve it."

"Doesn't sound like that would work," I muse.

"It didn't."

I stare up at the chart on the wall in the break room as Milo steps behind me to get into a box of something. Everyone's names are listed on the left, all of them with at least one black X on a day when they were running more than five minutes late, and a few with a red X on a day when they were more than fifteen minutes late.

The single red X in the row with my name might as well be cut into my arm.

A blemished reputation hurts that bad.

Milo steps up and looks at it with me.

"You still have the most perfect record out of everyone. You should see the row in *our* breakroom. I have seven tardies."

Most people here at the café have two or three black Xs for the month. But at least he has a good reason for having so many.

"You're taking care of your mom," I offer. "Pretty sure people there understand that."

"Boss hasn't said anything," he says, still staring up at the poster, his mind clearly somewhere else.

"You good?" I ask.

"Yeah," he says, refusing to look at me.

Okay, something's definitely not good, but I won't press.

"So," I say, desperately searching for some way to change the subject, "dig up any dirt on Jodelle lately? Any ideas for

THIS BOOK MIGHT BE ABOUT ZINNIA

the next clue? Maybe we should DM her after all. See if we can get any new info on her. Does she have open DMs on any platform?"

He smirks, half chuckling, eyes suddenly pinned to the floor, like he does when he's irked.

"Milo, come on, talk to me, what is it?" I finally say.

"No, no it's fine," he snaps, lighting up his phone screen and opening Instagram. "Just noting that we're escalating to the next level of desperation here. Closed DMs." He opens the bird app. "Closed." He types as I look over his shoulder, navigates to Jodelle's author website, where her gleaming face smiles up at us, teeth perfect, blond hair curving over her forehead in a side part.

"God, she's so pretty," I marvel. "If she *were* my mom, she could've been saving up seventeen years of skin care tips for me."

"Your skin's already perfect," he says, his voice unreadably even.

"Thanks," I say, hoping my uneasiness isn't audible. I look over his shoulder again as he navigates to a page titled "Tour Dates."

And then I see it: *Union Hall. Brooklyn, NY.*

"Holy shit, she's going to be in Brooklyn tomorrow?"

He looks up at me in total confusion.

"Why are you excited like that's close to here?"

"It's two hours away! We can take the train!" I exclaim, my

whole body buzzing at the prospect. "We'll make a day trip of it! You and me! Mom will only lose her shit about things she knows about, remember? We'll just tell her we're going to a school homecoming gala or something with past homecoming royalty and *boom*. We're good to go for the evening!"

He stares at me in silence for so long, and goes so pale, I worry he's about to pass out.

"Milo?"

"That's tomorrow," he says flatly.

"Yeah, tomorrow's Saturday!" I remind him. "Free day! Neither of us work tomorrow, right?"

"Wrong," he says with a smile, but there's no light in his voice. "*You* don't work tomorrow, Zinn."

I have no idea what he's talking about, so all I can do is guess.

"You mean AP Lit?" I ask, the only difference between our two schedules. "Did Ms. Jarhill give you a paper this close to holiday break?"

"Nope, no paper," he says, arms folded, challenging me to guess again.

This isn't like Milo to be so closed off. And I don't have time to play these head games. I have two minutes left in this break, while he just got here. If he wants to play around, he can do it by himself.

"Fine," I say, stepping past him. "Guess you'll talk to me when you're ready."

"Did you read *The Well* before you gave it to me?" he asks from behind me. I turn to look at him, my whole body going cold.

"No?" I say sheepishly. "I . . . didn't."

Oh God, what was in that book?

"I understand the title now," he says. "It's a play on words. It's not about a literal well. It's about the well, as in the well-to-do, and how affluenza plays such a major role in narcissistic traits, which . . ."

He pauses for a minute, holding back the floodgates, like his thoughts about this are ready to burst out of him.

"Which makes the not-so-well-to-do . . . the well."

Whoa. Wish I'd read some reviews first.

I stay quiet, staring at him as I *know* the clock is ticking into black-*X*-number-two territory for me. But a thought hits me.

"Milo, are you saying I have affluenza?" I ask.

"I would never diagnose you," he says, "but I will say the book made me realize that every conversation we've had in the last few days has been about you and your essay, and your life, and your problems, and your mom."

The bite in that last word grabs me by the throat and threatens to shake the life out of me.

"What?" I ask, begging him to explain.

"Your mom," he says again, nodding bitterly, "and your backup mom, and the mom you get to pretend is your mom, for funsies, for the sake of an essay. I don't get to do that. I only have one, and she's dying. So forgive me for not being a beacon of light for you with this one."

Here stands this boy, this boy that I will love till my dying breath, with a mom wasting away in an easy chair at home, and here I am complaining about the mom who plucked me from the collection of adoptable kids available in 2006, casually deciding if I want to pursue the mom who left me with an agency the same year.

But is that really fair of him?

"Milo, if I don't ace this essay—which is due *tomorrow*, by the way—I won't get into Harvard—"

"Is everything you do for Harvard now?" he growls.

"Milo, are you . . . jealous?" I ask, regretting the words the minute they leave my mouth. "I mean, if you want to apply, you can still apply! You've got the grades for it!"

"This isn't about grades," he says, his eyes wilder than I've ever seen them, "but I guess that's all you can see."

That catches my attention.

"What's that supposed to mean?" I ask.

He smirks in pain, half chuckling, eyes suddenly pinned to the floor again.

"It just means I'm happy for you," he says. He smiles up at me now. "I mean, sorry about your perfect attendance. Some of us are busy remembering to buy adult diapers on the way home."

Where the hell is this coming from all of a sudden? I search

THIS BOOK MIGHT BE ABOUT ZINNIA

Milo's eyes for any clues, and for the first time in our ten-year friendship, he's totally unreadable.

"Milo?" I ask. "Be real with me, did something happen—"

He sniffs, cutting me off, and reaches up to his eyes, pressing his fingers against them.

"Mom's . . ."

His voice crumbles, and it breaks me. My heart is racing. Seeing him like this, in a pile of a million pieces in front of me, makes me want to run, hug him, and scream at him to tell me what the hell is going on, all at once.

And that question that's sending razor-sharp aching anxiety along my jaw burns my chest.

What about your mom?

"Milo . . ."

"Mom's not doing great," he says, cradling himself with his arms. "Natalie texted me to come home while we were at the park, and I stayed to help you out, and now I *really* need to go home."

"Go home, then," I encourage. "I'll call your team and let them know you're out sick tonight, and you can go home and make sure your mom is okay, and then . . . maybe she'll be feeling a little better by tonight?"

He stares at me in disbelief.

"Don't you get it? Mom is *not doing great. Chronically.* I can't just up and leave for Cambridge, or Sacramento, or anywhere else for college. Not like you can. And I sure as hell can't come with you to New York on a whim. So go track down your 'pretend' mom tonight if you feel like it. I'll be busy taking care of the only one I have."

The hiss of the steam wand fills the silence between us, but it doesn't help. His eyes speak clearly now, hurt and frustration swimming in his tears.

"I'm . . . sorry."

What else can I say? How can I make this better?

I never meant to hurt him like this, cut so deeply. There has to be a way to fix it.

"Could I . . . buy you and your mom dinner? I could order some pizzas and—"

"Zinn," he snaps, then after a moment of consideration, he gives up. Slings his backpack over his shoulder and drags his arm across his eyes. "You're still trying to buy answers to your . . . well, I'd say problems, but you like to pretend you don't have any."

His eyes drift from me, up to the schedule, and back to me.

"But I guess when the rest of your row is used to being perfect, one blip looks worse than it does for most people."

He reaches into his pocket and pulls out a small gray box I haven't seen in weeks. No, months now, isn't it?

He slips the little mouthpiece into his mouth, and I look on in horror. When did he start smoking again? Today? I swear I haven't smelled it on him since he quit. He was doing so well.

THIS BOOK MIGHT BE ABOUT ZINNIA   141

"My mom is actively *dying*, and all you want to talk about is your essay. You're only asking now because you feel guilty and you know you should."

"Milo . . ."

But he's already turned to leave, vape pen in his free hand.

I feel a tear roll down my cheek, and I quickly wipe it away, knowing what it would take for Milo to pick up a vape again, after all this time, after all the work he put in and all the self-help books he tore through to prepare himself.

I did this to him.

I squeeze my fists to calm my trembling hands, just as Harlow leans in through the door with her waterfall of red hair.

"Hey, you okay?" she asks.

I nod, afraid to speak in case my voice betrays just how not okay I really am. When I look at Harlow, I can tell she doesn't believe me. She looks me up and down and asks, "You ready to come back?"

I nod again, but she asks—probably because she still doesn't believe me—"Do you, uh . . . want control of the music?"

I find my phone in my pocket and follow Harlow to the front, pulling up the first playlist I find that might take my mind off all of this: 2000s throwback club hits.

First up is "Promiscuous" by Timbaland and Nelly Furtado, and I breathe a sigh of relief. It's not a sad song. It's not a breakup song. It's not a song that will catapult my weepy self off a cliff into sobby-mess territory.

"Numb" by Linkin Park is farther down, but I'll cross that bridge when I come to it.

In the meantime, I shut my eyes and drink in the pounding bass line, wondering what it might have been like to be at a concert in the 2000s. I asked Mom about it once. She said people just listened. And I was like, okay, but what else? Did they at least hold up their phone lights? Did she take videos? I know they didn't post them anywhere, because the internet was apparently good for nothing in those days. She told me once that early YouTube was just comedy shorts and music videos.

Was that all a concert used to be too? Were people just there to listen and enjoy the music and make out with strangers and—

Oh, and drugs. She said there were lots of drugs.

So, not so different from now, in ways.

I open the internet browser and click a new tab, wiping out one of my existing five hundred somewhere, and type in Jodelle's website. I wonder if she was the concert type in the 2000s. If she ever listened to this exact song while in a dark room with thousands of people all enjoying the same song. I wonder if she ever took drugs. If she'd ever tell if she did.

Her face is so perfect, staring up at me with a confident smile.

"You good to take this one?" asks Harlow, elbowing my arm gently as she tamps a little mountain of ground espresso.

THIS BOOK MIGHT BE ABOUT ZINNIA   *143*

It jolts me back into the real world, and it takes a moment before I notice the man standing at the end of the counter, looking on while Harlow prepares the coffee and I stand idle by the milk pitchers.

"Uh, yeah," I say, slipping my phone into my apron pocket and crouching to get a jug of milk from the fridge.

I operate on autopilot for my whole shift, totally unable to focus. By the time 4:00 p.m. rolls around, the time I was originally supposed to be off, before Harlow asked me to stay an extra hour, my brain is totally fried. After playing round after round of scenarios that *could* happen in New York tomorrow.

Jodelle's signing line could be so long, I never even get to the front. Actually, I've only heard that's how it works. I've never been to an actual book signing. Once, we had a local author in here signing books in the corner, but not a single person came, so I'm not even sure that really counts.

What if people in line get emotional and it takes *hours* to get to the front? What if Jodelle rushes me outta there so fast, I don't even have time to ask her whether she had a child seventeen years ago? That's not exactly something I can lead with.

Hi, Jodelle Rae West, bestselling author of three novels, including one that sounds like it's about me, but I promise I'm mentally stable and not a delusional fan who wants your money.

I pull the steam wand lever, grateful that the hiss masks my heavy sigh.

What the hell am I thinking going all the way to New York to meet a celebrity? That letter asked me for a more interesting story, not chronicles of a stalker. It's like sending in the opening chapters of the sequel to *Misery*.

I could stay here and write an essay about how my journey to find my birth mom through a novel led me to a dead end some other way, but I'm actually a better person for it because it brought me that much closer to my best friend in the whole wide world. That would work, right?

Or would I just be using Milo again?

My chest wells at the thought of asking him—maybe he'll forgive me and be willing to put this whole thing behind us—and then, at the perfect time, Harlow steps up and whispers, "You can take your last ten."

Yes! A ten-minute break is exactly enough time. I can't get my apron off fast enough.

I hurry to the back, where I fish my phone out of the pocket. As the screen flickers to life, my phone vibrates in my hand, and I read the message banner at the top. It's Mom.

Kelly: When will you be home? You're late.

I look at the clock. It's 4:37? I was supposed to be home seven minutes ago. She's even more uptight than usual today. Just as I go to text back something about picking up an extra shift and she needs to relax, I get another buzz.

Kelly: Did you leave your phone at work?? Why aren't you answering?

THIS BOOK MIGHT BE ABOUT ZINNIA

And then three more.

Kelly: Ok never mind, I see you're reading this.

Kelly: Maybe you doubled back for it?

Kelly: Anyway, be home soon. I made lasagna!

I grimace in annoyance, not at the prospect of lasagna—that's fine. Better than fine, actually—Mom's lasagna is delicious. But at the idea that Mom was *really* about to unleash her fury on me for being seven minutes late to the house. I resist the urge to block her on everything. I know she'd just call our cell provider and have my phone cut from the family plan.

So I do the only thing I can do. I text back.

Me: Hey mom, I took someone's shift. I'll be home late.

Kelly: How late?

Ugh, who the hell knows? Why is she riding me so hard about this? I'm seventeen with my own car. If I decide to pick up an extra shift, I should be able to without informing her about every waking moment I live and breathe.

And then one of the darkest thoughts I've ever had creeps in.

What if Mom is like this when I get to Harvard?

Holy shit, no. That can't happen. She wouldn't be like this, would she? Surely she understands that all the work she's been doing to prepare me for adulthood is so I can actually thrive as an adult, right? *Alone?* Calling her occasionally when I need to know how to schedule my own doctor's appointment or buy insurance or change a tire?

Surely?

No . . .

I *have* to go to New York tomorrow. I *have* to meet Jodelle. Not just for this essay, I realize. But because I need to do things by myself. For myself. I'm seventeen, and if I want to hop on a train to interview an author so I can have the best possible ending for this essay about looking for my origin story in a bestselling novel, then I should get to do that.

And if Mom finds out I went on a pretend quest to find my birth mom, I'll just tell her it's so I can schedule those doctor's appointments not just as an adult, but as an adult who's fully informed about her own medical history! Yeah! She'll believe that, right?

But Milo.

How can I abandon him? Would it be so bad to write this essay with a dead-end ending? Is that almost as bad as an it-was-all-in-her-head twist at the end, if it all leads nowhere?

Me: **6pm**

I text Mom back an exact time, not because it's necessarily accurate, but because I know if I don't give her one, she'll flip out and demand one. "For my safety," she says. Although if I'm not home seven minutes after she expects me, I don't know what the big deal is.

My phone flickers to life with a text from Milo that sends an arrow straight through my heart.

Milo: **Mom's gone.**

CHAPTER 10

Tuesday
2006

I searched high and low for answers but found none.

Not from Land.

Not from my people.

Nothing.

And with winter approaching, finding the tree again became less a casual pastime and more a dire search-and-rescue endeavor.

Normally, journaling helps, releases something in my spirit bursting to come out one way or another. But not today. Today I'm asking questions with no answers. I thought I'd steal a glance at the genealogy records at the library after work, but even they yielded nothing.

No marriage records for a Lorelai Walker, no birth records for a Tuesday Walker. As far as the library's concerned, none of us exist.

I know only one person who knows my father's name and what happened to him, and that's Mom. Another dead end.

I sigh and put the pen down while my headphones blast music into my head. Maybe I should let all of this go. Maybe it's none of my business. Maybe Mom's right and I'm putting her in more danger learning where she came from. But if I find out one day she's in trouble, and I could've done something to prevent it, I couldn't live with that.

The break room door swings open and in steps Justin. He locks eyes with me and nods hello. I nod back.

"Getting some good writing in?" he asks. I shrug. "That was the saddest no I've ever seen."

That gets a smile out of me. He steps up and rests his hand on the chair opposite me with a face that asks, *May I?*

I nod and slip my headphones off, the only sounds in the room those of the café.

"Writer's block?" he asks, sinking into the chair and folding his arms on the table.

"Something like that," I answer. "Things just aren't flowing right."

I leave out the part about me being on a quest to make sure my daughter isn't being hunted by the freakin' Mafia.

THIS BOOK MIGHT BE ABOUT ZINNIA

149

"You know," he says, holding eye contact for so long that it commands my attention, "might help to have someone else's eyes on it. Doesn't have to be mine. But sometimes it helps to put your thoughts somewhere else. They can start to look a little different."

"Different how?"

"Depends where you put them," he says, and smiles. "Long as it's somewhere safe, it's a great way to get some new perspective."

"Somewhere safe?"

"Somewhere judgment-free," he says, his eyes pleading. "Somewhere you can trust."

Silence settles between us, and I catch myself fidgeting with my sweater sleeves.

"Thanks," I offer, but when I look back up at his eyes, they flicker with pain. "I really mean that. I appreciate the company."

He manages a smile and nods.

"Well, I'm not on break. Gotta get back out there. I'll leave you to it."

He doesn't realize it, but I'm a minute overdue to return to the trenches myself. But I wait till he stands, turns, and leaves before I pack up. Moments later I pause by the door, staring at the backpack. *His* backpack.

I clutch the journal tighter against my chest. My heart is in here.

Justin would really love it, I think. I hope.

To him it's just a story about a princess, a king, and a queen.

My heart thunders as I consider it. What would be the harm? He knows how dear it is to me, and if I told him not to, he wouldn't share it.

What is *wrong* with me? I know his type, the cute ones who stay nice enough to get close, and once they're close enough to find out things about you that you regret sharing with anyone, they stab you through the heart and laugh with all your other classmates.

But . . . *Justin*?

He's different. I can feel it.

In the time I've been here, all I've sensed from him is kindness. I look into his eyes and all I see is soft, sweet sincerity. Tenderness where an ulterior motive should be.

"*Tuesday!*" calls Dario's voice from out on the floor. In one swift motion, before I can talk myself out of it, I unzip Justin's backpack, drop the journal in, and zip it shut again.

I'm back out to the bar in minutes, heart racing at the thought of the cute boy next to me maybe enjoying my story, even if he'll never know what it means.

And hoping, praying, he really is as safe as he says.

CHAPTER 11

Zinnia

2024

NARCISSIST: A PERSON WHO HAS AN EXCESSIVE interest in or admiration of themselves. *Webster's.*

Narcissistic personality disorder: a personality disorder characterized especially by an exaggerated sense of self-importance, persistent need for admiration, lack of empathy for others, excessive pride in achievements, and snobbish, disdainful, or patronizing attitudes. *Oxford.*

What's the difference between a narcissist, a snob, a diva, and a harmless person with confidence? They all sound confusingly, dangerously close, and clearly I've crossed a line.

Narcissist.

Am I really?

I check my phone again to read my last text.

Me: **I'm sorry. I love you. Text me back when you're ready.**

Read at 8:27 p.m. Yesterday.

It's 4:45 p.m. now.

Seven hours and fifteen minutes left till the essay deadline.

I sigh and pull my legs up to cross them. I sit farther upright against my headboard, fold my arms, and shut my eyes.

Have I messed up so bad that I've lost Milo completely?

Surely not. I messed up, sure. I could've asked about Brandy. *Should* have asked about Brandy. I should've made sure Milo was okay, should've asked him more often, *Are you actually okay?*

But is that really my responsibility? Is it my job to read into Milo's assurances that he's okay? To pry? To ask the same question over and over again in case he's withholding the gory truth?

Is that my responsibility, or that of a therapist?

I open my eyes again and stare down at what I have for my essay so far.

My name is Zinnia Davis, and last week I thought my birth mom was trying to reach me via the strangest communication method of all time: a bestselling novel.

I sigh.

Not my strongest opening.

Does Jodelle ever feel insecure when she starts writing a

THIS BOOK MIGHT BE ABOUT ZINNIA

novel? Hesitant? Anxious, even? Or do the words just flow right out of her fingertips as she types, as easily as they do for me when I'm telling a story out loud?

I've seen professional writers talk about having writer's block, but somehow when I'm reading Jodelle's work, I can't picture it. Everything's written so smoothly, the thought of her bungling over notes from her editor just doesn't compute.

I take a deep breath and keep typing, because I read somewhere that the cure for writer's block is to type without thinking. I stream-of-conscious my way through the next paragraph:

You may think this narcissistic of me. Who am I that a bestselling novelist would write an entire book about me, just to find me again seventeen years after giving me away?

I pause, wondering if my real birth mom ever did consider keeping me. I guess it shouldn't matter if she gave me away for my own good or threw me away like a freshly clipped hangnail—either way I ended up in the loving arms of Kelly and Ben Davis, typical white couple in the suburbs.

But I do wonder if I can confidently use the words "after giving me away" if I don't know if she did.

I hit backspace and type *after saying goodbye.*

That sentence at the beginning of the prologue crops up again. *I lost her far too soon.*

I spot the book sitting on my vanity, and I imagine Jodelle sitting at her writing desk—or with the kind of money she makes, more likely her writing yacht—thinking of me. Even if she didn't, I have to sell the fantasy here.

I delete *after saying goodbye* and type *after she lost me.*

There we go. I can feel the inspiration flowing now.

Her words, not mine. It's right there at the beginning of the prologue, after Jodelle has already described the "her" in question by the heart-shaped birthmark on her forehead. You can see why this book piqued my interest. A girl lost at birth and named after a birthmark the same shape and location as mine? One coincidence is happenstance. Two is an anomaly. Three is a pattern. I had to investigate.

And then I'll go into detail about that first clue—Land as my Black father, Sky as my white mother, and the possibility of them creating a little flower child together named Zinnia.

It all works!

So why is there a nagging sense that I'm missing something?

I open my phone again to check for a text from Milo.

Still nothing.

A pang of guilt washes over me, wondering if he'll ever text me again. What if this is goodbye forever?

I take a deep breath and close out of Messages because, *We're not gonna think about that right now, Zinnia. Put your feelings in a box, where they can't get to you.*

I lean my head back against the headboard and shut my eyes again.

THIS BOOK MIGHT BE ABOUT ZINNIA

Do I go to New York tonight?

Do I meet Jodelle in her signing line?

I open my eyes again and stare down at my phone.

Do I leave Milo?

A text lights up my phone screen, sending my heart soaring with hope and then plummeting again as I read the text from my mom letting me know it's time to socialize and pretend everything's all right.

Kelly: Dinner's ready!

CHAPTER 12

Tuesday
2006

"I'M ALMOST FINISHED READING IT, BY THE WAY," HE says simply.

Oh God.

"The journal?" I ask.

"Course! Just got to the twist. It's a beautiful story! Gorgeous prose. Your dialogue is pretty poetic too. Slow and meandering, like smooth jazz."

"So the book equivalent of elevator music," I say, and smirk. "Thanks."

"You know what I mean," he says with an eye roll. "It was comfortable. Cozy. Like a daydream."

"Thanks," I offer, my voice and my hands shaky.

He's *reading it.*

THIS BOOK MIGHT BE ABOUT ZINNIA

Justin is . . . *reading it.* My thoughts, my hopes, my memories, and he said they're like a daydream. Warmth settles into me like a welcome embrace, and I can't force my face out of a smile.

The front door jingles, and I duck behind him and toward the storeroom, because I can't deal with another customer right now.

"Psst," he hisses behind me. "Customer at two o'clock."

But I'm already gone.

"Welcome in!" comes Justin's cheerful voice. He's mastered the art of pivoting. My trembling hands find the box I'm looking for marked DARK ROAST. I'm going to stay back here for as long as I can get away with and focus on breathing. I'm afraid if I go back out there and one more customer asks if I was born on a Tuesday, my social-agreeability facade will start to crack.

I yank the box cutter across the tape, gritting my teeth and unleashing all my pent-up energy on it, when I feel the sharp, searing sting across my finger. I jump back, stifling a yelp as the box cutter falls to the ground with a *clang!*

"Dammit," I mutter, sucking on my finger until the taste of blood permeates my whole mouth. I take it out and look at it—a long cut, but shallow. I won't need stitches, but I will need a Band-Aid and a glove for food safety. Which means . . . ugh, here I go back out to the bar, where we keep the first aid kit.

I click the box cutter closed before I head back toward the café, where a crisp, highfalutin voice rips straight through me, commanding my attention.

"Yes, Anders, I know—I told you I'd get you the next draft soon, and I will have the next draft *soon*."

A woman stands at the counter with a BlackBerry to her ear, cradled with her shoulder while she fumbles around in her Burberry bag for something. She pulls out a clutch-size wallet, unzips it, and slips out a gleaming silver card, then hands it to Justin without even looking at him. She's white. Blond, short hair just past her earlobes. Lips a tasteful berry. Nails to match. She repositions the phone, totally lost in whatever phone call she's on as Justin slides her coffee over the counter to her.

"Anders, have I ever missed a deadline?" she asks, clearly affronted.

A long pause while she waits for an answer. She picks up the coffee. Turns to the seating area, where she finds her table.

"Well, yes, *moved* a deadline. That doesn't count. Look, you know I make clean first drafts, and I will have something respectable for you by May. I just need another month, okay? Don't be such a hard-ass. Rome wasn't built in a day."

She takes her seat, and I keep my eyes on her as I move back to the bar. I can feel Justin looking at me.

"Do you know who that is?" he whispers, his eyes huge with shock.

THIS BOOK MIGHT BE ABOUT ZINNIA

"Um," I begin, "Barbra Streisand."

His mouth is a sarcastic flat line.

"Jodelle Rae West," he says. "*Huge* author. Very famous. Probably never had to shop for herself in her life. I'm sure she'd love to hear about your writing."

Every ounce of blood in my body seems to evacuate to somewhere else, and I feel my head grow cold at the suggestion.

"What?" I manage.

"People do it all the time! You should ask to send her your manuscript! She might take a look, send it to her agent, and get your name out there! You could get a book deal out of this and never have to deal with us café riffraff again—"

"No," I say definitively.

"What? Why not?" he asks.

How do I explain this to him?

How do I explain that my journal is my most personal thought bank? It was a leap of faith even to let Justin read it, let alone hand it over to a woman I've never met. Let alone see it on shelves. Let alone sit at the end of a signing line, looking people in the eye who will no doubt have endless questions about my deepest, darkest thoughts and insecurities.

It's more than a simple story about a princess and her parents, who lose her in the woods as winter falls. It's an exploration of everything I wonder about motherhood and daughterhood. What makes a good mom? What makes a good daughter? Are mothers allowed to set boundaries and say *Hey, I don't think I can actually take care of you—please go live with the family you deserve* without being shamed and made to feel like they've failed? Would I have been a better mother if I'd kept her? Raised her myself? When she could've gone to live with parents who make more than nine dollars per hour plus tips and actually *want* a child? Are daughters allowed to say *Hey, I don't like the way you're raising me—I feel suffocated and isolated and guilty for being mad at you*?

I'm sure Justin missed *all* of that. Maybe because he's a boy. Maybe because he's neither a mother nor a daughter. Maybe he'll never get it. Maybe the world will never get it. Maybe whoever reads the book will misunderstand what I'm trying to say with it. Maybe they'll think I'm not just a failure of a daughter and a mother, but a monster.

My throat is hot. Breathing is hard. My forehead feels damp as I imagine someone looking me in the eye and asking, *So, what was the inspiration behind the princess in the story?*

Even with all the time in the world to actually finish the story, I couldn't possibly share it. Couldn't possibly relive everything that's happened.

How could he understand?

"I just can't, Justin," I say, pulling out the dark roast bags to stock them. "Sorry."

THIS BOOK MIGHT BE ABOUT ZINNIA   161

Justin: Sorry if I said something I shouldn't have. I just think you're really talented.

That was the last text he sent me, and I've read it and reread it about fifty times now, trying to figure out what to say back.

I've typed and deleted, and typed and deleted, and typed and deleted.

Me: You didn't say anything you shouldn't have.

But he did. Delete.

Me: Thanks.

For the apology or for saying I'm talented? Delete.

Me: It's ok.

But it's not.

I sigh, flip my phone closed, drop it on the bed, and bury my face in my hands. My entire body is buzzing, tripping over the millions of options I could text back. I'm not ready to text back, and it's been too long, and he's probably wondering what's taking me so long, or where I went, or if I fell asleep. And I mean, after a morning shift and a whole day of school, that might be believable.

Bzzt. Bzzt.

I flip it open again, cursing the butterflies it sends fluttering. Justin saves me with another text.

Justin: Do you want the journal back? I'd offer to stop reading it, but I just finished it.

My heart stops.

He knows the end. He knows the twist.

Me: What did you think?

Moments pass. Too many moments. So many moments that I wonder if he hated it.

He must have hated it. Otherwise, why wouldn't he just text back a simple *I loved it!* Or an *It was great!* I'd even take a *With some editing, it could be a real book!* But then he finally answers.

Justin: I thought it was gorgeous.

My face grows hot. *Gorgeous?*

Justin: I really think you could be famous one day.

Now he's just flattering me.

. . . Isn't he?

Before I can even type a thank-you back, he texts again.

Justin: Someone out there can help you make a career out of it.

Me: Thanks.

Justin: I'm serious!

Me: Why are you so stuck on this?

What's with him and trying to show random people my work? Famous or not, what would they even do with it? My journal's not even a typed manuscript yet. It's handwritten scrawl with notes in the margins—*nobody* is going to read it.

Nobody professional, anyway.

Justin: You know Eminem got discovered after sending in a mixtape, right?

THIS BOOK MIGHT BE ABOUT ZINNIA

Except Eminem is actually *good*.

And me? I just write from my heart.

Me: Let me edit it first. Can you give it back tomorrow?

Maybe after I get it back, I can keep putting this off until he forgets about it. Maybe he'll lose interest.

My bedroom door handle turns and clicks open, startling the phone out of my hand. Mom leans in and locks eyes on me, clocking my surprise. Glances at my phone.

"Who were you texting?"

"Not Ezra," I say, sitting upright and grabbing my phone again, flipping it closed. Her eyebrows lift just a touch, and I quickly recover with "Promise," and further when the suspicion lingers on her face, "It was from work."

Which isn't a lie. Just an omission of the truth.

"It's okay," she says, and smiles suddenly. "I trust you."

She . . . *what*?

The suspicion must show on my face now, because she laughs. But not her normal laugh. It seems to explode from her, bursting through cracks in a wall she's desperately trying to keep up.

"Don't look at me like that," she says, folding her arms and leaning against the doorjamb to try to play it off. She sighs and looks at the floor, lost in thought.

I consider asking her if she's okay, but I already know the answer. First, a *Hmm?* to indicate that she didn't quite hear me, but really it's to give herself time to think up a selfless response like *Oh, I'm fine, honey*, when she knows I know that she's not fine, that she's visibly tired, and that everything she does is in the name of self-sacrifice, because she's a mom and she's not allowed to complain about being tired.

But why not? I've always wondered. You can complain about being tired without expecting something in return, right? Why can't moms?

Does it make someone a bad mom if she says out loud that she's tired? Is there some unspoken rule that you can't do that as a parent? And how do moms everywhere know this?

She must sense me staring, because she looks up at me, inhales sharply, and rubs the back of her neck.

"Have you eaten yet?" she asks.

What a weird question. No *I made X for dinner because it's super healthy and you don't want that waistline getting out of hand and . . .*

"No, I haven't," I say.

Her face changes. She knows it was a weird question.

"There might be some leftover spaghetti in the freezer."

Might be? Okay, now this is weird to an alarming degree. Mom knows exactly what's in the freezer at any given time, especially the leftovers inventory. I have to ask it.

"Mom, are you okay?"

"Hmm?" she asks predictably. "Oh, yes, I'm just a little, um . . . Well, go ahead and come out to eat when you're ready."

She turns and tries to leave, but I can't let that last sentence

THIS BOOK MIGHT BE ABOUT ZINNIA 165

slide either. When I'm ready? Dinner is never eaten when *I'm* ready, only when *it's* ready.

"Mom, is something wrong?" I have to ask. "You're acting really weird."

She stops halfway down the hallway and looks over her shoulder at me. Then her face melts into the *My baby* face.

"You just focus on being a kid, sweetheart. I've got it."

She turns and journeys to the kitchen, disappearing around the corner, and I brush off that first predictable part about focusing on being a kid, but I have to wonder . . .

She's got *what*?

CHAPTER 13

Zinnia

2024

MILO STILL HASN'T RESPONDED. I SHOULD SAY SOME-thing.

I'm the only one at this dinner table who hasn't said a word. I should *definitely* say something.

Mom and Dad occupy chairs on either side of me at the dining table, making conversation about nothing.

"There's no reason for the silent g in 'lasagna,' and you can't convince me otherwise," says Dad, pointing at Mom with his fork.

"Take it up with the Italians, Ben, I didn't choose how to spell it," she says, and smiles back. "Oh, I read an article today? Apparently, record labels are now *engineering* songs just for TikTok."

Dad's brow furrows. "What?"

THIS BOOK MIGHT BE ABOUT ZINNIA

"I *know*, I said the same thing," she says, shocked at the news the rest of the internet learned years ago. "Songs that are easy to duet with, I guess. Catchy ones."

"I thought all music these days was engineered to be catchy," says Dad.

I pick at the lasagna between tiny bites, only halfway listening.

"Well, yes, but . . . well, I've just heard it's different." Mom slices another bite of lasagna and lifts the fork to her mouth. "Mmm, I'll say that extra egg in the ricotta makes this *sing*. You all right, Zinnia? You've barely touched your food."

"Yeah," I lie. "I'm just thinking."

I leave out the fact that I'm thinking about Milo and what I said to him. God, it's all been so misconstrued. He knows I didn't mean that I'm so focused on finding my mom—I mean my birth mom, maybe—that I don't care what happens to his.

I wondered how she was doing, but it never felt like the right time to ask. If we're together, we're happy. I never want to bring down the mood. I sigh, wondering if that's a part of perfectionism too, wanting every conversation to be a happy one.

Mom and Dad exchange a glance, revealing silently that they don't believe me.

"I'm not really hungry," I say, standing before they start asking questions. "I'll be in my room."

"Honey," says Mom, "you know you can tell us anything. Did something happen between you and Milo?"

"Huh?" I ask, hoping I sound surprised and not defensive. "No, I'm about to go call him right now."

What I wouldn't give to call him. To apologize. To tell him this is *not* how I wanted our conversation to go, that I care. I care about him and his mom so much that I'm willing to miss the one chance I have to make my college essay something to turn the heads of the Harvard admissions committee or club or whatever conglomerate is up there making decisions.

I reach my room and shut the door gently behind me, sighing a deep sigh and sinking into the swirling war inside my head.

The book signing is tonight. At 8:00 p.m. In three hours.

Even thinking of throwing away the opportunity stings.

Am I really ready to do that, and for what? To stay here while Milo ignores me?

What if this essay bombs, and I go through the rest of my life wondering what would've happened if I *had* gone to the train station tonight? I could still make it. . . .

It's only five o'clock. . . .

I'll call him one more time.

If he answers, I stay and talk. If he doesn't . . .

I'll take that as a sign from the universe that I'm meant to be on that train tonight.

I slip my phone out of my pocket, and the screen lights up with a selfie of the two of us at the coffee shop. My smile is bordering on a laugh as I squeeze Milo in close to me. His smile is

THIS BOOK MIGHT BE ABOUT ZINNIA

just as big, but I look into his eyes and realize they're far away. Like he's got something on his mind. Thinking of something else. How long has he looked like that? Does he always look so distracted?

Is he always thinking about her?

Wouldn't I be?

Jodelle Rae West is my *pretend* mom, and I can't stop thinking about her. If my own mom were as sick as Milo's mom was, wouldn't she consume all my thoughts?

Just as my phone rings for the last time and triggers the recording "I'm sorry, this person has a voice mailbox that has not been set up yet," my door handle clicks behind me and in squeezes my mom.

"Zinnia?" she asks. "Can I come in? I just want to make sure you're okay."

It almost breaks me, my jaw burning from holding back tears, but I steel myself and nod, refusing to look at her.

I feel her weight sink into the bed behind me.

"You don't have to tell me what's wrong," she says, "but I want you to know that we love you. And I know that, you know, our experiences are different. We've known they would be since the day we got you. But we're here for you."

Okay, steel dissolved. Two tears fall.

"Thanks," I croak. I know what she's talking about. Mom and Dad are both white. *Very* white. Like, German and Irish heritage somewhere down the line, strawberry blond hair,

Mom with blue eyes, Dad green. I'm half Black, my dark 3A curls thick and loose. When I was three, Mom and I dressed up for Halloween as Marilyn Monroe and Dorothy Dandridge. I've always known I am half Black, the other half probably white.

My parents, I have to say, were *very* prepared to raise me. I've always been told I'm beautiful. Mom used to compliment me as she ran the brush gently through my hair with the Cantu line she learned how to use, bobbles tied just tight enough to hold all day. She's told me since I was a kid that my experiences would be different from hers and Dad's. She gave me the talk about the police when I was around ten.

They were prepared to adopt a Black girl. But in the right context I'm mostly white-passing.

I don't think they were prepared for that.

I feel her warm hand inch over and squeeze mine.

"You're our angel," she says. "Whatever's happened, you can talk to us."

"Thanks," I say again. In the silence I can feel her pain. So I offer more. "This isn't about race, though, Mom."

"It doesn't have to be about race to be influenced by it," she says. "I want to be sensitive just in case."

"You don't have to be. It's not about that this time. Promise."

"Tell me what it's about, then," she invites. "I'm here to listen."

I wipe away the tears that are pooling in my eyes again and take a deep breath. Maybe it's time to tell someone about all of

THIS BOOK MIGHT BE ABOUT ZINNIA

this. Normally, that would be Milo, but I've never had a fight with him before. Is this even a fight? I spot *Little Heart* on my vanity, and I picture him standing in the only bookstore left in town, looking over the face-outs with Jodelle Rae West's name all over them—purple and gold books with their own display, probably with a matching cardboard poster at the front of the store—thinking of me. Maybe he picked up a couple of copies with bent corners or misprinted jackets where the spine text was a tad slanted or the formatting was just slightly off, and he put them back in exchange for the *perfect* one.

Maybe every decision he's ever had to make about me has had to be *perfect.*

Have I really put that much pressure on him?

Have I been the problem this whole time?

"Mom," I begin, "am I'm a narcissist?"

Silence.

Total stillness.

I don't even feel her move behind me.

"Mom?"

"Well, um," she says, assuming her professional voice, "I'm no mental health professional, so I can't say. But . . . you do have perfectionist tendencies."

Perfectionist tendencies.

Is that the same thing?

"Like what?" I ask, afraid of what she'll say back.

"Well," she says, reaching and giving my hand another

squeeze. "You hold yourself to an impossibly high standard sometimes. I know we've talked about Harvard since you were a kid. Hell, I still have one of your baby onesies with the logo on the front. Your dad and I have always said you can do *anything* you put your mind to."

There's a silent "but" at the end of that, and after a long sigh, she continues.

"I don't want you to think less of yourself if you're less than the best. You are perfect enough, Zinnia."

Perfect enough.

"That's a paradox if I've ever heard one," I say. "Perfect enough?"

"Yup," she says. I can hear her nervously running a hand over her jeans as her voice grows shaky. "You know, when I was a kid, um . . . actually, when a lot of millennials were kids, we were told we were special. A lot of us were put into gifted programs early and funneled into college as if there were no other options, but the truth is it caused us—*me*—a *lot* of anxiety. Even to this day."

I turn to look at her in surprise.

My mom? Anxious?

"Really?"

"Yeah," she says sheepishly. "I just hide it well. But when I had you, I promised myself I'd never create an environment where you had to hide it well. But I think, somehow, I inadvertently have. Maybe it's because you're an only child, or

THIS BOOK MIGHT BE ABOUT ZINNIA   *173*

because you go to the best school in the state. Or maybe I've just said the word 'Harvard' too many times."

"Mom, you're not a failure," I assure her. Maybe a little helicoptery, but I could have it *so* much worse.

"No, no!" She panics, turning and gripping my hand with both of hers. "This isn't me asking for validation. This is about *you* and what you need. I just really, *really* wish you'd tell me so I can help."

I think after everything Mom's just shared, I can tell her exactly what's going on without ridicule.

Okay, with minimal ridicule.

"See that book over there? The one Milo got for me?" I ask, nodding to *Little Heart.* Mom follows my gaze, goes to the vanity, and picks it up.

"*Little Heart?*" she asks. "I didn't know Jodelle Rae West had a new one out. She's one of your favorites, right?"

The favorite, but I don't correct her.

"Yeah," I say. "Except this one is . . . kinda . . . about a girl who has a heart-shaped birthmark on her forehead."

She looks at me blankly for a minute before blinking.

"Wow, that's . . . an interesting coincidence," she says, flipping through pages curiously, as if the book's changed in her hands somehow. "And so . . . what?"

"So," I say, getting to the totally deranged part, "it's about a girl whose father abandoned the family and a mom who . . . gave her away."

"Really?" asks Mom, her eyes flickering.

I nod.

"Wow," she says, her voice breaking, "that, uh . . . that *is* a coincidence."

She stares at the first page in silence, her fingers trembling as she holds the book aloft.

"Mom," I begin, easing into the hardest question I've ever had to ask her, "can I ask you about my birth mom?"

She sighs the shakiest sigh I've ever heard as she sits back on the bed for support.

"Oh, well, uh," she says, "we never met her, remember? Don't even know her name. The agency worker just brought you to us. Straight from labor and delivery, all wrapped up in a little white swaddle blanket with green and burgundy footprints all over it. You had the chubbiest, reddest little face."

"Is that why you named me Zinnia?" I smile.

"No, actually," she says, her face stoic and stone-cold, "*she* named you that. If she was going to relinquish full custody with zero visitation and zero contact, the least we could do was keep the name she chose for you. Besides, we liked it enough, and it was easy to tweak in case you decided on a different persona or gender. Zinn leans more masculine, Zane even more so, Nia for a shorter version—"

"*She* named me?"

Why didn't anyone ever tell me this? Why didn't it ever come up? I mean, I guess I never asked, but . . . I guess I should have.

THIS BOOK MIGHT BE ABOUT ZINNIA

"Yes," says Mom. "If she'd gone and named you something outlandish, that would've been one thing, but . . . it was the one part of her we chose to keep. It was the only thing we *could* keep. The doctors said she wouldn't say a word at the hospital, just kept writing in a little journal. So she wrote your name on a page, ripped it out, and sent it to us. In fact—"

She cuts off her own sentence, bolts up from the bed, and darts from the room, before I hear a resounding follow-up from down the hallway.

"Wait right there!"

I think of all Jodelle's characters. Daisy and Poppy Ridgefield from *Westland* are both flower names. Sisters. Maybe Sky and Land, mom and dad, king and queen, could be an allegory? I could say they're the personification of vehicles for creating a flower. Tools of photosynthesis. My heart pounds in my throat as I realize that it wouldn't be totally far-fetched for Princess Little Heart to have a flower name.

If she does, there's my essay linchpin—the thing that makes all of this a believable excursion, convincing enough that the Harvard admissions board could understand why I might go all the way to New York to talk to Jodelle, at least.

Mom steps back into the room, unfolding a tiny piece of faded purple paper. She sits back on the bed.

"I knew this day would come," she says, holding it out to me. "I haven't looked at this since the day we brought you home."

I stare at it for a moment. An item my birth mom held. Wrote on. She thought of me when she wrote down my name. Did she miss me? Does she miss me now?

How would she react if she knew I was turning the moment she wrote my name into a commodity to be sold to a college admissions board?

Guilt rattles me.

"Zinnia?" asks Mom, snapping me out of it.

"Sorry," I say quickly, reaching out for the note. I take it in my hands, the paper soft and faded yellow at the edges. I unfold it and see it written in all caps.

ZINNIA.

I take a deep breath.

This is her handwriting.

A page from her journal.

"Guess you get your love of words from her," says Mom warmly. Love of words? I look at her questioningly.

"I told you she had a journal." She nudges me. "Sounds like she loved to write."

She loved to write.

No way. There's absolutely no way.

I picture Jodelle's face. And I wonder . . . do we look a little bit alike? I mean besides my tightly curled brown hair and my big brown eyes. I have her cheeks, don't I? And that nose . . .

I reach up and touch mine.

I picture a young Jodelle sitting in a hospital bed, knees

THIS BOOK MIGHT BE ABOUT ZINNIA

pulled up to her chest, scribbling my name. And I wonder if it would be so far-fetched for her to have grown up, written two bestselling novels, and taken a chance writing a third in the hopes that maybe, just maybe, her lost daughter would use it to find her.

I've been so focused on this damn essay that I didn't see the clues right in front of me. Jodelle is old enough to be my mom, she's got a propensity for flower names, and what are the chances she'd give her character a heart-shaped birth-mark *exactly* where mine is?

"Can you hand me the book?" I ask, my voice shaky.

"Sure, why?"

She hands it to me, and I thumb to where I stopped reading about a third of the way through.

"I mean, nothing serious," I say, trying to hide how *very serious this could be.* I flip to the last page of the book, hoping for an ending. An answer.

> She fled to the woods from whence she came, into the icy jungle that had frozen over with the king's heart, taking shelter in the trunk of the Wise Old Oak.
>
> How was she to grow there, this spring child? To flourish in times of cold stubbornness was not in her nature. She was too new and too soft, not yet hardened by

years of rejection or disillusioned by long winter nights.

Even as her mother, though I could see all from my dwelling in the sky, I could do nothing to help her.

I'd lost her to the snow, afraid I'd never see her again.

I feel my forehead beading with sweat.

"Zinnia?"

But I barely hear her.

Too new and too soft? That sounds like a flower to me. *To flourish in times of cold stubbornness was not in her nature?* Definitely could be a flower. Likely a flower, actually. In fact, I can't think of what else the princess would be *besides* a flower.

I flip through the book until I reach the last page, and a stiff envelope pokes out, pressed deep between the pages. One I didn't see before.

I pull it out and flip it over, and I find my name scrawled in Milo's signature third-grade handwriting.

Zinnia.

I can't open it fast enough.

"Is everything all right?" asks Mom.

"Yeah," I say. "It looks like Milo left me a note or something."

She pauses before venturing into new territory.

THIS BOOK MIGHT BE ABOUT ZINNIA 179

"How *is* Milo these days?" she asks. "I haven't seen him here in over thirty-six hours. Are you two all right?"

"Are you two all right" sounds like we're a couple, and I know Mom knows we're not. But it still stings like a breakup would.

I unfold the letter and read.

> *Zinn,*
> *I've started and thrown away like 10*
> *of these, so if you're reading this letter,*
> *there was a lot of work behind it.*

I swallow, guilt washing over me at the realization that I didn't even *find* this note until days later. I read on.

> *I've tried to picture life without you.*
> *Waking up, going to work, maybe*
> *even going to Bean Rock even*
> *though I know you won't be there.*

My eyes prick with tears. I can feel his sadness through the page. And it's written like he's saying goodbye to me, like he had to say goodbye to his mom. He's losing two of the most important women in his life in the same year.

> *I know you'll get into Harvard,*
> *whatever it takes. You're probably*

*expecting me to ask you to stay
friends with me, to stay in touch,
to keep space for me in your life,
but the truth is, you won't. Not
because you don't want to. I believe
you do. But you'll outgrow me. It's
happening already. There will come a
moment when you'll realize I'm not
good enough for you, and when that
happens, I want you to know that I
saw it coming, and that I've already
accepted it. I care about you, Zinnia.
And I wish you the best.*

"Zinnia? Are you okay?" comes Mom's voice. The first tears roll down my cheeks as my heart shatters into a million pieces.

Milo doesn't think we'll make it. Not only that, he's *banking* on us not making it. He thinks I'll run off to Cambridge and forget all about him, drift away, make new friends. *Richer* friends. *Better* friends, according to him.

I just . . . I can't believe he really wrote this and left this in this book for me. And maybe . . . maybe he assumed I'd seen it already. That I'd read this note already and moved on with my life without even talking about this. And why would I do that if I hadn't already accepted it myself?

THIS BOOK MIGHT BE ABOUT ZINNIA   181

No wonder he's disappeared. He's licking all kinds of wounds I had no idea about.

"Zinnia?" my mom asks, afraid now. "Are you okay? Is Milo okay?"

"His mom is gone," I say, because it's all I can muster.

"Brandy? Oh my God. Um. . . ." She scrambles for the right words. "We'll have to send a gift basket. I'll call Harry and David. Or is that too . . . I don't know . . . maybe just flowers would be better. We can take them over to their house tomorrow if you want."

Gift baskets. Flowers. Money.

It all feels wrong now. All at once, it feels like too much and not nearly enough.

Tears well in my eyes as it all sinks in, what Milo was trying to tell me.

"We can't throw money at this, Mom," I say.

Not when all Milo needs, all he's been asking for this *entire* time, is a shoulder. A cuddle. An embrace. Some assurance that he's not alone in feeling the way he feels, and that he won't *be* alone once we graduate. Some comfort in knowing someone else will ache with him as his world falls apart.

No parents at just seventeen. Technically a ward of the state since sometime last night.

How did I not know how insecure he was about *us*?

How could I just assume?

How can I make this right?

I jump to my feet.

"I have to go. I have to find him." My hands can't find what I need fast enough. Purse. Wallet. Keys. Phone. SEPTA pass.

Mom stands in silence as I dart around the room looking for my things. Then I hear from behind me, "Tonight's your resubmission deadline," she says. "Are you . . . almost done revising it?"

I pause, keys in hand, and I know what I have to do. I can't go to New York tonight. There's just no way anymore. I'll risk it all—New York, the essay, Harvard—just to reassure Milo that he doesn't have to endure this, *any* of life, alone.

And as for Jodelle—she'll have more books. More tours. There will be more chances to meet her. Probably. I hope.

I just don't know how Mom is going to take it. I turn halfway, unable to look at her as I admit what I'm about to.

But I don't.

Mom steps up. Her hands grip my shoulders, stilling me, and I look up at her with questions written all over my face, I'm sure. Hers is bending into the Mom face, the *My babyyyyy* practically bursting from her. She pulls me into a hug and squeezes me tight, and I can feel her heart thundering. Or is that mine?

"A narcissist," she begins, "wouldn't care to make things right, especially at their own expense."

She pulls away and smiles down at me.

"Mom?" I ask. There's no way she's giving me her blessing.

All those years of swim classes? All those hours of community service, all the documentation of societal contributions and records of accolades, awards, and accomplishments, put at risk?

"I've given you tools for success," she says, "and I've raised you to be a good person. And I always hoped you'd never have to choose between the two. But here you are. And the choice is yours."

Two more tears fall from my eyes, and she pulls me against her again.

"Thank you," I say, feeling the weight of Harvard lifted from my shoulders. She's given me permission to make a choice she might not have, and, God, does it feel good.

She kisses my curls and says, "I want my hourly text, though. And be home by nine."

Yup. Same Mom.

I fire off a Hail Mary text to Milo, hoping, praying, he sees it.

Me: **Catching the next train to your house. Don't go anywhere.**

CHAPTER 14

Tuesday
2006

WORKING IN A COFFEE SHOP ON AUTOPILOT IS A DAN-gerous game.

I yelp as the sting of searing hot milk lashes both my hands, and I yank them away and press them against my apron. I shut my eyes, waiting for the pain to subside. I realize I'm clenching my teeth, and I take a deep breath in through my nose and back out through my mouth, just like they taught me at the hospital.

It works, just as Justin comes up next to me.

"Hey, are you okay?" he asks.

"I'm fine," I lie, stepping back up to the counter. The skin on the backs of both my hands tingles with pins and needles, and I examine them closely. The faintest tinge of pink fades into both of them.

THIS BOOK MIGHT BE ABOUT ZINNIA

He turns and leans in close and speaks so softly that the handful of concerned customers gathering at the bar can't hear.

"You go run them under cold water. I've got bar and register."

I stare up at him in surprise. Bar *and* register? At eight in the morning on a Saturday? Does he have a death wish?

"I'll be fine," I insist as I reach up and pull the steam wand lever. There's no way he can handle himself out here, not when we're about to get a rush of pre-soccer-game parents sneaking in a coffee before they have to be screaming on the sidelines.

He reaches across my counter and flips the steam wand back up.

"Hey!" I exclaim, rage pulsing through me.

He rests a hand on the counter and looks me square in the eyes with a determination I haven't seen in him before. He looks so serious. I didn't think Justin had a serious bone in his body.

"I won't let you blister your hands," he whispers. "Go."

It's not a suggestion anymore.

He wedges himself between me and the counter until I have nowhere else to go, unless I want to stand in the middle of the place empty-handed, or stock cups and grounds.

But damn, this is starting to really hurt.

"Fine," I surrender.

I slip off my apron and head for the back room, where the

handwashing sink provides cool, delicious reprieve for my singing skin. I breathe a sigh, basking in it for a moment. When I look out to the floor, Justin is flying from fridge to pitcher to steam wand to espresso machine to cup to Sharpie to register.

I stare down at my pinking hands, flip them over under the water. I would've stayed out there with Justin, carrying bar while he ran register and we both waited for a teammate or two to arrive before the lunch rush. I would've sacrificed my comfort for the good of my team. Isn't that what motherhood is, anyway? Sacrifice?

I could have kept her.

I could have worked here while Mom took care of her at the house. Maybe she would've had someone else to dote on, to dress up, to command around like a puppet, to pray with and cook for. Maybe it would've given me a break in more ways than one, and maybe it would've kept baby girl out of the arms of the Terrenis.

Now I don't even know where she is. Have no way of finding out. The agency burned to ashes. Mom told me last night over dinner when I asked about it. She said it was a shame, too, since they were in the middle of digitizing their archive of records. Then she followed it up with, "Get some more greens, sweetheart—the postbaby weight will come on quick if you don't lay off that pizza."

I sigh, wondering how she expects me to worry about my

THIS BOOK MIGHT BE ABOUT ZINNIA

weight when baby girl might be out there falling into the hands of the very people Mom told me to stay ten miles away from. Maybe I'm overreacting. What if they're nice people? I've seen *The Godfather*. The Mafia wouldn't hurt their own flesh and blood, would they? Actually, according to *The Godfather*, she wouldn't even be involved in crime, she'd be a traditional wife taking care of the home and whatnot, reminding her husband to remember the cannoli.

A thought grips me.

What if by letting her fall into the hands of the Terrenis, she marries a man who's also involved in the Mafia, thereby dooming her to a life of misery or even widowhood. What if by choosing Ezra as her baby daddy, I've doomed her to an eternity of chaos and stress like me and—

Bzzt. Bzzt.

My Razr rings in my pocket with the classic ditty, followed by "Hello, Moto." God, I thought I turned that off. My fingers have gone from feeling like they're coated in lava to going totally numb from the cold, and I decide they could use a break from their bath.

I plop down into the empty chair by the utility closet back here and flip my phone open.

My heart goes cold.

Ezra: I'm sorry I didn't tell you about Amy.

Just when I was getting used to the idea of going to school every day until graduation and seeing him holding hands with Amy Sullivan in the hallway and giving her little pecks on the cheek between classes, sharing graduation photos and whatever. I'll bet they IM every night, and if I checked each of their Myspaces—even though I would rather die—they'd be in each other's Top 8 for sure, and—

Ezra: My parents kicked me out. I don't know how much longer I'll be on this plan.

I glance up to where Justin is now standing at the register, laughing with a customer. A woman's voice by the sound of it. Good, he'll be occupied long enough for me to text back. My fingers fly as I type *444607777666777*77799909442804427*73 36633*3*, which yields the letters . . .

Me: im sorry what happened?

Did the Terrenis find out about her? Do they know? Do they know what we did? Otherwise, why would he be texting me instead of his new girlfriend?

I'm really glad the text message makes it look like I'm totally calm and keeping it together while I'm literally clenching to keep from shitting myself.

Ezra: They found condoms in my drawer. And Narcan.

Oh, he uses condoms now, huh? Could've used one of those when he was with me. Then we might not be in this mess. I want to text him exactly that so bad, it hurts. But I take a deep breath, summon restraint, and type something I hope is more rational.

Me: Why the Narcan?

THIS BOOK MIGHT BE ABOUT ZINNIA

Ezra: Actually it was for my cousin. He told me he uses, and it scared me, so I keep that in my drawer, because he's not dying here.

Damn. My heart flutters just a bit at the heroism of it. He kept that in his room, knowing his own parents. And then he texts something else.

Ezra: They didn't kick me out because I had it. They kicked me out because I wouldn't tell them who it was for.

Me: I'm sorry.

Ezra: It is what it is.

Me: Where are you staying?

Knowing Ezra, he's sleeping at a campsite somewhere, or he's built his own in the woods behind his house. He's always loved nature. While most of us have posters of our favorite bands—I have one of Destiny's Child and one of Lifehouse—or sports greats we look up to (mine being an action shot of Bethany Hamilton that's actually an ad for Roxy, but whatever, it counts), Ezra has shots of several outdoorsy places he's been to.

The one with him standing on the bridge in front of Multnomah Falls in Oregon is my favorite. He's swimming in a huge blue poncho with his arms lifted into the air like he doesn't have a care in the world up there, basking in the trees and the ferns and the fresh air. That poster was burned into my mind after that night, since it was on the wall next to his bed.

I'll probably never forget it.

Ezra: The park.

What?

Me: Why not Amy's house?

Amy Sullivan's parents have a house so big, the driveway is longer than the block we live on. I was there once in middle school for her American Girl–themed birthday party, pleasantly surprised that she must have thought we were close enough friends to invite me. And then when I walked through the door in costume, I remembered there was only one Black American Girl doll—Addy—and I was the only Black girl in the room. She didn't invite me because we were friends. She invited me because she needed an Addy.

Which, it's whatever. I guess it was nice to be invited at all, but at least I knew why.

At least she was nice to me. And I'm sure she's grown up since then.

She has to have, right?

Ezra: I don't want Amy to know.

But he wants me to know?

Me: Why are you telling me this?

Ezra: I can't talk to Amy like I can talk to you.

My heart is thundering as I read that last one over and over and over. He can't talk to her like he can talk to me? What does that mean? She's his girlfriend, after all.

Ezra: We're still friends, right?

My throat closes. Friends?

How can we be friends after that night? Did I imagine the

THIS BOOK MIGHT BE ABOUT ZINNIA

light in his eyes before he kissed me? Before his hands moved over me? Something electric buzzes within me, and I shut my eyes against it. I can't do this. I can't be friends with someone I still . . .

Still *what*, exactly?

I don't know.

I just know I can't do *this*. Talking to him behind Amy's back, being a dumping ground for his feelings, an ear to listen when he's sad, a shoulder to cry on. Not when Amy gets to have him when he's at his best. But then, what do I text back? Yes? No?

A loud clang pulls me back into reality, and I look up with a gasp to see Justin flinch away from the counter as milk explodes from the metal pitcher still bouncing across the floor.

Me: Gotta go.

I lunge for the mop and dart for the bar, where Justin is pressing his burned hands into his apron. I reach for his shoulder and then jump back. What the hell am I thinking, touching him? Instinct, I guess?

"Are you okay?" I ask.

He looks up at me with the most pained smile I've ever seen, his normally piano-key-white cheeks now a deep shade of pink.

"I just need a minute with the sink."

God, that sounds worse than I'm sure he meant it.

"You've got nerve forcing me to take a break when—"

"I'm sorry."

His breathing is heavy, from the pain, I assume. Until

moments pass and he shuts his eyes, grips the sink we're only supposed to use for bar dishes, and says it again.

"I'm so sorry, Tuesday."

"For . . . what?"

I'm terrified to ask.

Is this where it happens? When I find out he's been lying to me this whole time about enjoying my company and wanting to be my friend? That he was only nice to me because he made a bet with his friends that he could get me into bed within a month?

When he straightens and looks at me, his eyes are glassy.

"Justin, what happened?"

Is Dario going to fire me? Am I getting written up for something? What the hell is going on? I need Justin to start talking *now*.

"I . . . Jodelle was . . . here the other day. I . . . I didn't know what to do. I didn't want you to lose your chance. . . ."

I can't feel my hands. My legs feel like they might collapse underneath me, and the room is spinning.

"So . . . ," I begin, not wanting to know the answer, "where is my journal?"

His lips purse, and he stiffens.

"Tuesday," he begins, reaching up to touch my shoulder.

"I need to go home," I say, recoiling. My journal, my most treasured thing . . .

Gone.

THIS BOOK MIGHT BE ABOUT ZINNIA

He nods.

"Okay," he says simply. "Okay."

I can't get my apron off fast enough. My body is buzzing with unwelcome electricity, wearing me out, sapping the energy from my bones as I dial my mom's number.

"Tuesday?"

"Please come pick me up."

"I'm kind of in the middle of someth—"

"*Please*, Mom."

I shut my eyes and take a deep breath as I wipe away more tears. I don't know what I need right now. A shoulder to cry on? An ear to listen? I really don't know. All I know is that I can't do this. I can't be here.

"I can't keep coming to get you because you're having a bad day, Tuesday. Was someone mean to you at work?"

Was someone *mean* to me at work?

Someone *robbed* me at work.

But I know I can't say that to Mom. She wouldn't understand. I doubt she'd care. *It was just a journal,* she'd say. But it wasn't. It was *my* journal. It was my rock. The blank page was my place of escape. Now I'll never get to go back and read the story I wove about my girl, and me, and Ezra, and the kingdom we could have had.

"Yeah."

A sigh comes through the receiver.

"Fine. I'll be there in an hour."

Click.

I flip my phone closed and slip it into my pocket, then cradle myself in my arms. I grit my teeth as a sob bubbles up, threatening to consume me.

Weeks go by before Jodelle returns to Café Alba. She's bold to show her face anywhere near me again. Standing at the counter, waiting for her coffee like she isn't carrying the stolen pages I bled on.

"Now's your chance," I hiss at Justin, not taking my eyes from her as she slides into a chair and pulls out an expensive-looking, ultrasleek gray Apple PowerBook. She's going to be here for a while.

"I want it back, Justin," I demand, turning to him now. His face is stone, but I watch him melt.

"Tuesday, I can't—"

"You said you wanted to make it up to me? Now's your chance. Get my journal back, and I'll drop all of this."

My heart pounds as I glance back out to where the woman sits alone in the corner, typing, phone sandwiched between her ear and shoulder.

"I am in the coffee shop *now*, Anders. I'm literally working on it this morning. . . . Yes, I will do the *Good Morning America* interview. I can be back in New York tomorrow morning."

THIS BOOK MIGHT BE ABOUT ZINNIA

My chest thunders. She's going home tomorrow.

This *has* to happen today.

"You talk to her or I will," I hiss, leveling my eyes at him until he realizes I mean it. He clears his throat and turns to the seating area.

"Ma'am?" he asks. Her head whips around so fast, I'm surprised it doesn't twist off and fall on the floor. She looks around the empty coffee shop dramatically.

"You must mean me," she chuckles.

Finally she notices me standing just a few feet away, her smile hiding a layer of ice underneath. I've met people like her before. Not everyone who smiles is a nice person.

"Yes, ma'am," he says to her, glancing at me. I keep my face even, hoping he understands the gravity of this conversation. If he ever wants any chance at mending our friendship, at earning my trust again, he'll get the journal back. "I, uh, wanted to ask if you've tried our new seasonal blend."

I busy myself with the calluses on my palms, picking at them and tossing pieces into the garbage one by one by one.

"I haven't," she says warmly. "Are you offering me a sample?"

"Yeah, I'll whip one right up for you. Care to come up to the counter so you can see how the magic happens?" On the word "counter," he nods to me as some kind of cue and then clears his throat.

As the woman shuts her PowerBook and all but floats back to the coffee counter, eagerly awaiting whatever bullshit Justin is about to put in a cup and call it art, I stare at her blankly, studying her face. She'll give it back, right? She doesn't look like a thief, I guess. But then, what does a thief look like, anyway?

I clear my throat, and her eyes find mine. She offers a flat-mouthed *Oh, I didn't see you there, but I'll acknowledge your existence with an awkward half smile that implies you should probably be doing something besides staring at me* face. I offer one back.

"Um," I begin, my voice cracking. "I like your bag."

She lets half a chuckle escape before she catches herself. Every hair on my arms prickles once her mask cracks, revealing the condescension underneath.

I knew it.

This is not a nice woman.

"Thank you," she says.

Just ask her already, Tuesday. You've got nothing to lose, and you might never see her again!

"I've seen you in here a few times," I continue, busying my hands with pouring—and steaming—milk for a drink that nobody even ordered. "Do you live around here?"

"No," she says with half a laugh. I wonder if that was condescending too. One of those *As if* laughs. "I live in Manhattan. I'm just here for the week to get some of this Philly inspiration. It's just bursting with creative energy."

"Yeah," I say. And she's probably right. I wouldn't know. Farthest I've been from Philly is Allentown. Seventy miles away.

THIS BOOK MIGHT BE ABOUT ZINNIA

Manhattan must be a magical place. I imagine everyone's well dressed and buttoned-up like this woman, marching down the busy streets with all the other New Yorkers bound for greatness. Everyone who comes in with a Jersey or New York accent seems to have it all together. Or at least they act like they do.

I guess no one really does in the end.

Justin joins me at the counter with a small steaming cup of black coffee.

"Presenting: liquid gold. This is our Matagalpa blend. Medium body. Mild acidity. And just a *touch* of caramel notes."

"Ooh," she says, and grins, taking the cup gently, with one hand supporting the bottom like she's at some kind of ultra-fancy wine-tasting party. "I did a yoga retreat in Matagalpa once. *Gorgeous* views."

Actually, I have no idea how someone would fancily hold a cup, but if I had to picture it, this would be it. She takes a sip. A slurp, actually.

"Oh, that's smooth."

"Right?" he asks, leaning on the counter and glancing at me. He points at her with a slight tilt of his head that says, *Go on, now's your chance!*

What does he expect me to say—*Hey, I want my journal back*?

"Um," I start, like I start every sentence. Why can't I just spit it out? Why was it so easy to fight Justin about this? To accuse him of giving away my precious journal when I confided in him about the whole process?

She stares at me in total confusion as I continue, unable to still my shaking hands.

"I, um . . . gave Justin," I say, helpless as my own voice crumbles away, quieter and quieter, "my journal, and—"

"Oh!" she exclaims, pulling out her BlackBerry again and holding a single apologetic finger in the air. "I have to take this. It's my agent, I'm sorry."

My heart shatters as she leaves the coffee on the counter and darts for her things.

My eyes burn with tears, knowing this is my last chance.

But she's on the *phone*, for crying out loud. I can't interrupt her. What if—

"Anders? Yes, I totally forgot about the dinner tonight. And that the trains are on a Sunday schedule. Just call me a cab when I get to Penn Station, and I should be right on time."

She checks her watch, slaps her PowerBook shut, slips it into her Burberry bag, slings that over her shoulder, and heads for the door.

"Miss West?" I call after her, but she's still on the phone, and the door opens, and the bell jingles, and she steps outside and turns.

And she's gone.

I stare at the glass as my vision blurs, my cheeks on fire. I don't even notice I'm clenching my fists until I feel Justin's

THIS BOOK MIGHT BE ABOUT ZINNIA

fingers embrace one of them. I jerk away so fast, I slam hard into the syrup rack, rattling the bottles and making him jump back too.

"Don't *touch* me!" I shriek, and I sprint for the only place where I feel safe here.

The bathroom.

I slam the door behind me and lock it, flipping the light switch so I can be alone with my thoughts in this pitch-black room. I lean back against the wall, and I crumple to the floor, clutching my knees as the tears roll. As I come down, my elbow taps the toilet, reminding me of the moment I sat staring down at the test that would change my life. And that more than once I knelt over one, heaving, wondering if I was doing the right thing.

I'm still not sure.

I text Mom.

Me: **Please come get me.**

I choke on a sob as the darkness pulls me in. Sinking, sinking, sinking. I gave her away once, and now . . .

I've lost her all over again.

"I'm sorry," I whisper to her, shutting my eyes hard against how much it hurts, a deep, searing twisted mess of guilt and regret. "I'm sorry."

Maybe she's better off without me. I've made a mess of my own life.

I hope I at least gave her a better one.

CHAPTER 15

Zinnia

2024

THE SEPTA STATION IS *FREEZING*.

It's not even nightfall yet, but even against the last remnants of sunset, the chill in the air is bitter, whipping through my jacket as I squeeze my fists over and over in my pockets, looking in both directions for train headlights. I sigh, my breath a cloud that spills onto the platform. I'm alone out here.

I shiver, and as I stare down the platform, I feel something cool and soothing settle in my chest; a peace I didn't know I could have comes over me. An assurance that as much as it hurts to let go of potentially the perfect essay ending, it hurts so much less knowing I'm on my way to be the friend Milo deserves.

I missed so many clues.

THIS BOOK MIGHT BE ABOUT ZINNIA

201

I was so preoccupied with this essay. With Jodelle. With Little Heart. With me.

And now, whether she's actually part of my origin story or not, I'm walking away.

Returning to the boy who's had my back all these years. Who deserves my time, attention, love, and care.

I'd do anything for him.

Jodelle will be there.

Harvard will be there.

Someone clears their throat behind me.

I whip around.

A figure sits on the edge of the covered bench in a huge black peacoat and hat, matching black turtleneck pulled up over the mouth. All I can see in the sea of black are piercing dark eyes staring up at me.

At first I'm not sure I'm seeing what I'm seeing. Then I venture his name.

"Milo?"

My throat is scratchy from holding back so many tears, and I want to hold him, to collapse into him, I want to tell him how much he means to me, and how sorry I am, and how I can't believe I missed it. So many signs. Even now as he stands and steps forward, I notice a pink hue to the whites of his eyes I didn't see before. A faint purple under his bottom lids. How does someone look so . . .

So tired?

"Milo," I say again. He stops only a few feet from me. What do I even say? *I'm sorry?* That seems so pointless now. I'll be lucky if he ever speaks to me again.

His eyes narrow for just a moment before he purses his lips, and I notice them trembling. His eyes well.

"Milo—"

He reaches for me, wraps his familiar arms around me, rests his head on my shoulder, and I feel him trembling. I reach up to touch his hat, to cradle his head tight against me. I embrace him back, holding on so tight, I never want to let go. He squeezes me harder as a sob racks him.

Then another.

And another.

And as the sunset darkens around us, and no train comes, my heart breaks.

"I'm sorry, Milo," I whimper. "I'm so, so sorry."

He gives me one last squeeze before pulling away, eyes glued to the ground as he drags his sleeve over his cheeks and rasps out, "Thanks for doing this. For coming to find me. I wasn't sure if you would. Or if you cared. But now I see you do."

"Of *course* I do. I wouldn't be here if I didn't. Harvard will be there, Milo, and so will Jodelle. But our friendship? I don't want to take that for granted ever again. I *won't*."

"I haven't been there for you, either, Zinn," he says. "And what I said about you being too rich to understand what I go through, or to care about me . . ."

THIS BOOK MIGHT BE ABOUT ZINNIA

He cuts himself off and tears his eyes away.

"Well, that was just shitty of me."

"No, you were right," I admit. "I didn't realize it before, but I've always gotten by with throwing money at problems. I didn't even see that for what it was. I realized today that . . ."

Do I really want to admit the next part out loud?

"It's all I've ever been shown."

A gift basket can't fix everything. Flowers can't fix everything. I don't even know if Mom or Dad would know how to fix a problem without throwing money at it. Friend's mom died? Order flowers. Can't find the wrench? Buy another one. Thanksgiving's coming up and everyone's preoccupied with other stuff? Cater! And then a thought bubbles to the surface like a clog from a drainpipe.

Isn't that what they did when they adopted me? When they found out they couldn't conceive?

Am I the thrown money?

"At least once you've sent in your essay, you won't *need* to find Jodelle. I mean, unless postpone your application."

And then I realize there's something he should know. As my best friend, as my brother, as my ride-or-die.

"Milo, my birth mom liked to write."

I pull the small piece of purple paper from my pocket and unfold it, revealing my name in all caps: *ZINNIA*.

"She wrote this," I explain.

He marvels at it. Takes it in his hands carefully, like he's deciphering letters on a sheet of toilet paper.

"Your birth mom gave you your name?" he asks. "How do you know?"

"Mom told me," I say. "And that's not all. You know how in *Eastlake* and *Westlake* the characters have flower names? And how we've found several weird links between my life and Little Heart's?"

Here's the part where he'll think I'm crazy. He looks up at me, his face full of questions.

"Zinn—"

"I know, I know. I just want to ask her one day, you know? Or at least . . . get confirmation that it's not her."

So much silence passes between us, Milo's eyes glued to the paper again, that I can't read him. At first I see confusion, then I see wheels turning, then I think I see something else . . . something fleeting and rare for him.

"Let's go," he says finally.

"What?"

"We can catch the six thirty Amtrak to Brooklyn if we catch the SEPTA from here to Thirtieth Street Station in a few minutes."

His words process so slowly, his face turns from determined to confused as he stares at me.

"Milo, what?"

"Yeah!" he says with more surety than I've heard from him

THIS BOOK MIGHT BE ABOUT ZINNIA

in years. "Talking about finding a woman to be your stand-in mom for the sake of an essay was one thing, Zinn. I'm not going to let you lose an *actual* chance at finding your birth mom just to help me through a rough time. I'd never forgive myself."

I stare into his eyes and realize he's serious.

This is all too much. One minute I'm debating whether to go to New York or be there for my friend, and the next thing I know, I'm on my way to New York with said friend to possibly find a woman who merely hours ago I was pretending could be my biological mom, come to find out she could *actually* be my biological mom.

It's all very, *very* too much.

I look down at my clothes. The simple wool leggings, sweatshirt, and peacoat, the winter hat on my head. It's so basic. My face is clean but makeup-free. Is this how I want to meet her? Jodelle Rae West? At the very least, my favorite author, and at the most, the woman who gave me away? What if seeing me like this reassures her that giving me up was a good idea?

Woo-woo! A train whistle in the distance jars me from my trance, and when I look at Milo, he cocks an eyebrow.

"Was your brain in the bad place again?"

I nod.

He puts an arm around my shoulder.

"We can talk about it on the train," he says. "That is, if you're okay with this trip possibly not being perfect."

. . . Am I?

I look down at my boots and realize the socks poking out of the tops are slightly different. Both are beige with black polka dots, but one sock's dots are slightly larger and spaced farther apart.

How did I not notice?

And do I care?

And why?

Both my feet are warm and dry, and nobody's going to notice the difference but me.

Am I okay with being unperfect?

Should I be?

Narcissist or not, what if the key to not noticing imperfections about myself is to stop centering myself in everything?

"Thanks," I say, "but I think I've talked about myself enough today."

He nods, and the whole train ride is spent in blissful silence, me leaning my head on his bony shoulder with my eyes closed. Just knowing he's here keeps my brain from going back to the bad place, for now. People board here and there until the speaker announces we're nearing Thirtieth Street Station, which will connect to Amtrak.

CHAPTER 16

Tuesday
2006

"I JUST DON'T UNDERSTAND, TUESDAY, HOW YOU'RE still struggling to function," says Mom. "I don't ask for much, do I? Just a little independence from you? You're sixteen now, supposed to be on your own. Hold down a job. Focus on school. Bring home . . . not even straight As—Bs are fine. Do you know what my mother would have said if I'd brought home Bs?"

I try to block out her voice as we drive through the night, staring at the city flying by. *Anything* to distract me from this conversation. I didn't ask to be picked up to be lectured to. I asked because I was falling apart at work.

But not only can I not tell Mom about Jodelle stealing my writing, because she'd press a lawsuit, and we would absolutely lose, and I don't want any more attention from my classmates than I already have, but I also can't tell her about the journal. Because she'd tell me to be more careful and not hand out my work so carelessly.

And I *absolutely* can't tell her about Justin.

I don't even know what I was thinking. I don't even know if I like him like that. He was just . . . so warm and kind. He made a mistake. He gave away the journal to help, and I know if he could, he'd march right up to Jodelle's front door and demand it back.

I thought part of me would hate him forever, would never be able to forgive him.

But now, when I think about it, all I feel is a blank space where hatred should be.

Maybe I'm too tired to hate him anymore.

Where is the line that divides being too tired to hate someone and loving them?

Something in me stirs, remembering his touch, and I look around for anything to distract myself. At some point between Mom's complaints, she pauses and glances up at the rearview mirror.

She glances again.

That's entirely too many glances.

Curiosity grips me, and I turn to look over my shoulder through the rearview mirror, where I see an SUV tailgating us.

"Shit," she mutters, which jolts me. Mom *never* swears.

"Mom?"

THIS BOOK MIGHT BE ABOUT ZINNIA

"*Shhh*," she hisses. "I think this is a cop. Seat belt on?"

"Of course," I say as red and blue lights flicker in all our mirrors like a Christmas tree.

"Great," she says through a quickly summoned smile. "Act normal."

Act normal?

Are we not normal?

"What's going on?" I finally ask.

She pulls the car over and we crawl to a stop.

"Mom?" I ask, fear now creeping in. She's frozen in the driver's seat, her hands balled in her lap as she stares straight ahead, a million thoughts running through her mind, I'm sure. "Talk to me," I beg as the officer walks up to the window.

A Black man, average height and build, with a surprisingly warm smile after pulling us over.

"Morning, ma'am," he says with a grin as Mom rolls down the window and returns the smile. He nods kindly at me. "Miss."

I try my best to smile without looking as petrified as I feel.

"Morning, Officer," says Mom.

"You have any recording devices on you this evening?" he asks.

"Just our phones," sings Mom, her voice raspy as she says it.

Panic hits me. Why would he ask that?

He glances down at his scanner.

"This your vehicle, ma'am?"

"Of course," she says, and smiles.

"You realize you have a broken taillight and ran a stop sign back there?" he asks.

"I must have been preoccupied," she chuckles sheepishly, gesturing to me. "Plus, I've got a bit of a distraction. Do you have kids, Officer?"

"Yes, I do," he says with a smile in his eyes.

"Then you must understand what it's like." She smiles again. His fades, and he glances into the back seat.

"Your car smells like gasoline. Did you know that?"

"Oh, uh," she says, glancing over her shoulder, "really? Must be a leak somewhere."

"Maybe," he says, his even gaze telling me he doesn't believe a word of what she's saying. "Mind stepping out of the vehicle?"

Holy shit, what?

Mom stares at him for a minute, and though I can't see her face, I know what it looks like when she speaks. It's her poised voice. Her resolve voice. Her *Don't mess with me* voice.

"Do you know who I am?" she asks.

Oh God, really? She's going to pretend to be a celebrity now? Of all the ridiculous strategies for getting out of a traffic ticket, this is probably the *most* ridiculous I could think of. I look down at my Volcom hoodie and jeans that are torn at the heels from dragging on the ground. There's no way he'd believe we're celebrities, or even rich. What the hell is she

THIS BOOK MIGHT BE ABOUT ZINNIA

211

thinking? Heat creeps into my cheeks, and I want to disappear in a puff of smoke.

The officer looks just as shocked at the absurdity of this approach, and he busies himself with his scanner screen again, before Mom talks.

"Why don't you run my plates?" she asks.

"Sure, step out of the vehicle first while this processes."

She pauses again, her hands gripping the wheel now.

"Trust me?" she says. "It would be in your best interest to run the plates first."

He cocks an eyebrow as his scanner lets out a faint beep. He stares at it. Blinks a few times. Then he looks up at Mom with new eyes.

"Oh, uh," he says, glancing at me. "I, um . . . I'm sorry, I didn't realize this vehicle belonged to one of our own—"

"Understandable," she says. "It's been decades now. But I'd appreciate being allowed to go."

What the hell is she talking about?

My face must show my utter confusion, because the officer gives me one last glance before gathering his scanner and clipboard in his arms and nodding apologetically.

"Of course, ma'am. Miss. You both have a blessed day."

And then he *leaves.*

Mom rolls up the window again and busies herself with adjusting the radio dial and flipping one of the heat vents shut. Then she puts the car in drive and merges back onto JFK

like that wasn't the *furthest* thing from a normal police inter-
action.

Nah-uh, we're going to talk about this.

"Mom, what was that?"

"What was what?" she asks, obeying a detour sign and smacking her lips. "The construction down here is just awful. Just let me get on Market Street, for God's sake." She catches herself. "Lord, I apologize," she says, lifting a hand in the air.

"*Mom*," I demand.

"Yes?" she asks, glancing over at me in shock, like *I'm* the one being outrageous.

"Why did he let us go?" I ask. "And what do you mean, 'it's been decades'?"

"Like I told the officer," she says through gritted teeth, "I will talk about it with you when you're ready."

"I'm ready now," I insist, feeling the anger bloom in my chest like a thorny weed. "Tell me what the hell is going on!"

"You watch your mouth," she spits. "You can't even handle a day at a regular job, let alone what I have to do all day."

The hell is she talking about? She doesn't work. And even when she did, it was remote work for a call center.

"You said the most boring job in the world. That's literally all you've ever said about it."

And that it's confidential. Not quite the FBI, probably, but just as sensitive. So I was never allowed to ask anything more. I never noticed the gasoline smell in here—probably because

THIS BOOK MIGHT BE ABOUT ZINNIA

this hatchback is older than I am and always smells like a mechanic shop. But now that an outside nose that's not smell-blind mentioned it . . .

She glances up into the rearview mirror again, like she did a few minutes ago. She's been doing that so much more recently. How have I not noticed?

Maybe she's right about me being distracted. I've been so preoccupied with Ezra, and the coffee shop, with Jodelle, and now *Justin*, of all people. I never realized she started acting weird after she picked me up that night in my gown, after we saw smoke billowing from Oak Park Adoption Agency.

"You just focus on what you need to focus on, and my legacy will be yours one day."

Legacy?

"Mom," I begin shakily, unsure I want to know the answer. "You've been acting so weird lately. Just *tell me* what's going on before I have to start guessing."

"You focus on letting go of that baby, all right?" she snaps. "Apparently, that's all you can handle right now."

It stings like a flaming arrow through me.

That baby.

That baby was *my* baby for a moment in time.

How am I supposed to let go as long as I don't know if she's safe? That journal was my only outlet for putting down my memories of her, and now it's gone. Sure, I could start a new one, but it would be only half the story. Sure, I could start over, but it wouldn't be the same. How can Mom be so callous about all of this? No answers from Ezra. No answers from the agency—

The one that burned down.

The gasoline smell.

Mom acting weird since prom.

"Mom," I say again, "what happened to the agency?"

"Oh, Tuesday, stop interrogating me. Haven't I been through enough for the day?"

Deflecting. What she always does when she knows she's wrong about something. There's something she's not telling me.

We circle around past the boba tea place and merge onto Market Street.

"Finally," says Mom, glancing over her shoulder before accelerating again. "Just let me focus on the road, okay? Sit there quietly and pray if you're so pressed about *my* business."

My business. My legacy.

. . . The Terrenis.

This vehicle belonged to one of our own.

"Mom, was my dad a cop?" I ask hesitantly, barely able to form such a ridiculous question.

"*Tuesday*," she snaps.

"And why all the secrecy around him? What does he have to do with us now? And what's with your hatred of Ezra's family? Did they run together or something? Was Dad a crooked cop?"

THIS BOOK MIGHT BE ABOUT ZINNIA 215

"No, Tuesday, he wasn't," she hisses. "You will not slander his name. Your father was a good man." Her voice hitches as she continues, "God, why can't you just leave the past in the past? As a mother, I'm trying to protect you."

Her eyes give up two streaks of tears as she looks at me.

"Please understand that. I'm protecting you from *so* much you don't want to know."

"I *do* want to know," I insist. "Everything's been so weird and all over the place lately. I don't know what life is or who I am or who I can trust. Not Ezra or his family, not my classmates, not my coworkers, not my boss, and now not even you?"

She laughs a laugh that's supposed to make all of this sound absurd, but I know that laugh. That's the laugh that lingers a little too long, is a little too forced. The laugh that says, *Stop asking questions about grown folks' business.*

That's all the answer I need.

My mind drifts back to the gasoline smell as I catch another whiff of it.

What lengths would she have gone to to cover all of this up? Lying to her own daughter is one thing, giving up her own granddaughter to the state is another. Straight-up arson?

"Mom, you . . . Did you . . . burn down the agency?"

Her eyes are wild as she drives, zeroed in on the road.

"You wanted to keep me from ever finding her," I continue, my voice choked with tears, "and you wanted to keep me from the Terrenis so I couldn't find out about our family—"

"I did what I had to," she spits. "I left Ezra's father for a reason."

She . . . *what*? Before I can even ask, she continues her tirade.

"He's a monster. A horrible man with a horrible bastard son to carry on killing in his name. It's not just Ezra, Tuesday, their whole family is destined for hell, and I won't let them take you with them!"

"Ezra is *not* his family!"

"He's a Terreni as much as you're a Coo—Walker! This is why I wanted to wait to tell you all of this until you were old enough to understand. You're still ignorant! Still determined to fight what's been spelled out for you, what's right in front of your eyes!"

I'm frozen where I sit, my heart pounding.

All this time I've been looking into Ezra's family history to make sure she's safe from them when I should have been protecting her from my own family by staying away. Maybe it's better that I leave her alone after all, forget she exists, for her own safety.

If I want her to be safe, I have to keep her from *me*. And here I thought I might have made a good mother.

Angry tears well in my eyes as I remember my dream of Ezra standing by our living room window, cradling that little footprint-covered bundle in his muscular arms, his

THIS BOOK MIGHT BE ABOUT ZINNIA

black curly hair disheveled as he glances over at me.

Not only can that dream never happen because Ezra's family is dangerous. But that dream can never happen because *my* family is dangerous. I thought maybe *one* of us would have been a decent parent, but how could I ever think so, given where I come from? What I've been born into? My mom's out here burning down buildings in the name of burying the past.

How can I *ever* think about bringing a baby into this mess, now or ever?

No wonder Mom wanted me to get rid of her.

"I suggest," she says, "you forget about the baby, forget about the Terrenis, and forget about whatever you just heard, and let me focus on the road—"

"*No*, Mom," I holler now. Her eyes flash with rage.

"What did you say to me?"

For all the hell she's put me through, for the secrets she's kept, for the lies she's told, for making me give her up *knowing* I didn't have the full story . . . I said no.

"You don't get to control me anym—"

"You listen to me—"

"No, *I'm* talking, and you're going to listen!"

That's it.

My veins surge with venom as we fly down Market Street, and I can feel I'm about to do something reckless. I want to hit her. I want to jump out. I want to scream.

But I don't do any of that.

"Stop the car!" I scream, every muscle in my body hot with rage.

Mom doesn't move.

"I said, *stop the car!*" I shriek, lunging for the wheel with both hands as we fly over Market Street Bridge.

"*Tuesday, let go!*" hollers Mom, her voice shattering as she elbows me in the chest, which shoves me backward, pulling the wheel with me. It all happens so fast in the dark behind my shut eyes. Forces pull us forward as the screech of tires rings in my ears, a crash like a million bones crunching under our car, feeling light as air, and just as I manage to open my eyes, the windshield goes black, I fly forward against my seat belt, and water crashes around us.

We're in the Schuylkill River.

CHAPTER 17

Zinnia

2024

AS THE SEPTA SLOWS TO A STOP, MILO CHECKS HIS phone.

"Looks like we've got a little time," he says. "Should we get coffee first?"

After a moment I nod, realizing how nice it'll be to get a cup from a coffee shop that's *not* Bean Rock.

"Coffee sounds perfect." I smile, taking his hand in mine.

We step off and my phone buzzes with a text.

Kelly: **Time for my hourly text! You ok?**

I roll my eyes.

Me: **Yup. Just talking.**

It's not a total lie. We *are* talking, I just didn't say where. She thinks we're in Milo's room, when we're really about ten miles away in downtown, walking up the steps of the café halfway down the block that looks so old and crumbly, it might be a historical site. With the *A* in the name unlit under the evening sky.

Café Alba.

CHAPTER 18

Tuesday
2006

IT'S BEEN THREE WEEKS SINCE MOM DROWNED IN the Schuylkill River.

The investigators didn't ask whose fault it was. I was apparently found unconscious and couldn't remember my own name, let alone details about what happened.

But I know it was my fault.

All I remember from that day is my rage at finding out who I am and what I was born into.

I roll over on the mattress and look up at the clock on the wall.

Twenty minutes until my next shift.

There's a knock at the door.

"Come in," I call.

Justin peeks in and then steps inside, shutting the door behind him before slipping his apron off over his head.

"I was just about to come wake you up for opening."

"Couldn't sleep," I say, sitting up and leaning back against the wall. I tuck my knees up and stare at my feet. Anything to distract me from the fact that he's walking closer. And stopping at the edge of the mattress.

And lowering himself to sit on it.

I shut my eyes, wanting to absorb the tears back into my head.

"Thanks for the spare room," I say.

"Course," he croaks, tightening his hands and opening them, over and over. He clearly doesn't know what to do with them. He clasps them in his lap and continues, "Took some convincing with Dario to let you sleep back here, but given the circumstances, he understood. And as long as you can stand the smell of caramel and mocha sauce twenty-four seven, you can stay as long as you need."

I don't know what to say.

The fact that I've spent all this time hating him when he's been nothing but warm toward me since I walked in for my interview . . . there's not much I *can* say.

"Thank you," I repeat.

Without him, who knows where I'd be? In foster care? Not the same agency that took Baby Girl, but I've heard they're all the same. At least, that's how they're shown in movies.

"Hey," he says, turning to me. I return his gaze, and my

THIS BOOK MIGHT BE ABOUT ZINNIA

heart skips as I realize he's leaning closer. "You can sit this shift out if you need to, okay? I know morning customers can be . . ." He grunts a noise of extreme discomfort that conjures a smile out of me. "But I can take it."

Something about the way he says "I can take it" sends something warm through me, and I look away.

"Thanks," I say again, realizing I have to say more this time. "I . . . really appreciate it. Everything."

He stares at me in the dim light, and when I look back up at him, his lips are pressed tightly together like he's afraid that if he opens his mouth, too many thoughts will spill out at once.

"Tuesday," he finally says, my name rolling so gently off his tongue, like he's afraid he'll break it, "I know you've been through a lot lately, and I know I've messed up. Big-time. But I want you to know"—he keeps his fair eyes trained on me, piercing through mine—"you can lean on me for whatever you need. No strings attached. No catches."

"Boys only want one thing," Mom said.

Several times. All the time, actually. She said it when I started middle school, and again when I started high school, and even though she'd drilled it into me by the time I met Ezra, I didn't believe her.

And I still don't.

Not when Justin is looking at me like . . . *this*.

I melt.

Is he leaning closer?

He is.

"Justin," I half whisper, closing my eyes and leaning in. I feel a kiss on my forehead and then feel his forehead press against mine.

"Not now," he breathes, and I can tell he's holding back.

Even I don't know what the hell is going on with what I'm feeling, but I know one thing. That kiss *did* mean something. And I want him to kiss me again. *Really* kiss me this time. I want with Justin what I had with Ezra, just once.

I open my eyes to meet his.

"Please?"

I just want to forget it all for a while. I want to drown out everything else and be unable to think about anything but how warm he is.

But he pulls back. Looks away. Swallows. Pushes himself to his feet.

"Wouldn't be right," he says, and then he rushes to elaborate before I assume this is, of all things, a question of race. "You're in a crazy place right now. You just lost your mom. And your daughter."

I stand to meet him, glaring up at him.

"Don't."

"I don't want to take advantage—"

"You *wouldn't* be, Justin. I know what I want. . . ."

There's silence where the words "and I want you" should be.

A torrid concoction of rage and desire burns through me. I want him, and I hate what he's saying.

THIS BOOK MIGHT BE ABOUT ZINNIA

"Don't do what my mom did," I warn. "Don't treat me like a baby, Justin. You may be older than me, but you don't know everything."

Not *that* much older either. Nineteen.

I'm eighteen.

His cheeks have a faint tinge of pink, and he shakes his head.

"There's a difference between babying someone and respecting them. And I don't like to speak ill of the dead, but it sounds like your mom didn't know the difference either, so how could she teach you? Especially when teaching you to conflate the two gave her power?"

My whole body hums with anger. I want to throw something. I want to storm out and quit right now like I should have done when Justin gave away my journal.

How *dare* he speak of my mother like this?

His eyes go wide as he realizes what he's just said, and he shrinks.

"I'm sorry. I just hate seeing you mistreated," he says, looking at me again. "She didn't treat you right, Tuesday. She never listened to your feelings. Respected your boundaries. Did she even *let* you have boundaries around her?"

It stings and sends the first tears finally rolling down my cheeks. But he doesn't stop. He steps closer, making my heart skip a beat.

"She never let you be your own person or make your own

decisions. *Everything* you did was forced, wasn't it? All those times you tried to tell her how she was failing you as a mom, did she *ever* listen?"

He pulls back again, restraining himself. But he can't hide the veins in his neck, the red in his face. Even his voice fights to get out.

"She made you think *you* were crazy for even suggesting she could do better. There should be a word for that."

I bore into him with my gaze, feeling my eyebrow twitch as my heart pounds. Fighting him in silence like this is borderline painful, not because he's being cruel, but because I know he's right.

Every conversation with my mom ended with her in the right. Me backing down.

"She made you give her up, didn't she?"

It's like I've been hit by a freight train.

"What?" I ask.

There's no way he could know that. How the hell did he know that?

"Medical procedure?" he asks. "Won't happen again?"

"Justin—"

"Tuesday, every page I read of that journal bled *right* off the page. I could feel the sadness in every word, and I knew it was something special. Something real, something raw. I knew you'd been hurt, and I wasn't exactly sure how, but now . . . it all makes sense. All you've said about your mom is that she's

THIS BOOK MIGHT BE ABOUT ZINNIA

strict, and it's *obvious* from the story that you didn't want to lose your princess." He nods, narrowing his eyes. "And that should've been *your* choice."

"Justin, stop." I can't take any more of this. I turn and find my apron on the wall and charge for the exit, but he steps in front of me and leaves me with one last thing.

"Tuesday, wait." He sighs. "All I'm saying is if you never want to see her again, I understand. But just make sure it's on your terms."

"And how the hell should I do that, Justin? I don't even know where she is."

"That's never stopped any mother I know," he says, his mouth hinting at a grin.

And I realize the full weight of what he's suggesting.

I *do* have a way to make sure she's safe. An open door that I thought was closed until just a little while ago. A door I tried to close but maybe shouldn't have.

I have Ezra.

I stare at Justin, wondering if he's really suggesting what I'm thinking he is, and he nods to tell me yes.

"Go find him," he says, opening the door and stepping back out onto the floor. "I've got this place. And I'll be here where you get back."

Am I really ready for this? To find Ezra Terreni and make sure he and his family aren't going to find her and drag her back into whatever bloodstained feud lies between our families? Who's to say if I would've given her up if my mom's voice hadn't drowned out my own? What I do know, though, is I would give anything to keep her away from this legacy of secrecy and questionable ethics.

She deserves better.

I nod at Justin, gather my things, and step outside to catch the train to Ardmore. My fingers fly over the keyboard.

99966688#28#84433#7277755#8666*66444*4*448?

Me: you at the park today?

Ezra texts back immediately.

Ezra: Yeah. You around?

I find my seat on the train and let out a sigh, hoping this is a good idea, regardless of what my mom would say about this. If the Terrenis really are as dangerous as Mom said, I could be walking into a hornet's nest. Even if they've kicked him out of their house, he would never really be out of the family. I know how much family means to people in crime syndicates. At least, I've seen movies about it. I hope I'm doing the right thing.

Me: I will be in twenty minutes.

I step off the train onto the platform and read the new text from Ezra.

Ezra: I'm tuning my guitar by the swings.

THIS BOOK MIGHT BE ABOUT ZINNIA 229

My heart skips, picturing him sitting there, strumming away.

Just a block from the train station, there's an outdoor patio area. Actually, that's an exaggeration. It's just a few oversize outdoor couches under a pergola. And five blocks beyond that is the entrance to the park. It's as pretty as I imagined a park in Ardmore would be. The sunrise has turned the sky into a brilliant sorbet of colors, and the early-morning mist has settled over the grass. The mist and massive trees surrounding this place make it look like something out of *Jurassic Park*. And it's totally empty, totally motionless, until I spot him.

My heart flutters at the sight of him, rocking back and forth with his guitar in hand, plucking away at a tune I'd know anywhere. He pauses, presses his hand to the strings as I step closer. He hums the bridge, and the minute it ends, I'm ready with the first verse.

"'I remember when,'" I sing, drawing his gaze. That smile could melt ice, but I somehow find my voice again. "'I remember, I remember when I lost my mind.'"

I'm not the best singer. I won't be going on *American Idol* anytime soon, but at least I can carry a tune.

He grins and sings the next lines with me.

Maybe it's the fact that our voices are married out here in the otherwise quiet, or maybe it's just because it's Ezra, but something prompts me to hum the parts between lyrics.

And then, just as I get comfortable, I realize I don't know the next part. . . .

But Ezra does.

Silence as he presses his hand against all the strings at once. His eyes begin to glisten.

"'I just knew too . . . much,'" he sings.

And then he just . . . stares. Without looking away, he nestles the guitar down gently on the bark chips next to him, leaning it against the swing set pole.

"Hi," I say, my voice as awkward as I feel.

"I lied to you," he says suddenly, finally breaking his hold on me and staring down at his hands. He clicks his nails together in thought, and a million questions tumble through my mind, none of them good. I feel my face going cold.

He lied to me?

"About what?" I swallow, not sure I want to know the answer.

"About my family," he says, glancing over his shoulder toward the trees before looking back up at me with his brown eyes flashing more intensely than I've ever seen. It sends a chill through me. "You should stay far away from me, Tuesday. You don't know what they're capable of."

"No, Ezra, I—"

"Tuesday, *please*," he says, standing now. "At prom I couldn't—still *can't*—tell you everything. You have to understand—"

THIS BOOK MIGHT BE ABOUT ZINNIA

I cut him off before I can think.

"I know about your family," I say.

But do I?

I'm not nearly as confident as I hope I look as I hold his gaze.

"My mom told me everything," I say, in a sick way relieved that I don't have to worry anymore about tarnishing her reputation or disparaging her. What's she going to do? Lecture me from the grave?

Guilt hits me. How can I be happy my mom is gone? Is it wrong to feel this relieved? This free?

"You don't have to hide it anymore," I say, my fingers trembling. I knit them together to keep my nerves under control. It doesn't work. "You're not your family, Ezra."

"She didn't tell you everything," he says, his words heavy. "She didn't tell you about my father. What he's capable of. I can't tell you much, Tuesday, but I can tell you to stay *far* away from Matteo Terreni."

His father's name is bitter in his mouth, and when he says it, something in his eyes lights on fire, and I catch a glimpse of the boy who held me so close that night, who kept me so safe. The boy I could tell anything for a little while. Ezra Terreni, the boy who will probably always have a piece of my heart.

Maybe Justin was right.

I imagine how I'd be feeling right now staring at Ezra like this if I'd *actually* gone through with what I wanted to just an hour ago. Maybe I do have things to think through first before I get too close to anyone again. This is all just . . . *way* too much.

The overwhelming feeling of defeat crushes me as Ezra nods.

"You're right," he says. "I'm not my family. And you're not yours. I would never hurt you, or do anything to hurt you."

This doesn't make any sense. I can *feel* there's so much he isn't saying.

"Ezra," I plead in a desperate whisper and stepping closer, "what did your father do to my family? Please, I have to know."

He lets out the world's biggest sigh, which is followed by the world's longest silence, before picking up the guitar again and plucking a couple of strings. He glances around. In a voice so soft, it's barely there, he says, "Does the name Derek Foley Cooper mean anything to you?"

Why does that sound familiar?

I think back, suddenly realizing. The newspaper clipping in the attic. The officer who shot himself.

I nod, glancing around the park out of nervous habit. My heart races like I'm opening a file on Mom's laptop that she never wanted me to know even existed. With how jumpy Ezra is, I half expect snipers to be hidden among the trees surrounding us.

He plucks again.

"He's the reason you and I aren't siblings."

What?

THIS BOOK MIGHT BE ABOUT ZINNIA

I blink, thinking. What the hell does that even mean?

"Ezra—"

"My dad was with your mom," he explains plainly, his voice still soft, "before she left for your dad."

He stops plucking long enough to level his eyes at me and say, "You see the motive."

My throat closes. Dizziness overwhelms me.

Ezra's dad had it out for mine the moment he met him. All he needed was one good reason to kill him. The police statement. That's what did it.

He stands and closes the gap between us, offering another glance across the park, this time in the opposite direction, and he reaches for my hands, sending my heart thundering again.

"Ezra, what are you—"

He kisses me, hard, and my words have nowhere to go. I feel his hands on my forearms, and then around my back, and warmth floods me.

"Ezra," I muster against him. "Ezra, I can't. Please—"

He pulls away and smiles down at me, his eyes hungry and searching.

And then I remember Amy.

I yank away.

"You're taken now, remember?" I didn't mean for it to sound so venomous, but I can't help how I feel. What the hell is he thinking, kissing me like that when he has a *girlfriend*?

To my horror, he *smirks*!

"I can't help it, Tuesday," he groans as he sinks back down into the swing. "You drive me crazy." He takes up his guitar again, cradling it in his lap like a newborn baby, before looking back up at me. "For the record, I want nothing to do with my family."

He strums a single, gentle chord.

"You're lucky in a way, you know, not to have to deal with yours," he says. "You're free."

You're free?

That's what I was supposed to feel when I watched the nurse carry baby girl away, wet and kicking and screaming. I'll never be free of that sound.

But at least now, with Ezra's word, I know he won't be telling his family anything, even if he finds out about her.

She's safe from them.

As safe as I can ensure she is.

The adoption agency is gone, along with their records, so there's another avenue the Terrenis can't use to find her.

"'My heroes had the heart to lose their lives out on the limb,'" he croons. "'And all I remember is thinking . . . I want to be like them.'"

I sink into the swing next to him, and for a moment we both mourn the families we were born into, and *I* wonder, if we'd come from different parents, if we could have had a life together. If he could speak freely with me. If we could have looked at each other across a living room with a cooing baby between us, assuring each other with just a look that we'd be all right.

"'Ever since I was little,'" I sing, unable to hide the shake in my voice as the tears well. "'Ever since I was little it looked like fun.'"

His voice joins mine.

"'And it's no coincidence I've come
And I can die when I'm done.

But maybe I'm crazy
Maybe you're crazy
Maybe we're crazy
Probablyyyyy.'"

I burst through the back door of Café Alba like a hurricane, my heart pounding as my eyes search the dimly lit space, my mattress on the floor in the corner.

"Justin?" I ask into the dark.

"Tuesday?" comes a gentle voice, in stark contrast to my mom's, from out at the bar. Justin appears in the doorway, his strong arm up with his hand resting on the doorframe, sleeves halfway rolled up, looking at me with glistening eyes. "Are you—"

"I'm okay," I say, my eyes burning with tears.

Silence settles between us as he looks me up and down, questions all over his face.

"Really, I am. I'm okay. And she'll be okay."

"You talked to Ezra?" he asks.

I nod as the first tear rolls down my cheek, and he steps closer, faster, until—

I'm in his arms faster than I can realize, holding on to him like he's the only thing tethering me to this reality. He envelops me and holds me tight.

"I'm so sorry," he says, his voice cracking. "I could say it over and over again forever and still not say it enough. I'm *sorry* for what I did. I just wanted someone to see what a great writer you are. I *know* how much you want to write. How much you love it. I just . . . I couldn't see you just throw your dreams away. You deserve to have your work read, but if I could go back in time, I never would've—"

"I know why you did," I cut in.

God, he's so warm against me. And he smells like the faintest vanilla now that I'm this close to him. I've *never* been so close to him.

"You should probably get back to the counter in case someone comes in," I say.

"I've locked up."

I pull away and look up at him in shock.

"What? Why?"

"I couldn't make coffee for people knowing you might be

in trouble out there, with Ezra. I didn't know what he would do," he says, nodding to the back door. "I don't care about Café Alba losing a few bucks while we're both falling apart. The coffee doesn't matter. The customers can wait. All that matters is . . ."

He cuts himself short as he stares deep into my eyes. He swallows, deciding what to say next. My heart thunders in my chest, and I stand frozen in his arms as I realize what he's not saying. Until he finally, *finally* says it.

"All that matters is you, Tuesday."

He asks without asking, his eyes darting down to my lips, before I lean in and he pulls me close and, *finally*, kisses me.

CHAPTER 19

Zinnia
2024

TURNS OUT CAFÉ ALBA IS PRETTY COZY INSIDE. COZY enough to make me want to take off my jacket and hat, but we'll only be in long enough to grab a cup before catching our train. It's cozy, all right, although it's *obviously* old. Smells like coffee, pastries, and old books. The walls are a dingy yellow, were probably once the color of sunshine, and there's a Tuscan air to the whole place. Very early 2000s. In fact, the only thing *not* old about this place is the huge TV mounted in the corner, so high that it's almost touching the ceiling, playing CNN.

Just under the TV there's a wall with photos of famous people through the years, probably because it's right by the Amtrak station. I'm sure people of all walks hop off the train

THIS BOOK MIGHT BE ABOUT ZINNIA

from New York and stop by for a cup. I don't recognize most of these people.

"Welcome in." A bearded man in flannel greets us from behind the counter, warm but rehearsed, a hello I know all too well.

"Hi," I trill, still examining the celeb wall, where I spot— oh hey, Timothée Chalamet! This seems like his kind of place. Oh, and Zendaya was here! My heart flutters at the thought of even breathing the same air as her.

Milo steps up to the counter and asks, "Do you have any almond milk?"

The man shakes his head sadly, and I notice his name tag: JUSTIN.

"Ah, sorry, I think we're out," he says. "My wife just went in the back to check for more." He nods toward the door to his left, which I assume leads to a back room.

"That's all right. I'll just have an Americano," says Milo, glancing back at me. "We're kind of in a hurry."

"Catching a train?" asks the man, who picks up a hot cup and flips it over once one-handed. Yup, he's been doing this awhile.

I'm giving the celeb wall one last glance when I notice it—a picture of a woman with a blond bob posing by herself in front of the espresso machine with a smile and eyes I'd recognize anywhere. I squint, realizing . . . *No way . . . Is that . . . ?*

"You had Jodelle Rae West in here?" I ask, reaching up and scratching my forehead under my hat.

The man behind the counter doesn't look up from the machine as it drips its hot elixir into Milo's cup, but his pursed lips and quick blinking before he says "Yup" tell me there's something he's not saying.

Clearly, Jodelle is a sore subject. Maybe they had a fling or something once upon a time. If Justin were Black, I might be wondering if he was my birth dad.

"We're actually headed to New York to see her," says Milo as I step up to the counter.

"Oh, no kidding?" asks Justin, although his voice is flat and dull.

"Could I have a twelve-ounce vanilla latte, please?" I ask, an obvious attempt to change the subject.

"Absolutely," says Justin, glancing up at me. There's kindness behind his blue eyes, his strawberry blond hair graying in streaks at his temples. He's handsome, in a dad kind of way.

"I've never been to the Big Apple myself," he admits as the Americano finishes and he pulls the steam wand down to start my latte. "Philly Center City is plenty busy for me."

"Fair," says Milo, picking up his Americano from the bar and taking a sip.

"Sorry again about the alt milk," says Justin, glancing at the back room door again. "If you want, I can ask her if she's found any."

"Nah, we're good," I say, glancing at my smartwatch for effect. We really can't miss this train, though, if we're going

THIS BOOK MIGHT BE ABOUT ZINNIA

to have a chance at getting to the front of Jodelle's signing line at all tonight. "That signing line will probably be a mile long when we get there as it is."

Justin pauses for way too long before finally saying, "Yeah. Probably."

I hear boxes shuffle somewhere in the back.

"You okay?" asks Justin, looking toward the door.

A muffled voice comes through from the other side.

"Yeah!"

The most exasperated "yeah" I've ever heard. Clearly, she's straining back there, holding or moving something heavy. Justin shrugs and gives us both a sheepish smile as he passes the latte across the counter.

"Can't help someone who won't admit they need it, am I right?" he asks.

"Tell me about it," says Milo, glancing back at me.

"Wooooow," I say playfully. "Feeling very attacked right now."

"Okay, let me stay out of the middle of that," chuckles Justin. "Safe travels. And, uh, have fun meeting Jodelle. She's . . ."

He pauses, seemingly searching for the perfect words.

"She's one of a kind."

Milo and I cradle our coffees, thank him for them—this latte is one of the smoothest I've ever had—and step out the front door and back into the bone-chilling air. As Milo takes my hand to help me down the icy steps, and we turn toward the station, my phone pings with a notification I haven't seen before.

Location services enabled. Disable?

What the hell?

I hit the disable button and slip the phone back into my pocket. No need to bring Big Brother along with me. Maybe someone accidentally tried to connect to my hot spot or something?

Before following Milo down the street, I glance up at the window and see Justin's wife step through the back room door, straining under the weight of a small but clearly heavy box, which Justin runs to scoop up. She smiles up at him, radiating gratitude that feels years deep.

Her warm brown skin glows in the yellow coffee shop lights, and just before I walk past the window entirely, she spots me, her eyes lingering before she gives me a smile too and a nod.

"Ready to meet your mom?" asks Milo.

I smile up at him.

"My *maybe* mom, remember?"

"I don't know. Bestselling-author mom? Harvard-bound daughter? Maybe success is genetic."

I let out a sigh. Guess I should focus on that. Whether Jodelle is my birth mom or not, after tonight I'll have enough material to write an essay interesting and compelling enough to get me into Harvard.

THIS BOOK MIGHT BE ABOUT ZINNIA

But when we finally board the train and settle into our seats, and Philadelphia starts flying by outside the window, my mind drifts, and I can't stop imagining how incredible it would be, and all that it would mean, if she is.

CHAPTER 20

Tuesday

2024
AN HOUR AFTER ZINNIA LEAVES CAFÉ ALBA . . .

I WIPE THE FRONT COUNTER FOR WHAT MUST BE THE fiftieth time today and heave the heaviest sigh I've heaved all week. My knees are screaming for a seat, and the ache in my lower back is ramping up. Just minutes left until closing, and I absolutely can't wait to lock that door for the day.

I feel Justin's hand on the back of my upper arm.

"You can take a break," he says, his voice as gentle and warm as ever. I smile, but I can tell by the way he looks at me that he knows it's forced.

"I'm fine," I insist.

"That makes a second reason why I think you need a break."

"What's the first reason?" I ask, turning to pick up a box

THIS BOOK MIGHT BE ABOUT ZINNIA

full of gum and cookies. We're getting low in front of the register. He rests his hand on the box.

"The first is that I love you." He grins, those eyes just as bright and earnest as the day we met. He takes my hand and leans against the counter beside me. "And you've never put yourself first. And we're getting to the age where we *both* deserve to put ourselves first."

Getting to the age, this guy says.

"Hilarious." I smile, flipping the lid off the box and pulling out a few packs of gum. "You saying we're old?"

"What if I am?" he asks. He leans forward and touches his nose to mine. "What if I'm saying it's time we sold this place and made off for—I don't know—Iceland or something?"

"Iceland?" I laugh, giving him an eye roll. I cross the floor to put the box away.

"Switzerland?" he offers.

"Warmer, please."

This might be the fifth time he's brought up the idea this month. Maybe he's serious. We practically live here at the café, after all. We spend more time here than in our apartment in Fishtown.

"Cancún?"

"*Too* warm."

"Los Angeles?"

"Closer. What about the Pacific Northwest?"

"You want to go where they pronounce it 'waw-ter'?" he laughs.

"Not really," I say with a smile, and I mean it. "I want to stay here with you."

"Well, the 'with you' part is perfect, but do you really want to run this place forever?" He looks up and around as if he suddenly doesn't recognize it, when we've been here almost every day since we bought it. Sure, there were moments when one of us would want to quit, think about leaving and seeing the world or going back to school or starting a family, but the truth is . . . I think we were both too happy with each other to make a change that might mess that up.

It's comfortable here. *Really* comfortable.

"You don't get tired of seeing the same four walls every day?" he asks, glancing at the front door to make sure we don't have any customers about to come in. "You don't get tired of the mundane, Tuesday? You don't want to see something new?"

"It's a privilege to be curious about the world, you know," I say, processing the idea as I say it. "I kinda *like* the mundane, Justin. It's safe. It's home."

He swallows and looks at the floor.

"You're right," he says, "but I want you to know, even though we've been married ten years, even if I have to tell you this every day until we hit *twenty* years, you are safe with me."

THIS BOOK MIGHT BE ABOUT ZINNIA

"I know." I nod. And I know it's true. I could go anywhere with him, do anything with him, and I would never be afraid. But something deep within me, buried since forever, tells me I still need to be. And I don't know if he'll ever understand that. I want the normal, the expected.

I want routine and reliability, and I wouldn't mind waking up next to him every morning in the same little home we've made together until the day I die, with no interruptions.

"Love you," he sings with a goofy grin.

It brings forth a laugh I didn't expect.

"Love you, too."

He looks up at the clock and then makes for the front door to lock it for the night.

Seconds later, after we've both breathed that end-of-the-day sigh every hourly worker in existence knows well, a whirlwind of hair and clothing with hands slams *smack* against the glass door.

A woman takes shape after I've had a moment to settle the adrenaline coursing through me, and she raps on the door, her eyes wide and panicked.

"Sorry, are you closed?" she cries.

I resist the urge to roll my eyes so hard that they get stuck at the back of my head. The door's locked, it's 8:00 p.m., the *exact* time the clearly written sign on our door says we close every day of the week, *and* our chairs are inverted on top of our tables.

How could she possibly think we are open?

I nod at her through the window, and the last glimmer of hope vanishes from her face.

"Please," she begs, tucking her blond curls behind her ears and scrambling to pull out her phone. "I'm looking for my daughter."

CHAPTER 21

Zinnia

2024

THE DELAWARE RIVER IS SO PRETTY AT SUNSET.

From my window seat, it feels like I can see all of New Jersey. I wonder where Jodelle is from. Her voice in my headphones answers the interview questions with finesse and poise, and I wonder how differently I would speak if she'd raised me. Probably not much different from Mom, since I don't hear an accent from either of them.

"Inspiration can come from anywhere, you know?" she says with a smile. "When writing *Little Heart*, I drew inspiration from nature. I often take my little mister for walks in Central Park in his little stroller with his favorite mouse toy, and I find inspiration all around me."

"You good?" asks Milo, nudging me.

"Yeah," I say, my mind stuck on meeting Jodelle. I hope she's kind. Her smile is kind. At least while she's interviewing. But even if she is, how the hell do I bring all of this up? Do I just . . . let her know how much *Little Heart* inspires me?

Hey, Jodelle, I'm a huge fan.

No, no, *everyone* in line is going to say that.

Hey, Jodelle, how many kids do you know with a heart-shaped birthmark on their forehead?

Nah, that's implying that she based Princess Little Heart on a real person, and as little as I know about being a professional writer, rule number one is to insist that all characters mentioned in the work are entirely fictional and any resemblance to real persons, living or dead, is purely coincidental.

Hey, Jodelle, did you, like, lose track of a baby seventeen years ago?

Immediate security deployment.

The interviewer on *Good Morning America* leans forward curiously.

"And so your little mister, that's your . . . pet?"

"Cat," Jodelle chuckles. "Benedict is the only man I need."

I smirk. I feel that.

I could probably go my whole life with just a cat. But then the interviewer says something that breaks my heart a little.

"Cats make the best children, too, don't they?"

"He's the only child I really need, and spoiled like one. He even has a baby monitor in his room." And then Jodelle *laughs*,

THIS BOOK MIGHT BE ABOUT ZINNIA

along with the interviewer and audience. She's clearly happy with Benedict and zero kids. Maybe I'm making a mistake. Maybe this whole trip was a bad idea. "Whaaaat?" she asks playfully. "What if I step into my walk-in fridge and can't hear him?"

My phone pings with a text.

Kelly: Zinnia Michelle, where are you?

Ugh, God, why is it any of her business? I'm seventeen and about to be out of her house, when I'm going to have to travel alone—*gasp*—*all the time.* How avant-garde and daring! I let out a grunt as I fire a text back.

Me: I'm still with Milo.

If only Mom could appreciate all the pain I've spared her through lying by omission. I could've just told her I'm on a train to New York and turned my phone to silent. But instead I watch as a typing notice pops up. She's replying.

Kelly: Are you at his house?

What the hell? Why does she care so much? I feel rage course through me, and I jam my phone back into my bag without answering. I shut my eyes against the pulsing anger. Who the hell does she think she is, interrogating me like this? All I've ever done is gotten straight As and stayed out of trouble. And as a mom, those are all the details she should really care about, right?

Milo takes out his own headphones and peers at me as I slump down in the seat.

"It's your mom, isn't it?"

Can she just stop for a while and be my friend sometimes? Isn't that what she's supposed to become after I turn eighteen anyway? Transitioning from a mom to a friend? How are we supposed to share mimosas on some rooftop brunch as adults one day if she's always going to monitor my alcohol consumption and track where I'm—

"Oh my God," I say, realizing what happened. I pull out my phone again as Milo asks, "What's up?"

"I didn't tell you," I say, finding that "location services enabled" notification from earlier, and finding a whole string of others like it that have been cropping up in the background. "I . . . I got this notification, at Café Alba, and . . ."

"And what?" he asks. "Zinn, talk to me."

I scroll through notification after notification as the full realization sinks in.

"My mom's been tracking us."

"What?" he asks.

"She knows where we've been going. The coffee shop, homecoming . . ."

The park?

Hell.

"Milo, I need to ignore my phone," I say. "If there's an emergency, you need to be ready to call someone, okay?"

"Okay," he says, shrugging, with a tone that questions how in the world we would have an emergency out here. Maybe he's right. We're almost adults now, on a train to New York at

THIS BOOK MIGHT BE ABOUT ZINNIA   253

sunset, going to a book signing by a famous author in a public location with plenty of witnesses.

Why would we have an emergency?

"You in the bad place again?" he asks. I can feel my fingers going tingly with anxiety, and my stomach twists into a knot. I nod.

"Yeah, I am."

"Can I hold you?" he asks, and I nod. He puts a lanky arm around me and pulls me close, and we both sigh against each other. I wonder if he needed this closeness too.

"Milo," I say.

"Yeah?"

"I'm . . . still really sorry about your mom. She was—"

"It's okay."

"She was always so great to me."

I wish I could do more. I want to fill the silence with something, anything. But I realize talking might just make things worse, so I leave him with, "Just let me know if I can help."

"Just promise whether Jodelle is your birth mom or not, you'll remember you're awesome without her."

"Yeah," I say, "of course."

"And you won't forget about me at Harvard, even with your protagonist energy."

"Never." I have to smile. "Every protagonist needs a best friend. Especially one who's the protagonist of their own story."

I shut my eyes and take a deep breath, smelling the patchouli and vetiver on him. Why can't my mom be more like Milo? Content just to bask in the silence with me? Let me feel what I feel without asking too many questions? My phone vibrates again, and I happily ignore it. But at the same time, part of me wonders if I'm being ridiculous. It's my *mom*, after all. Of course she's being a little over the top. That's what a mom does.

Apparently.

Which is part of the reason why I can't see myself having kids. I can't imagine caring *that* much about anyone else.

Holy shit, I really do sound like a narc.

Is that what this is? Ignoring my mom's calls to galivant a state over to find my possible-birth-mom-who-may-have-written-a-book-about-me-but-hasn't-a-clue-who-I-am? What if I *am* a narcissist, and this is just one manifestation of my condition? Ignoring my own mom, who raised me as her flesh and blood, and for what? Some vain pursuit of association with a celebrity?

Protagonist energy.

"Milo," I ask as I sink deeper into the mire of panic, "can someone have protagonist energy without being a narcissist?"

After a moment of silence he shifts in his seat.

"I think so," he says. "Yeah, I think they can. Your mom's a great example."

THIS BOOK MIGHT BE ABOUT ZINNIA

255

"How?" I'm genuinely curious. *My* mom? Protagonist energy? Never really saw it.

"She's *really* into perfection. Like, effortless perfection?" he asks.

I don't get it.

"It seems really important to her to *be* perfect and *appear* relaxed and cool. Think about how many things she's signed you up for through your entire life. Everything she's pushed you toward is in pursuit of admission into Harvard. Has she ever suggested you do anything just for *fun*?"

Fun? Yeah! I've had fun in swim class and my AP classes and honor roll, and every summer we go to a different country for a two-week vacation. She always suggested museums or cultural tours, but . . . that's just . . . what moms do, right?

"I don't know," says Milo, his voice now strained. "Remember when my mom showed us how to bake cookies and then ate them with us in the playhouse? Things like that never appear on résumés, but I'll remember that day forever."

Milo's body trembles just enough for me to notice, and my hand finds his.

"So will I," I say. "I won't forget her, and I won't forget you. I promise, Milo."

More buzzes.

More ignoring.

I had no choice, I realize, but to take this trip to New York.

If not for the essay, then to find out from my possible would-have-been mom what it's like to spend time together without steering the ship toward an Ivy League admission.

Buzz.

Buzz.

Buzz.

Milo looks at me, and I feel him squeeze my hand.

"I'm, uh," he says, and sniffs, dragging his wrist along his upper lip, "I'm gonna go find a bathroom. Need anything?"

I shake my head as he stands and slips his hand from mine. He disappears down the aisle, and I feel another set of buzzes in my pocket.

Buzz.

Buzz.

I need a distraction.

I pull out the book and examine the cover. Maybe I should skim the rest, absorb as much as I can before I actually meet Jodelle. I've pieced together enough clues already that talking to her about this won't sound weird, whatever the outcome. Whether she's actually my birth mom or not.

So why is my heart racing?

Maybe it's the idea that I could be the daughter of a best-selling author? In fact, the only essay ending better than venturing on a fruitless quest to find my birth mom through clues in a bestselling novel is venturing on a fruit*ful* quest to find my birth mom through clues in a bestselling novel.

THIS BOOK MIGHT BE ABOUT ZINNIA

I run my hands over the cover like I'm looking at it for the first time.

What if this all ends in a yes? Am I ready for that?

Am I ready to possibly *actually* find her?

I guess I have to be. For Harvard.

Anything for Harvard.

Someone walks past my arm down the aisle, and I glance up at a tall man in wool slacks and shiny black shoes. He looks over his shoulder at me and offers a warm smile before turning toward the seat across from me.

He unbuttons the only fastened button on his heavy wool winter coat and sits, facing me and smiling with a kind nod.

I nod back warmly and look down at the book again, flipping it open to where my Penn Valley High bookmark sits with a gold tassel hanging over the top.

"Pretty bookmark," says the man, his voice so deep and rich, it almost hums out of him, a thick Italian accent curving his words.

"Thanks," I reply, although I'm immediately wondering why this guy is talking to me. I'm a girl traveling alone on an Amtrak train, and there are a million other seats open in this car alone.

I focus on the book instead, finding the paragraph I left off on.

But then he interrupts again.

"I'm reading that same one," he says, reaching into the bag on his hip and pulling out his own copy.

"Oh!" I smile warmly now. No wonder he's talking to me. Just making conversation.

His hair is dark ringlets nearly long enough to cover his ears, and his dark eyes smile at me as he continues.

"How far have you gotten?" he asks, leaning forward to get a closer look.

"Oh, um," I say, shutting it instinctively, "I'm in the middle of the rising tension, I think. Sky is finding her way to Little Heart while Land sinks into the earth's crust."

"Fascinating scene," he says, opening his hands in thought. "Are you a fan of hers?"

"Jodelle?" I ask, noticing the lift in my own voice at her name. "Yeah, I read her duology when it first came out. I'm glad she's branched into adult."

"That's how it works with many authors, right?" he asks, sitting up again and leaning back against his seat with a smug smile. "Their audiences grow up into adults, and their material evolves with it."

Yeah, I guess he's right. Musicians do it all the time. Even children's characters address their adult former fans sometimes now. Had never heard of Steve or *Blue's Clues*, but everyone my mom's age was in tears listening to him tell them they did a good job that day or whatever.

"Matteo," he says with a nod hello. "And you?"

I know better than to give my real name to a stranger on a train across state lines.

THIS BOOK MIGHT BE ABOUT ZINNIA

"Kelly," I say reflexively.

Weird that my mom's name popped up first, but whatever. I'll go with it.

"Hmm," he says pensively. "Kelly."

He's thinking about my name for a touch too long, and staring.

"Yeah, just . . . Kelly," I say, hoping the *duh* comes through my tone.

"Apologies, you just . . . look familiar. Are you sure we haven't met before?"

He's probably been through Bean Rock before at some point. Maybe he saw me while I was on break in the café or something. If he'd seen me at the counter, I'd remember him. I lock in faces like no one else.

I study his face for a minute, really trying to think if I've seen him. Now that I look close, the shape of his eyes, his thick arched brows, and the dark curly hair all remind me of someone just out of reach in my brain.

"Maybe?" I shrug.

He smiles, opens his copy of *Little Heart*, and thumbs through the pages.

"You must be going to her signing," he says, kind of like a question, kind of not.

"Oh, when is that?" I ask.

He stares at me curiously.

"You and your friend don't talk quietly."

Embarrassment creeps up the back of my neck at the realization that he knows I'm lying.

"You don't have to tell me your real name," he says with a smirk as he gets to his feet. "I don't blame you. But when you see Jodelle, could you ask her something for me?"

I nod reflexively. Anything to get this conversation over with faster.

He extends a hand to me for a handshake, I take it hesitantly, and he tightens his grip a little firmer than a squeeze and leans down to me so he can speak lower.

"Tell her Matteo Terreni wants to know why she kept her from Ezra."

A smile and nod later, he lets go and steps down the aisle toward the back of the train.

CHAPTER 22

Tuesday

2024
TWO HOURS AFTER ZINNIA LEAVES CAFÉ ALBA . . .

I LOOK AT JUSTIN, WHO'S LOOKING AT ME.

He shrugs.

"She doesn't look like she's here to rob the place," he whispers.

I rest the broom against the wall and make my way around the counter.

"They never do," I grumble.

I step up to the door and look at her through the glass. There's no way I'm opening this place up without a damn good reason, because of safety and because, for fuck's sake, I'm tired.

"Your daughter isn't here," I announce, hoping it's enough to make her give up. If her daughter is truly missing, she's wasting time hanging around here looking. Can't she understand that?

Unless, I think, *she's not actually here to find her daughter but to demand everything we have in the register.*

She shifts her weight from foot to foot and looks down at her phone nervously. She motions with a single finger for me to wait a moment, and I sigh a huge sigh. I just want to go to the back and sit. And then go home and lie down.

Maybe Justin's right. Maybe we *are* getting too old to be on our feet all day.

The woman holds up a photo of a teenage girl in a sparkly lavender prom gown with a corset in the middle, and I recognize her as the girl who was in here earlier with that tall black-haired lanky kid. She walked in all bundled up with her beanie plunging over her forehead, so I could barely see her face, but in this photo, in that purple dress, which I might've worn to my own senior prom if my mom hadn't forced me into that scratchy black number, she's absolutely radiant.

"Dark hair," says the woman, "dark eyes, birthmark on her forehead. Just not in this photo. Her curl is in the way."

Well, her beanie was too low on her head for me to see anything like that last bit, but I look up at the woman through the window, and her blue eyes come to life again as I nod yes.

"She was in here earlier with her boyfriend."

Her face contorts into a bitter laugh and she shakes her head.

THIS BOOK MIGHT BE ABOUT ZINNIA 263

"Not her boyfriend. Just a friend."

I wouldn't be *that* naive about it. That's word for word what I told my mom before I went to Ezra's house all those years ago, that I was visiting a *friend*.

The woman glances down the street and rakes her fingers through her hair. Then she turns back to me, clearly desperate for answers I can't give.

"Did she tell you at all where she might be headed?"

I glance at Justin, who's taken up the broom and busied himself with sweeping up some of the sugar from around the self-service bar in the corner. We exchange a look, and I hope he understands what mine is asking: *Should we tell her?*

I remember my childhood as clearly as if I'm still in it—all the gaslighting my mom did, now that I know the word for it. All the times she made me feel so small in her house, so insignificant, so clueless, like I had no idea what was good for me.

Well, I *did* know. Or at least, I figured it out eventually. I've found it. With Justin.

Even though I got it wrong with Ezra the first time. And if I'd listened to her, I would have kept shutting Justin out just because Ezra hurt me to my core.

I study this woman in the window, her blue eyes hopeful I can give her any detail. But I don't know what kind of mother she is, if this whole thing isn't a hoax to begin with. I don't know why her daughter was in here earlier. She could be on the run from her, and when I think of all the times someone could've called up my mom to out me for whatever innocent thing I was doing, I'm eternally grateful they didn't.

I know what I have to do.

"I'm sorry," I say with a shake of my head. "Like I said, she's not here."

CHAPTER 23

Zinnia

2024

PENN STATION IS JUST THREE BLOCKS FROM FILA-ment Bookstore.

It's 8:00 p.m.

"Isn't this kinda late for a signing?" says someone nearby as Milo and I walk side by side through the thin layer of snow building on the sidewalk. I glance over my shoulder as a woman and young girl slip past us.

"Scuse us," says the mom with a smile before she turns back to what looks like her daughter. "I don't know," she muses, "I guess different authors have different signing times. If they all happened earlier in the day, they might not have time for them all."

The girl seems satisfied with that logic, and she cuddles

up under the woman's arm. And then I see it. The line. The *massive* line that wraps around the building at least halfway, from the looks of it. We join at the very back, behind this mom and daughter as they embrace in the cold.

Milo puts his arm around my shoulders and squeezes.

"You excited to meet her?" he asks.

"Yeah," I say, and then, "No. . . . Kinda?"

I've played it out ten thousand times in my head. What will she be like? What will she do if I start asking her questions about Princess Little Heart?

What was your inspiration for that heart-shaped birthmark? I'm sure she's heard that one a million times.

Who was your inspiration for her? I'm sure she's prepared with a legal answer for that one. Any resemblance to real persons, living or dead, is purely coincidental.

Did you lose track of a baby seventeen years ago?

A wave of panic washes over me.

If she *wanted* to find me, wouldn't she have brought it up by now? Wouldn't she have mentioned in that interview about her cat, Benedict, that she's always *wanted* a daughter? Or that she *had* a daughter and lost her, and *will the real heart-shaped-birthmark girl please stand up, please stand up, please stand up*?

Wouldn't she have put out an APB on me if she wanted to find me?

The line inches forward.

THIS BOOK MIGHT BE ABOUT ZINNIA

"Milo, this is batshit."

"Yup."

"Why the hell did I think this was a good idea?"

"Because you're *also* batshit, and I'm here with you doing this because *I'm* batshit. And because how many people have an opportunity to find out if their favorite author is actually blood-related to them?"

I let out a sigh, my breath white clouds in the chilly air. I guess he's right. The worst thing she can say is no.

The line moves again.

"But how will I know if that's a *real* no, or if she's—I don't know—telling me off? What if she *is* my birth mom and . . ."

Oh my God, what if this becomes a race thing?

What if she can tell I'm Black just by looking at me? What if she spots my Black features, and I don't look enough like her for her to accept me, like some kind of animal instinct? What if I'm like one of those baby birds that get scooped up by a human after falling out of a nest and get rejected by the mom because they no longer smell like her?

Logic barrels through my brain like a snowplow, shoveling the mountain of thoughts accumulating by the second.

Calm down, Zinnia, you're overreacting. Jodelle isn't an animal. She's a human. And if she's worth knowing, she won't care what you look like.

A deep breath helps slow my heart back to normal.

The line shuffles forward again.

But I'm not so naive that I don't realize Jodelle might want to leave a spontaneous encounter with a man in her past. And if she's secretly a racist piece of shit, *especially* a man of color. Something sour curls in my stomach at the thought.

What if my birth mother is a racist?

"Zinn." Milo's voice cuts through the noise.

"Hmm?" I ask, still barely here as the line keeps moving.

Shit, does that mean Jodelle is shuffling people so quickly through the line that I won't have time to ask her anything?

"Did you finish the book?" he asks.

"Not yet."

He's quiet, and I hope I haven't hurt his feelings.

"It's just that I've been so busy studying the first half for my essay—"

I stop right there and it sinks in: I've taken Milo's gift and turned it into a tool to rocket my Harvard application into the accepted pile.

"Sorry, Milo. I really am. I'll read it on the train back, okay? Promise."

"I think you'll really like the end," he says.

"Wait, I didn't know *you'd* read it."

"Yeah, I picked it up after I finished *The Well.*"

I gasp.

"You finished it and you didn't talk to me about it?"

He pulls away and looks down at me with the most confused face.

THIS BOOK MIGHT BE ABOUT ZINNIA

"When would I have had time to talk to you about it?"

"Fair," I concede as the line moves again.

We shuffle and shuffle, the line grows shorter and shorter, and the night grows colder and colder, and I wonder how many more readers Jodelle can stand to meet. I'm sure she loves this part of her job, or she wouldn't do it. With so many copies flying off shelves, she must be raking in enough money to rest on her laurels forever away from all of civilization if she wants to, right?

Okay, maybe not forever and ever, but long enough to go without public appearances for a while.

Soon we're through the front doors of Filament Bookstore, and the bookseller at the front closes the glass doors behind us to keep the heat in until the line moves again. My fingers, even as I slip off the winter gloves, are totally numb and red, thawing in this warm book palace. I look up and around at its majesty. Books line every wall and table, and when I look ahead, I realize the line to Jodelle is only ten or so people long, and in the gaps between readers, I see her.

Her blond bob hangs just past shoulder length, a brilliant contrast to her burgundy turtleneck. She's smiling up at the next person in line, who's just bouncing with energy as they regale her with everything they felt as they turned the pages she wrote.

I swallow, and I suddenly feel warm and clammy all over.

There's only one word I can think of to describe Jodelle Rae West in person—vibrant.

She's totally electric sitting at that table as she picks up a bookmark and pin and hands them to the next reader in line. "Oh my God, I *loved* the ending!" they exclaim. "What made you decide—"

They cut themself off before leaning down and asking their question too quietly for anyone else in line to hear. Milo and I are only three people away now, but I still can't hear them. Jodelle looks up at them with a hearty chuckle and says, "I've always preferred happy endings, you know. Everyone deserves to find their forever place."

Their forever place.

We shuffle closer. Two people left. My eyes are trained on Jodelle. Maybe she'll understand this whole situation. Maybe she'll stand with tears in her eyes and welcome me into her arms and tell me how she's spent her whole life looking for the daughter she lost. Maybe we'll be . . . I don't know . . . friends?

Like my real mom and I are supposed to be at this point?

As if she's heard me, my phone buzzes in my pocket again, and unexpected rage surges forth.

How dare she track me? And without me knowing!

When have I *ever* given her a reason not to trust me? When have I drunk or done anything that could remotely be considered a drug? When have I brought home anything less than an A? When have I ever stayed over someone's house without telling her first? I've *always* been trustworthy. I

THIS BOOK MIGHT BE ABOUT ZINNIA

might be the most trustworthy kid at all of Penn Valley High.

So now? She gets what she wants to pretend she's had this whole time: a daughter who makes her worry.

I slip my phone out and hold the off button, then swipe so the screen goes completely dark. I look to Milo to see if he notices. He doesn't.

He's observing, like he always does in a new place.

"Shopping?" I ask.

"Maybe. Just wondering if they have this many new and shiny books in Trinity Library."

Why the hell would he be wondering that?

"In Dublin?" I ask, trying not to get distracted by the line that's not really even a line anymore.

"Is Trinity Library in Dublin?" he asks, shocked. "Stop capping."

"Um. No. Definitely Dublin."

"Must be thinking of Trinity College."

"That's in Connecticut." I chuckle. "Are you okay?"

"Yeah." He sighs in confusion, shoving his hands into his pockets.

One person left.

"You're thinking of Trinity Church," I realize. A gorgeous historical landmark, with towering spires and buttresses that look straight out of a fairy tale.

"Or I'm trying to distract you from the bad place," he says, taking my arm, squeezing it, and leaning in close. "Did it work?"

I smirk up at him because, yes, it did.

And the only person in front of us says, "I just came to grab a bookmark for my daughter, thanks," and dips.

Leaving me and Jodelle here, eyes locked. I wonder if she recognizes me. Her smile doesn't waver, even though I've already been staring at her for *way* too long.

"Hello," she says, inviting me forward with a nod.

"Hi," offers Milo, elbowing me so slightly that I almost don't notice.

"Hi," I begin, "Jodelle, um . . . it's an honor to meet you."

An honor? *Come on, Zinnia, you're meeting a bestselling author, not the Dalai Lama.*

She reaches for a copy of *Little Heart* from the dwindling stack to her left, already bookmarked to the signing page.

"Uh, no, no," I say with a jump, scrambling to get my copy out of my bag—God, what was I thinking not taking it out earlier?

It tumbles out of my hand, and I kneel to pick it up, horrified that I've just dropped something precious right in front of its creator, even though it's hardly one of a kind and I'm sure Jodelle doesn't even keep track of how many of her books have been sold, let alone how many are in print, let alone care if one gets a little beat up.

Still, my face is hot, and I clear my throat and try my absolute damnedest to save this encounter.

But I have no idea what to even say. Jodelle saves me.

THIS BOOK MIGHT BE ABOUT ZINNIA

"It's great to meet you," she says, her voice so warm and soft, I forget how nervous I am. It's like talking to royalty.

"You too," I reply.

"Uh, would you like me to personalize?" she asks.

"Oh, right, yes, um . . . Zinnia," I say, spelling it slowly for her, looking for *any* sign of realization. *My birth mom named me.*

She writes my name across the title page at a medium pace, I guess. How many Zinnias are there in the world? Maybe I was wrong? Surely she'd remember the name she gave me. . . .

"Such a beautiful name," she marvels, making my heart skip.

"Thanks," I say. "My, uh . . . my mom gave me that name."

Stupid, of course my name came from one of my parents, and historically and gender-binarily it's assumed to be the mother.

She cocks an eyebrow and nods.

"Your mom has great taste."

I glance up at Milo, who raises his eyebrows and gestures to Jodelle with his gaze like, *Well?*

"Um, can I ask you something?" I ask, clasping my hands so tightly, I'm sure I'm cutting off circulation. "Why did you give Little Heart her birthmark?"

"Oh, uh—" she begins, before Milo jumps in.

"She hasn't finished the book just yet. Almost."

Aw, shit. The answer to that question must be in the book. I really am an idiot.

Jodelle opens her hands and sucks her teeth apologetically.

"Sorry, it really would be a spoiler," she says. "But I'll tell you what. When you get to that part in the book, you can let me know what you think of her birthmark."

And then it hits me. *The birthmark!*

It would explain everything! If she doesn't remember my name, if she doesn't recognize me by my brown eyes like my father's, or my wide nose like my father's, or my sharp chin like Jodelle's, she would *have* to recognize . . .

I reach up and take my hat off, holding her gaze as I pull my hair back enough to show my little heart. Jodelle freezes and then softens.

"Oh, you . . . ," she says, then pauses. "You drew a heart for *Little Heart*, that's so—"

"She was born with it," offers Milo. "It's . . . why we came to see you."

She looks to me again, her eyes going dull as it all sinks in.

"I thought . . . maybe I could talk to you," I say as I venture further into this wild new wilderness in which security could come snatch me at any moment. "Get some . . . answers?"

Jodelle looks from me to the rest of the line, glances up at the attendant leaning against a pillar in the middle of the room that I didn't notice until now. Jodelle swallows, some of the color drained from her face.

THIS BOOK MIGHT BE ABOUT ZINNIA

"Let's, um . . . ," she says, pushing herself to her feet and nodding at the attendant, before smiling back at me. "Let's talk over dinner. I had to cut this line short anyway—it's getting late. Are you hungry?"

CHAPTER 24

Tuesday
2024

SOMETHING TICKLES MY TOES, AND I FLINCH IN MY sleep.

The harsh blue glow from the TV assaults my eyes, and my body craves a stretch, which I indulge in.

"Hey," groans a voice playfully from the other end of the couch, "get your icy feet off me. Damn, you sure you're not hypothermic?"

"You wanna rub them for me?" I ask. A big, strong pair of hands wrap around my toes and begin massaging. I roll onto my back until he and I are lying with our feet next to each other's shoulders. I take up his feet and reciprocate.

Then I sigh.

"You okay?" he asks.

THIS BOOK MIGHT BE ABOUT ZINNIA

"Why do you always ask that if you know the answer?" I ask.

"Because I keep expecting you to get better at hiding it," he chuckles. "And I keep hoping you don't. Way more convenient."

I smirk. "I just . . . keep thinking about that woman in the window."

"Yeah," he says. "Just conjures up memories?"

"Exactly."

I think of baby girl. How old would she be now? Definitely a teenager. Seventeen or eighteen? I've lost track of time. Would she be applying for college yet? Maybe she doesn't even want to go to college. Maybe she ended up with a family that owns a multibillion-dollar company with overseas accounts, and she'll never want for anything. Maybe they changed her name, and my child is actually a celebrity that I've seen before on TV and just didn't know.

I let out a heavy sigh, and Justin stops massaging, giving my feet a gentle squeeze.

"What do you need?" he asks.

God, I love when he asks that. It's such a simple question, but it's one of the things I appreciate most about him. In all my childhood I don't ever remember my mom asking me that. No teacher ever asked me that. Very few of my friends.

"A distraction," I say, reaching for the TV remote and switching the channel to the news, where there's a featured story about a local teen from right here in Kensington helping to paint the front of the library with twentieth-century Black icons. Peace settles into my chest like a welcome salve, and I recline back on the sofa.

But it's not to last.

"And now for a developing story coming out of Center City," announces the reporter earnestly. "A local honors student has gone missing after reading a bestselling novel."

My heart skips as her picture appears on the TV, clearly the daughter of the woman in the window, beanie and all.

"So she wasn't lying," marvels Justin, pulling his hands away and pushing himself to sitting as the reporter continues.

The name under the picture makes my breath catch.

Zinnia Davis.

Her name is Zinnia? The woman in the window and I really aren't so different, settling on the same name for our daughters. I remember the nurse's face as she leaned over the hospital bed with the birth certificate application.

"The adoptive parents have asked that you suggest a name."

Me? I thought. *Who am I to her anymore? Why should I get to name her?*

"It's just a suggestion," said the nurse. "The final choice is up to them."

I thought for a minute, and the name Zinnia just came to me. It was pretty, since it was a flower, after all. It was simple and unexpected, not as common as Rose or Daisy or Violet. I . . . liked it. And I hoped she would too. But I knew they'd

THIS BOOK MIGHT BE ABOUT ZINNIA

change it. Nobody was naming their kid Zinnia. They'd probably go with Madison or Hailey or Sophia. Something normal.

The reporter continues.

"Zinnia Davis is a senior at Penn Valley High, looking at college prospects. Her mother says Zinnia is on the straight and narrow, and this just isn't like her."

The report cuts to an interview of that frantic woman with the blue eyes as she tries to stay composed for the camera.

"She's never done anything like this. She's always home on time, always texts me where she is. Please, if anyone has any information, we'll pay you whatever you want, just bring her home," and then she breaks, her face contorting into a grimace before her tears fall and the camera cuts away, the reporter's voice taking over again as a slow pan of the Amtrak station begins.

"Zinnia Davis was last seen leaving her home late this afternoon. She is five feet seven inches tall, roughly one hundred twenty pounds, with a slender build. Distinguishing features include a heart-shaped birthmark on her forehead."

Another picture of Zinnia, this one with her hair tucked up into a swim cap, appears, that little brown heart peeking out clear as day.

I bolt upright so fast, I nearly fall right off the sofa.

"Justin, oh my God, it's her!"

I sit up and stare at the screen as her picture appears again, gasping so hard, I almost choke. Her cheekbones, her smile, her nose . . . They're . . . they're perfect.

I feel the tears welling as I study her eyes, dark and glittering, the color of mine. Open and beckoning like Ezra's. In the next photo, she's sitting happily on a swing at a playground that looks clean, colorful, and new. Her head is tilted to one side playfully, her bell-shaped head of curls just barely touching her shoulders. Her teeth are perfectly straight—does this mean she was adopted to a couple who could afford orthodontic care? Did she ever have braces?

Was she ever self-conscious about them?

Is she one of the popular kids at her high school, like her father, or is she awkward and wallflowerish like me? Does she ever wonder if I was like her when I was younger?

Does she ever think of me?

Justin reaches over and wraps his big, warm arms around my shoulders, and I immediately feel the tension ease from them.

"What do you need?" he asks again.

The problem is I don't know what I need. I needed a distraction, but clearly *that's* not happening. Another need is taking over, winning: the primal need to make sure Zinnia is okay.

"Zinnia," I say aloud, the name sounding foreign on my tongue, even though I'm the one who gave it to her. A wave of dizziness overtakes me, and I suddenly crave fresh air. "I . . . I need to think."

I stand and dart for the front door, taking my coat from the hanger.

Justin's voice is sweet and warm behind me.

"Remember that day in Alba," he begins, "when I said I've got this place?"

I nod, feeling tears well in my eyes, remembering how he told me to go find Ezra, to say goodbye to him and to her, to make sure my daughter was safe. He nods now, with a smile.

"I'll be here when you get back," he says. *"Always."*

I press my lips together against the tears, but it doesn't help.

I nod and squeak out the words, "Thank you."

Then I open the front door.

There's a man standing there in a dark peacoat and scarf. He jumps back, startled out of his mind, losing his footing completely and falling on his ass in the snow.

"Oh my God, are you oka—" I begin, kneeling to help him. He looks up at me, and those captivating brown eyes I'd recognize anywhere bring me right back to that day in the park when we sang side by side on the swings, the last time I saw him.

"Ezra?"

A smile curves the corner of his mouth, and his glittering eyes look me up and down briefly.

"Tuesday," he breathes. "You haven't aged a day."

CHAPTER 25

Zinnia

2024

I CAN'T BELIEVE IT.

I am *sitting next to Jodelle Rae West.*

The back of this private car is lit up so bright with all the New York lights glittering through the windows, and I try my best to stop looking at her, but . . . oh my God, what if she really *is* my birth mom? She hasn't said so yet, but would she—*the* Jodelle Rae West—really invite me to dinner somewhere . . . Actually, that reminds me. . . .

"So where are we headed?" I ask. In all the fuss, I forgot to ask.

She looks up from her phone with a smile and shrugs.

"Well, I was thinking of heading to my *favorite* restaurant, Tercer Acto, but then I remembered my private chef was actually

THIS BOOK MIGHT BE ABOUT ZINNIA

hired *from* Tercer Acto, so"—she waves her hand like everything she just said wasn't a big deal—"we can go to my place. I've already texted him to whip us up something. Any allergies?"

"No allergies," I say, thankfully not having to stretch the truth this time.

My phone buzzes with a text.

Milo: I'm right around the corner from the bookstore if you need me.

Me: Thanks. She's taking me to her HOUSE!

Milo: ??? Glad you added me to your Find My I thought you were going to dinner. U sure this is safe?

Me: Of course!

. . . But am I really?

I glance at Jodelle, who's still typing away on her phone. Have I been too naive? I've seen enough movies, read enough books, to know this could go sideways. Serial killers never jump out with a knife at first meeting, right? What if she's taking me to some secluded cabin in upstate where she's hired a whole team of henchmen to scrub the bloody scene after I'm gone? What if that's who she's texting now? Her next question catches me off guard.

"So, since you're only seventeen, do your parents know you're here?"

"Uh," I begin, thinking. But it's already been too long of a pause, and she looks at me with a cocked eyebrow. I let out a sigh that I hope is believably heavy. "My dad isn't around." Not a *total* lie—he's literally not here. "And I never knew my birth mom." Also not a lie. "To be honest, it's . . . kinda why I'm here to see you?"

Her face remains even, but her fingers freeze and she lowers the phone.

"Aw," she offers. The driver lets out a shallow cough, and we both glance up at him as he averts his eyes back to the road. She clears her throat and turns back to me. "Dear, I have a feeling you and I have so much to talk about."

My fears dissolve instantly, and I take up my conversation with Milo again.

Me: I'm sure.

It turns out Jodelle Rae West doesn't live in a cabin in upstate New York, nor a high-rise in Manhattan, although she owns one of each of those. She spends most days in her favorite white armchair at her desk in her office, upstairs from exactly where we're sitting at her dining room table.

She explodes into laughter at me explaining that the main character from her book *Eastlake* was my very first crush, a tiny spray of wine bursting from her lips as she rushes to dab her mouth with a napkin. I can't contain my giggles either, and I'm glad I was between sips of sparkling water when I chose to deliver that news.

THIS BOOK MIGHT BE ABOUT ZINNIA

"But he's a literal sociopath," she chuckles. "*How* could you have a crush on him?"

"Listen, sad self-deprecating characters are one hundred percent my thing," I explain with a helpless shrug. "Didn't say I wanted to *marry* him, just, you know, give him kisses."

"Ahh," she groans, squirming as if she's smelled something rancid, "don't want to knoooow, don't want to know."

I roll my eyes and sip my water, and she sips her wine, and we both leave a gap where words should be. The plates between us have been scraped clean, the Cape Cod mussels with pimenton aioli settling delightfully in my stomach. I don't think I've ever tasted something so delicious. She said she'd hired her chef from Tercer something? I'll find it. I *have* to go sometime. But for now it's time to get to the reason why I came.

"So," I venture, glancing at my phone and realizing it's already 9:00 p.m., "about *Little Heart* . . . did you . . . write it about anyone specifically?"

She clears her throat.

"Oh, yes, *Little Heart*," she starts, resting her wineglass back on the table. Her eyes linger on it for half a second too long, like she didn't want to let go. "Yes, I took inspiration from a little of everywhere. You know, there are a million and one princess stories out there. But when I thought of one who came from the sky and from the land, who ran away and . . ."

She stops, narrows her eyes at me.

"Have you read it till the end?" she asks.

I choose to be honest this time, since I *hate* spoilers, and shake my head.

"Ah," she breathes, looking almost . . . relieved? "Well, just know that she . . . goes through some things toward the end. As we all do."

. . . Do I even *want* to know?

"Things like what?"

"Well—"

Zzzzt, zzzzt, buzzes her phone. *Zzzzt, zzzzt.*

She practically leaps out of her seat, scrambling for it.

"Uh, if you'll excuse me, it's my agent, I have to take this." She hurries from the room, still wearing her burgundy turtleneck, her blond bob swinging as she jogs across the dining room. "Oh, um, help yourself to some more sparkling water or, uh, juice—do you like juice? No, you're too old for juice. Well, just help yourself."

And she vanishes around the corner.

Leaving me alone in this palace.

I look up at the chandelier, the glass of which I notice is tinted turquoise at the edges. Vintage. Fifties, maybe? And it's huge. There has to be a hefty price tag on that. In fact, this whole place screams money.

I tip up my glass and down the last of my seltzer, realizing that more *would* be nice. I look at the hallway where

THIS BOOK MIGHT BE ABOUT ZINNIA 287

Jodelle disappeared, and stand. Maybe she really won't mind me going in her kitchen. In her fridge. Seltzer would be in the fridge, right?

Only one way to find out.

God, I can't believe I'm here. The kitchen is just around the corner from the dining room, and the fridge is a chilly walk-in cathedral of food. I find the seltzer among the endless bottles of different seltzer flavors and brands, next to the endless fridge shelves of fresh produce—whole heads of lettuce, berries, apples, autumn squashes, and lemons and limes. It looks like a miniature grocery store in here.

And I thought my family was doing well.

Jodelle's voice makes me jump.

"No, I *told* you, Anders, I need to know what to do *now*!"

What the hell?

I search the fridge for the source—Jodelle's voice is too loud to be coming through the wall. It sounds a bit grainy, like I'm hearing it through a phone. And then I spot the machine in the corner with the little red light. It looks like a tiny radio with a screen on it, focused on a huge fluffy cat bed tucked into a hutch built into the wall, where a tiny black kitty is curled up in a warm little ball.

Aww.

A man's voice comes through even grainier.

"Is she there in your house, Jodelle?"

"*Yes*, she's here!" Jodelle pauses. "I didn't know what else to do. I couldn't just let her go thinking I . . . you know, *based* the book on her."

"You absolutely could have, and should have. If it gets out, Jodelle, that you brought a reader to your *house*—"

"It *won't*, Anders. I'll just convince her she's mistaken and it's been a wonderful evening."

"Convince her?"

"*Tell* her."

"You said 'convince,' Jodelle."

What?

. . . So *Little Heart* IS about me?

I hear Jodelle sigh through the speaker.

"Jodelle, what are you not telling me?" asks Anders. "Do you know this girl?"

"*No*," she cries, her voice frantic now, "I . . . don't. I—"

"What the hell, just say it!"

"Anders, remember when you asked me for something with heart in it? Something you could sell? Seventeen years ago?" she hisses. "And you put all this pressure on me to produce, produce, produce, and *all* I asked for was some *space* to *think*?"

My chest tightens at her tone. At the raw pain in her voice.

"I found some . . . material . . . and loosely based *Little Heart* on that, but I changed so much over so much time, and so many editing rounds, that I never thought—"

"What kind of 'material,' Jodelle?"

She erupts.

THIS BOOK MIGHT BE ABOUT ZINNIA

"Oh, does it matter? Some teenager lost a diary in a coffee shop. I couldn't even credit the original writer if I wanted to. I found it, so I should have the rights—"

"Jodelle, you know that is *not* how this works!"

My heart is thundering as I clutch the ice-cold bottle of sparkling water to my chest. I can't breathe. There's . . . there's no way I'm hearing this right. Jodelle *stole* the idea for *Little Heart*?

The princess, King Land, the sky queen . . . it was all . . . Plagiarized?

So then that means Jodelle isn't . . . She can't be . . .

I've been on a wild-goose chase this entire time. And my *favorite* author in the whole world is a sham. And everything around me that she's built, down to this fridge, is money owed to some teenage barista like me. Or who was a teenage barista seventeen years ago. My favorite author . . . my idol . . . stole writing from a *child*?

Angry tears flood my eyes, but I barely have time to notice them before . . .

"Wait, this could work," comes Anders's voice. "Hear me out. You said she's seventeen and adopted, right?"

"Yes," sighs Jodelle, having simmered down a bit.

"*And* estranged from her parents?"

"Yes," she says again.

"Why not just *humor* her, then?" he asks. "Wine her, dine her. Well, don't actually *wine* her, she's not twenty-one, but you get my point. Show her around the city. Let your readers think *Little Heart* was based on a real baby with a heart-shaped birthmark, one you gave up seventeen years ago and never told anyone about."

"Anders, that's insane."

"This whole situation is insane, Jodelle, but at this point, if you *don't* do anything, she'll know where you live, and more importantly, she'll know that if you're *not* her mom, her real mom is out there somewhere, which means whoever wrote the book must be someone else!"

My heart skips at the idea.

Her real mom is out there somewhere.

But how the hell would I even find her at this point?

Keep it together, Zinn, I tell myself, but why am I hyperventilating in here? I should have what I came for: an epic story to put in my college essay about following *Little Heart* all the way to New York City to find Jodelle Rae West, who turned out *not* to be my birth mom, but it's okay, right? Because I took a risk and did something interesting and that's all that really matters.

That's all that should matter. . . .

But it's not.

I drag my sleeve across my eyes and pick up my phone to text Milo, when I find he's already texted me.

Milo: **You good? Haven't heard from you in a minute and your phone disappeared from Find My.**

THIS BOOK MIGHT BE ABOUT ZINNIA

I'm about to text him something like *You were right, I shouldn't have gotten my hopes up, Jodelle lied to me, I should've seen this coming, God, I feel so stupid,* but a gasp on the monitor stops me in my tracks. Jodelle's voice lowers to a borderline whisper as she says, "Oh my God, Anders, I have to go."

Click.

The monitor shuts off, and the one on my end announces in its robot voice, "Connection severed."

Shit.

I scramble for the fridge door, but just as I reach the gaping opening, Jodelle appears, inches from me.

I shriek and tumble backward, splaying ungracefully on the floor as the seltzer goes flying and shatters against the floor. I shuffle through my thoughts, looking frantically for an alibi. I spot another bottle of seltzer on the shelf beside me, snatch it up, and clutch it close.

"Found it," I announce with a chuckle. "The, um . . . the seltzer."

"How long have you been here?" she demands. "What did you hear?"

"Um . . . ," I say, thinking, as I push myself to my feet. "Just, uh . . . something about a guy named Anders. Something about him asking you to write something. Working on a new project? I didn't hear any story details, if that's what you're worried about. . . ."

Her eyes tell me everything I need to know.

She *absolutely* knows I heard everything.

A moment of silence passes before she glances up at the door, and I realize she could easily lock me in this fridge and I could die without anyone knowing where I went or why, besides Milo. Without really thinking, I lower my shoulder and slam right into her, knocking her out of the way, before I turn the corner, snatch my bag off the dining room chair, and bolt for the front door with the heavy-ass brass lock.

"*Zinnia!*" she calls behind me.

My trembling hands can't untwist the lock fast enough. I hear her footsteps behind me, growing louder.

"Zinnia, come back, let me explain! It's not what you think! I had to tell Anders—"

I lower my foot too fast in the snow, and the icy step doesn't grip my boot like I thought it would. I go flying, and *wham*.

Pain explodes through the back of my head like a nuclear bomb. I see white. All sound clips out for a minute, my vision blurry and swaying.

I hear a groan and blink my eyes open, realizing that groan came from me. Cameras surround me from above, and I remember where I am, and what I need to do. I spot a gap between them, widening and narrowing as they hover above me. The minute I have an opening, I bolt. My unsteady feet carry me through the snow in the frigid night air. I stumble once or twice but not enough to stop me. Brooklyn

THIS BOOK MIGHT BE ABOUT ZINNIA

is glittering and quiet away from the horde of story-hungry humans behind me. They don't give chase. They just let me go.

Where the hell do I go now? I need to find someone to help. Anyone. But here, among the brownstones, no one is out this late. Lights are on in most windows, but I know no one would help if I knocked. All businesses are closed, besides a nightclub a few blocks away with a line of people. I'm only seventeen, so they'd never let me in. Not a single pizza place or corner bodega is open, and I can't feel my fingers.

I need to find somewhere to call Milo to come and get me.

I stop to catch my breath, my head swimming.

There's a gap under one of the brownstones—the one on the corner. I walk over and look at it closely, glancing around before stepping down and under the foundation.

If what Ezzie said was right, about hiding under houses for warmth, this should be a good plan, right? I can already feel a change in temperature on my cheeks, and I'm so, so tired.

I crawl inside, just far enough to be encased in darkness. It's not much, but it's toasty, and it's completely hidden. My head feels like it's bobbing in water or something, and every muscle in my body is screaming for me to sit down. So I do.

Then I pat my pockets, searching for that familiar block of technology, my only connection to civilization right now in this moment.

But I don't have my phone.

"Goddammit," I hiss.

I breathe a huge sigh, feeling the tears come on again, and I shut my eyes against them.

I'm just so, so tired. Sleepy, in fact.

I'll just rest my head against this wall and . . .

Figure everything out in a few minutes.

CHAPTER 26

Tuesday
2024

SOMEHOW, AFTER SEVENTEEN YEARS OF HEARING nothing from or about him, Ezra Terreni is standing just inside my front door. He looks around the room, studying.

"Nice place," he says. His eyes are now creased in the corners, but his shoulders haven't lost their broad, sturdy charm, and his sparkling eyes are as captivating as ever. When he looks at me, it still makes my knees weak, and I'm suddenly that wallflower walking past him in the halls at South Philly High.

"How'd you find me?" I finally work up the nerve to ask.

He sighs, looks at his shoes.

"Seen the news?" he asks.

My heart pounds. Has *he* seen the news? And . . . does he

know what it means? I glance at Justin, who clears his throat and says, "I'll give you two some space."

"Thanks, man," says Ezra.

The door down the hall shuts behind Justin, and Ezra folds his arms and shrugs.

"Were you *ever* going to tell me?" he asks, his eyes full of hurt.

I try to keep my voice even, my face neutral. I don't think either works. "Tell you what?"

"About why you were really gone for so long senior year? What you really wanted to tell me that night at prom?" He's impressively calm for what he's implying. "I didn't say anything then because I didn't want a child, and clearly you didn't either, or you wouldn't have given her up."

There's a bite to his words I wasn't expecting. Surely he can't blame me for what I had to do.

"I think you made the right choice," he says, softening. "It was . . . impressively mature, Tuesday. I don't know if I would've been strong enough to do the same thing. I just want you to know that."

It washes over me like a healing balm, knowing Ezra's not angry, not hurt, not slighted, doesn't feel like I robbed him of a child.

"How do you know she's . . . ," I begin, unable to finish that sentence. He does it for me.

"Ours?" That word rips through me, and I will myself not to imagine him standing by my mother's living room window

THIS BOOK MIGHT BE ABOUT ZINNIA

holding her. It hurts too much. "I know, Tuesday, because I *met* her."

My chest tightens.

"You what?"

I suddenly want to kill him. All this work to distance her from our families, all the work I've put into moving on with my life without her, without Ezra, knowing she can never know me or him, or our families, and he *sought her out*?

"She found *me*," he explains, as if he can read my thoughts. "And it was before I even realized who she was. I was busking right there in Mountainview River Valley Park, and this girl walks right up to me with this book in her hand, singing along with what I was singing. Outgoing. Into music. After she left, all the connections were . . . pointed out to me," he says, his voice swelling again. "The king in the book is named Land. Which is weirdly close to Terreni. And the queen, who's of the sky. Tuesday. As in Tiu, the god of war and the sky? And I almost didn't believe it at that point, but then there's the twist. . . ."

My legs are growing wobbly underneath me, and I reach for the nearest dining chair to sink into.

This is too much. It's all too much.

"What I don't understand is how *your* writing made it into a bestselling novel without your name on it."

I look up at him now, leveling my eyes at him.

"It wouldn't have changed anything."

"Bullshit," he hisses.

"Why do you care?" I demand to know. "You haven't been

in her life or mine all these years, living your carefree wake-up-wherever-you-like, eat-whatever-you-want, no-worries, no-responsibilities lifestyle. You've never had to work a day in your life, have you? Your family's probably still paying for *everything*."

His eyes widen. Clearly, I've wounded him, but I don't care. Rage spews forth like venom, lifting me from the chair.

"I had to carry her, deliver her, hand her off to some stranger, sign papers, recover alone, miss almost a year of school, and then I had to watch you and Amy carry on with life as if *nothing* happened, and the whole time I couldn't tell anyone about any of it. My own mother wouldn't talk about it."

My cheeks run wet, and I drag the back of my hand across one, then the other.

"Everyone wanted me to pretend everything was okay. That giving her away would erase her memory. Well, it *didn't*. I carried pain you would never understand, Ezra."

He studies my face as I unload everything I've been carrying around all these years, and it feels so, *so* good.

"I had to put that pain somewhere. So I wrote it into a journal, and that journal was given to Jodelle Rae West, with the *best* of intentions. And now, seventeen years later—"

"It's been published with her name on it," he says.

"Maybe she thought I would've forgotten about it by now," I offer, running my hands over my hair. "Maybe she thought she changed enough of the details, or the important ones."

"But not nearly enough to hide from us."

Us.

His face tells me all I need to know. But I need to hear him say it.

"Why are you here, Ezra?"

"I'm here, Tuesday, because she's looking for us," he says. "And I need to know, for her sake, if you're willing to put this family history of ours aside permanently."

"Ezra—"

"I meant what I said all those years ago," he says. "I want nothing to do with my family. I don't want to carry on with the legacy they left. My mom is gone, my dad is getting up there in years, and I'm their only child. So after he goes, this ends with me. I'm here to find out if you're strong enough to do the same."

He holds out his hand to me, and I look from his hand to his face. His dark eyes, the ones that captivated me all those years ago, are warm, honest, strong. He's serious.

And I know he's right. I'm not my family, and I haven't really ever been. He's not his family either. And for the second time in my life, I promise myself quietly that however imperfect I am, however undeserving a mother, I'll be better than the one I had.

I take his hand.

CHAPTER 27

Zinnia

2024

I TRY TO FLUTTER MY EYELASHES OPEN, BUT THEY'RE crusted shut with ice. I reach up to rub them, realizing how cold my hands are as I press my fingers to my cheeks and feel nothing. I look down at my gloves, wondering if they're doing any good at all. I can't feel my toes inside my boots, either.

I have to get out of here.

I groan, peeling my trembling body from the wall. Every movement is agony. My feet somehow feel like they're boiling in my shoes. I resist the urge to take them off, knowing that would only make things worse. Ezzie was wrong—houses aren't warm underneath. Or at least this one isn't.

I grunt, planting one foot on the ground and then the other.

I know little else but this: I need shelter, and I need it *fast*.

THIS BOOK MIGHT BE ABOUT ZINNIA

301

I peek out from the opening in the wall where I came down and emerge back into the Brooklyn night, streetlights lining the sidewalk. Only one window is lit up this late at night. What time even is it? How long have I been out here?

How do I feel so lost without my phone?

I look up and down the street and find *nobody.*

A chill rips through my clothes and panic creeps in. If I can't find shelter soon, I'm going to freeze to death out here. I start walking, and I'm not even sure where to.

I knock on a store window, then the next.

A house, then the next.

The lit-up house has a cozy-looking vestibule at the front with a dog bed in the window. I've never been more tempted to curl up on an animal bed, but at this point, I'll take *anything.*

I hear wheels on the road behind me, and I turn around to wave down the car.

"Hey, stop! Please! I need help!"

They whiz by like they haven't seen me, and I look after them, tears brimming.

What the hell do I do?

I look back at the gaping hole under that house. If I follow Ezzie's lead, I'll die. If I go back to Jodelle's house around the corner, who knows what the hell she'll do? And that dog bed looks *so* very cozy.

I look around to make sure no one's watching, and I try the storm door leading to the atrium. It's unlocked! My heart pounds as I ease it open, further earning a possible breaking and entering charge. But what choice do I have?

"*Hey!*" cuts a voice so sharp that it startles me back from the door, which slams shut. Inside, at the top of the stairs, stands a youngish man with red hair in pink-and-navy-striped pajamas I'd recognize anywhere. My dad has the same ones. Brooks Brothers. Gotta be.

"Hi," I say, and wave gingerly. "Um, can I please . . . use your phone?"

"You don't have a phone?" he asks, eyebrows flat in suspicion.

"I left it at my mom's house," I say, the lie stinging like bile in my mouth, since not so long ago I *thought* that might be my mom's house.

"First time I've heard that one," he says, folding his arms. "Go find a shelter or something."

"Sir, I'm not from around here. I live in Philly and I got lost and—"

"Uh-huh," he says, reaching into the pocket of a coat hanging in the entryway. "Here, take this, find somewhere to sleep, and leave me and my house alone. I've got a sleeping baby upstairs anyway. Go."

He tosses a single bill down the stairs, and when it lands at the bottom, I hear the door at the top slam behind him. A fifty-dollar bill.

It stings.

THIS BOOK MIGHT BE ABOUT ZINNIA

Milo was right. Money really can't fix everything.

I look back to the house, my throbbing head spinning. I'm still so tired. Everything in me wants to sit, wants to lie down and shut my eyes again.

Maybe I did it wrong, staying too close to the opening. Maybe if I crawl deeper under the house, it'll be warmer.

It's my only shot.

CHAPTER 28

Tuesday
2024

I KEEP MY EYES GLUED ON THE ROAD AS WE FLY down the turnpike. The Brooklyn Bridge looms ahead in the darkness, tall and strange-looking, though I've seen it a hundred times by now. It looks different, and at first I can't tell why. Everything does. And I realize everything looks different because it exists in a world in which I can picture my daughter's face.

How do you conflate the phenomenon of a real person, a baby, growing up as a concept, an idea, a borderline figment of my imagination, with seeing a real face and realizing it's hers?

She's out there somewhere. And she's alive.

A shiver travels up my spine at the cold, and I reach over

and turn up the heat a tad. Ezra notices, and as if he can read my mind, he sighs and says, "She's going to be okay."

"How do you know?" I ask. "You said you haven't talked to her since the park."

He pauses for a moment in thought.

"I haven't," he says, "but if she's anything like her mom, she'll find a way."

Even now, after all these years, the butterflies are still there.

I look at him as he smiles back at me. He looks my age, thirty-five. But the years have been good to him. His eyes haven't lost their sparkle, somehow, after all this time.

"Ezra," I begin, still in disbelief that he's really here, with me. That I'm really saying his name again.

"You don't have to say anything," he says, freeing me from the burden of explaining that Justin and I are happy together, that I wouldn't do anything to jeopardize that, and that we're driving to New York on strictly business. To ensure the safety of a human being we both made together. That's it.

"There is something I need to tell you, though," he says.

Oh God. Do I want to know? If it involves Amy Sullivan, I hope he spares me.

"I think my family knows about her."

We fly down the turnpike toward the Brooklyn Bridge in silence as tiny snowflakes kiss the windshield.

There's silence between us where a lifetime of catching up should be. Ezra slouches in the passenger seat, arms folded, staring out the window absentmindedly.

What's he been up to all this time? I'm afraid to ask. But I know I have to.

"Why do you think they know about her?" I ask, a lump forming in my throat at trepidation about the answer.

He inhales deeply and sighs.

"I was doing my laundry a few days ago," he says, "at a laundromat on South Street, since my local one was closed. Dad found me."

That lump becomes harder to swallow.

"What did he say?" I ask, getting annoyed that he's making me ask. *Just tell me, Ezra.*

"He walked up and he said, 'Ezzie,'" he begins, donning his father's thick Italian accent, "'I have a problem.' And then he took a long drag of his cigarette. I asked him what he wanted. He asked me, 'You seen this new book out? *Little Heart?* About a lost little girl?'"

Oh God.

"He found out about her through the book?" I ask. "How did he even . . . ?"

I can't finish the question because I already know the answer. Matteo Terreni knew the book was about his family

THIS BOOK MIGHT BE ABOUT ZINNIA

because a story about a family named after terrain, with a wayward son who chose to be homeless rather than participate in the family business, with a missing baby given up to a tree with the same name as Oak Park Adoption Agency, was just too much of a coincidence.

Jodelle didn't change enough of the story. And who can blame her? If she kept the twist in the book, she really couldn't change much.

"Tuesday," he says, and still, after all this time, it makes my heart skip, "I knew I had to come find you and ask you what the hell is going on. I had my suspicions when you left school—"

"Then why didn't you ask about me?" I ask before I can catch myself, sudden tears pricking my eyes. "Don't act like you cared, Ezra—this is about cleaning up a mess for you, isn't it? Tying up a loose end? Why are you really here?"

When I glance over at him, his eyes give no indication of anger or even defensiveness. Just hurt.

"I'm here, Tuesday, because I fucked up. Because I was stupid. And because I know it must have hurt you. And even though it's taken me seventeen years to come around and make things right, I hope and pray you can forgive me. Or at least help me find this kid we made so she doesn't reap what we planted."

That I can do.

For Baby Girl? Anything.

Legal guardianship, whatever. Legal documents, whatever. She's my flesh and blood.

I grip the wheel harder as we sail under the scaffolding climbing high over the bridge.

"I'm sorry," he says finally.

It should bring comfort, but it twists the knife into an old wound we didn't need to reopen.

"I'm sorry for not being there for you. Even as a friend."

He was never my friend. He was everything to me for one night, and then he was nothing. That doesn't change just because we're driving together to find her.

"What does your family want with her?" I ask. Although I'm not sure I'm ready for the answer. "Do they need more soldiers? More plants around the city to be their eyes? She's not one of them."

I say "them" like Ezra isn't one of them either.

"The good news is they don't want her to be," he says. "Dad said he wants to meet his only granddaughter—"

"He can't have her," I cut in. "I don't want him anywhere near her."

There's a long pause before Ezra reaches over and gently covers my fingers with his warm, strong hand. My breath catches, and I look at him when he says, "She's ours, Tuesday, but she's not ours."

It's a pain I never wanted to feel again.

I know he's right.

THIS BOOK MIGHT BE ABOUT ZINNIA

"Then what are we doing out here?" I ask. "You and I? Why are we looking for her?"

"Because so is the rest of the city," he says, holding up his phone to me. I glance over long enough to read the headline: ADOPTED PHILLY HONORS STUDENT MISSING IN BROOKLYN AFTER SEEKING OUT BIRTH MOM.

The miniature scream that escapes my mouth is not human.

After seeking out birth mom?

She's lost out here looking for me?

A million thoughts race through my head, most of them dancing around the central obvious one: *Why?*

Why, when she doesn't know a thing about me? *Why,* when as far as she knows, I want nothing to do with her? *Why,* when she's already an honors student? Apparently has a great life? Probably friends? Maybe even a special someone?

Maybe she's her school's Amy Sullivan.

He reads the first few lines of the article aloud.

"'Zinnia Davis was last seen leaving her home in Ardmore for the SEPTA train at five thirty-five p.m. She may be traveling with a companion, seventeen-year-old classmate Milo Reeves. Her mother, Kelly Davis, says this is extremely unlike her and that she may be following the bestselling novel *Little Heart* in pursuit of her birth mother, who may or may not be the author Jodelle Rae West.'"

That sends rage ripping through me.

May or may not be?

Why hasn't someone tracked her down and asked her?

Before I can ask, Ezra reads on.

"'Fans of the book have already begun noting the connection between Zinnia, who has a unique heart-shaped birthmark, and Princess Little Heart, who is so named for her own birthmark of the same shape. In solidarity, TikTokers have launched the #NoShoes challenge, abandoning their footwear until Zinnia is found. Jodelle Rae West was not available for comment.'"

I bet she fucking wasn't.

I grip the wheel harder, but I notice Ezra shuffling his feet, kicking off his shoes one by one. I look at him questioningly and catch a hint of that winning smile of his.

"We'll find her, Tuesday. I'm not going home until we do."

CHAPTER 29

Zinnia

2024

Clearly, this is a dream, or there wouldn't be a twelve-foot-tall apparition of Jodelle Rae West sitting across from me at her dining room table, and her dining room certainly wouldn't be a vast mirrorscape in sepia.

Everything is bland—a beige-and-brown haze settled over the whole place. Even Jodelle looks monochrome—her skin, hair, and clothes all a terra-cotta hue. A chuckle escapes her mouth as she notices me.

"What are you doing here?" she asks, her voice cloudy and shrouded in my ears, like she's underwater, or like there's a body of water between us. "You really thought so highly of yourself? Convinced you must be born of a celebrity?"

I'm frozen in my chair, unable to move a finger. The plate

on the table in front of me is totally empty, and when I look back up at Jodelle, a mountain of food lines hers. She plucks a grape off the pile and chews obnoxiously at me, leaning on her arm in mock fascination.

"Milo was right about you," she says. "You *are* a narcissist."

It should sting more, to hear it said aloud like this, but she's right. I just had to seek Jodelle out to find out the truth. Not because it would really change anything, but to know if my lineage spouted from a royal American bloodline via a famous writer. How stupid I was to assume.

I *must* be self-centered. *Must* be a narcissist.

She plucks another grape and pops it into her mouth.

"It's a good thing you don't want children," she muses. "They might turn out as misguided as you. What help, what direction, could you offer a child if you can't even direct your own life? Look at you, baying at the ankles of Harvard admissions just for a seat at the table."

I shut my eyes and take the verbal beating, every word, knowing I deserve it.

"You're right," I admit.

"Sorry, what was that?" she asks, cupping her hand behind her ear to poke at me further.

"You're right," I repeat, sharp this time. "Coming here was a mistake."

A smile curves the edge of her mouth.

"If only you'd realized that before you worried your

THIS BOOK MIGHT BE ABOUT ZINNIA

mother sick," she says, ripping a chicken drumstick out of the pile so aggressively, it shakes the whole mass. "Not me, of course, who you've only just met. I mean the only mother you've ever known. The one who was too *regular* for your pedigree."

Tears prick my eyes at that last part.

Is that really what I've thought this whole time? Has my mother been *regular* when I've demanded *perfect*?

"That's not true," I argue, but now I'm not sure. Do I really feel that way? Do I even love my own mom?

CHAPTER 30

Tuesday
2024

Brooklyn is a zoo. More so than usual. And in the middle of the night, too. People shuffle around shoulder to shoulder, calling the name I gave her.

"Zinnia!"

And even, *"Princess!"*

And *"Princess Little Heart!"*

I don't bother finding parking. I put my car in park along the first open stretch of sidewalk I can find, right next to a hydrant. I'm here to find my daughter before she freezes to death or worse. What's a parking ticket?

Ezra and I move to jump out, but before my feet even hit the ground, a cop steps up and booms, "Ma'am, you can't be here. This is an active investigation; we're clearing the area."

THIS BOOK MIGHT BE ABOUT ZINNIA

I look from his face up to the crowd, a sea of hundreds looking for her. I realize I could use my father's name. "Derek Foley Cooper" might jog this cop's memory, even if my father was Philadelphia PD. But I won't be my mother.

I won't be a liar.

I look into his eyes, hold his gaze as I form a sentence I never thought I'd utter out loud.

"I'm her mother."

"What?" he asks over the noise.

"I," I begin again, doing my best to still my trembling hands, "am Zinnia's mother. Tuesday Christine Walker-Cooper. And I'm here to find her."

By now Ezra's made his way around the front of the car, and he steps up to join me as I step out. He interlaces his fingers through mine, his hand warm and comforting. I look up at him as he smiles down at me.

"And I'm Ezra," he says, turning his gaze back to the cop. "Ezra Terreni."

"Nice to know you claim the family name," booms a voice in an accent I can't pinpoint from my left. A man saunters out from behind the car in a thick, dark peacoat, an equally thick knit winter scarf, and a beanie. His shoulders are dusted with snow, like he's been standing out here for a while. Waiting. "Even if only when it suits you."

His dark features against his olive skin make him handsome for his age. But his smile isn't one of charm. It's one of assurance. One that says, *I know things you don't.*

Even the cop flinches when he sees him. His presence fills the space around us. People don't dare shuffle too close.

"Matteo Terreni," he says, his voice like butter. He extends a hand to the cop, who takes it hesitantly before glancing back at me and Ezra.

"My apologies," he says, pulling his hand away. "I'll let you all, uh . . . talk."

And then he slips away into the crowd.

My heart races as Matteo watches the cop go and then turns his piercing gaze to us. To me. To Ezra.

He locks eyes on our hands, still clasped, and I yank mine away.

"You know," he says, stepping closer as Ezra instinctively steps in front of me, "my wife, Alessia, was seventeen when she became a mother. She had four loving parents—two hers and two mine. She had a family. She had support. She had a circle."

He pauses for a moment to take a deep breath, sending a plume of mist into the frigid air.

"If you, Tuesday, had had such a system, maybe all of this could have been different. Maybe if your mother had chosen wisely, you could have had a part in the same circle. I am sorry for that."

"Leave Tuesday out of the circle, Dad," says Ezra, his voice commanding and sure. In fact, I don't think I've heard him

THIS BOOK MIGHT BE ABOUT ZINNIA 317

sound so sure of anything before. "She's not part of this."

"Zinnia is," he says. "It's in her blood. She is family."

The word "family" conjures up a wave of emotions in me that I can't even parse out before speaking.

"You had my father killed," I say. "Her grandfather. Family doesn't do that."

"Your father slandered the family. And family protect their own with the tools they have been given," he says. "Is that not what you're here to do, Tuesday?"

"She's no more your family than mine," I hiss. "She's an honors student. She's beautiful. She's loved by friends, and adoptive parents who love her so much that they crossed state lines and launched a televised search party. She has *everything* I sacrificed so much for her to have. And I won't let you take that from her."

He stares at me, his eyes boring into mine. I feel my forehead beading with sweat.

This man could shoot me where I stand and reap no repercussions. He knows it. I know it. Ezra knows it. I always said I would do anything for baby girl. Even standing up to a mob boss.

Then, to my horrified surprise, he smiles.

"Then we are after the same thing."

Ezra, still holding my hand, squeezes it.

Matteo continues.

"For tonight I'm not here for her."

I glance up at Ezra, who stares at him unflinchingly.

"I am here for the one who put Zinnia and the rest of my family in jeopardy. The one who published my family's story and profited from it without compensating the owner of the source material. I am here tonight for Jodelle Rae West."

Oh shit.

I swallow, and Ezra squeezes my hand again as Matteo looks from his son to me.

"I know you wrote it," he says, and I catch myself holding my breath, my hand shaking in Ezra's. "You put your thoughts somewhere you believed was safe. I cannot prosecute the musings of a child. But those who steal from children?" He nods and leaves the sentence there.

I swallow, wondering what his plans for Jodelle are.

But I can't worry about that now.

"We have to start looking for Zinnia," I say, pleading for him to let us go. He raises his hands in surrender.

"I will leave you to find your daughter. And, Tuesday, know that even under the circumstances, as the mother of my granddaughter . . . should you call upon it, you *always* have the protection of Matteo Terreni."

He nods and then lets out the faintest gasp.

"Oh," he says, pulling his coat gently away and reaching into his interior lapel pocket. "I believe this belongs to you."

My breath catches as he holds out a tiny little book I never thought I'd see again.

THIS BOOK MIGHT BE ABOUT ZINNIA

The pages are curled at the corners, worn to death at the edges, with the middle of the cover still the faintest purple, now faded closer to a dull gray.

My journal.

My lifeline for so many weeks so many years ago.

I look up at Ezra, whose mouth is agape as he stares at his father.

"How did you get this back?" he asks. There is hope in his voice, more to his question. *Please tell me you got this back without hurting anyone.*

Matteo nods with a smile.

"Matteo Terreni always gets what is owed him."

He rests his hand on his chest and offers a humble nod before turning to disappear into the crowd.

CHAPTER 31

Zinnia
2024

WHAT KIND OF MONSTER DOESN'T LOVE HER OWN mother? I feel tears leave my eyes, but my cheeks don't feel wet. I reach up and touch them, and my fingers come away red.

"Oh, but it is true," croons giant Jodelle, slipping the drumstick into her mouth and sucking all the meat off the bone in one swift hand motion. "You know you're only out here looking for your birth mother because you need a replacement once you go off to college. And who can blame you? Nobody wants Mommy tagging along behind them through adulthood." She shrugs. "So leave her."

I look down at my fingers again, which are now blood-free somehow, and I clench my fists to make sure they're real. This has to be a dream.

THIS BOOK MIGHT BE ABOUT ZINNIA

... Right?

"I can't leave her."

"*Sure* you can," she practically sings. "Everybody knows by now to leave toxic parents in pre-2010. You're the only one who's lagging behind."

"Zinnia!" calls a faint, fuzzy voice through the sepia sky, making the clouds pulsate into pinks and purples.

"Mom?" I ask, pushing myself to stand.

"See?" asks Jodelle. "There she is now, sneaking around, tracking your every location. She followed you all the way to New York City. If you don't cut her off now, she'll follow you all the way to Cambridge—"

"*Shut up*," I hiss, unbridled rage surging through me.

"Zinnia," comes the haunting voice again in the dark. "Honey, we're here for you!"

"She doesn't care about you," croons Jodelle. "If she did, she would give you space. Let you live your own life. Listen to you."

That hits a nerve I didn't know I had, and I turn to glare at her.

"Listen to me?" I ask. "When has Mom ever *not* listened to me? She let me quit swim lessons when I said I hated them. She respected my choice to get birth control without even telling her. She even heard me out when I asked her about my biological mom!" I let rage take the helm now. "Even when I thought that was *you*."

Jodelle's eyes are a tad wider than they were, her hands up, ready to get defensive.

"And to think I was excited to meet you," I hiss. "My favorite author. You know I actually *hoped* you were my mom? I thought of how amazing it'd be to have one who's famous. Who loves to read and write just like me. Someone who gets me. But you're just a liar."

Her brows drop as she realizes she's losing.

"My mom is a lot of things. Far from perfect. But she would *never* lie to me."

I turn my back and walk.

"Zinnia!" shrieks Jodelle, sounding miles and miles behind me.

I step into the light and feel a million hands on me from all directions.

"Oh my God, it's her!"

"She's all right!"

"Get her to a hospital!"

"Zinnia, can you hear me?"

My whole body is more tired than I can bear, and everything goes dark.

CHAPTER 32

Zinnia

2024

I BLINK MY EYES OPEN AND PEER THROUGH THE HAZE to find a room *not* in sepia, but in brilliant white light, and I wonder if I'm dead.

I'm dead, right? That's how this ends?

The last thing I remember is my hands reaching up to feel my face and feeling nothing. Did I lose my hands?

. . . Did I lose my face?

I reach up now to feel my cheek, and I feel flesh, just as there should be. And my fingers, when I squeeze my hands, feel functional at least, but my right hand feels resistance, and when I look down, I see tape on the back, with a tube escaping from under it.

Oh shit.

I'm in the hospital.

I look up and around and find a face to my right, and I jump, half a second before I realize who it is.

"Mom!" I exclaim as she leans forward and squeezes my non-IVed hand.

"Oh my God, Zinnia, you can hear me! You're awake!"

Her voice breaks as she unloads.

"I thought you were lost, or dead, or worse, and I lost track of your phone and couldn't reach you, and then Milo found us and said he couldn't find you either, and . . ."

Her voice fades into the background as I look around and survey the room. Something beeps in my left ear, and I look over and realize it's a machine tracking something about my body. Heart rate? Oxygen? Who knows. No alarms are sounding, so I must be all right to some degree.

And then everything comes rushing back.

"Mom?" I ask, interrupting her. "Where's Milo?"

She blinks in surprise as the question seems to ground her to where we are right now and what's really happening.

"Sorry, I was dumping, wasn't I? I'll let you absorb everything for a bit. Um, Milo left to get some—"

A knock cuts her off, and the door eases open as Milo steps inside and locks eyes on me.

"Zinn?" he asks, setting down the tray of food he's carrying and rushing to my other side.

He throws his arms around me and holds me tight.

THIS BOOK MIGHT BE ABOUT ZINNIA

325

"Milo," I say, feeling my cheeks burn with tears against his shirt.

"I'm so glad you're alive," he says, pulling away and staring at me like he's seeing a ghost. "You really took that twist and ran with it, huh? Dedication to the bit?"

"What?" I ask.

What's the twist? I just got to the part about Land and his weird origins; what the hell happens after that?

Milo and my mom exchange a glance, like they're quietly debating how much to tell me.

"Honey, I think it's time you heard the story from the source."

She and Milo exchange a smile, and Milo squeezes my foot before going back to the door. I watch Mom's face for clues, but she's a locked safe, staring down at her hands, lost in thought.

And then a crushing thought sinks in.

"Mom, did I miss the essay deadline?"

Her eyes meet mine now, hollow and searching, and before she can say anything, the door creaks open and Milo steps back inside.

Behind him I half expect to see Jodelle Rae West. Or Dad. Or the cops, even. But none of those people walk in. Instead a woman I've never met before, the same height as Milo, leans in. Her hair is pulled back into a puff, her face bare and fresh, her age just barely kissing her eyes. She blinks, seemingly lost, her mind clearly flying a million miles per hour. She purses her lips and clasps her hands, then opens her mouth like she wants to say something but thinks better of it and closes it again.

She stands there in the door, frozen, watching me.

I search her face.

Her dark eyes flicker as she looks to my mom, who looks over her shoulder and nods.

"Come, join us," says Mom, standing to meet the woman in the door.

She steps inside and Milo slips out, but not before I notice him and he gives me a wink.

I look to Mom, who gives the woman's hand a squeeze and turns back to me.

"I'll give you two some time," she says to me, before leaning in close and wrapping her arms around me and squeezing. "I love you so much."

I squeeze back, shutting my eyes even as I feel them brimming with tears. I don't know how she found me, how anyone found me, given that I was stuck under a house with zero access to the outside world.

Mom pulls away, glances up, and kisses my forehead, right where my birthmark is, brushes a wayward curl back from my face, and stands.

"I'll be outside if you need me," she says to the woman, before turning and leaving the room.

THIS BOOK MIGHT BE ABOUT ZINNIA   327

The door clicks shut behind her, and it's just me and this mystery woman, staring at each other.

"Hi," I say.

She remains frozen where she stands for a moment. Swallows.

"Hi," she says back, her voice shaky, so quiet I can barely hear her.

There's clearly so much that she has to say, and I wonder if she has the right person. I swear I've never met her before in my life. Is she part of Jodelle's PR team or something? Is she from Harvard's admissions department? Surely she's not a reporter. Not with the way Mom looked at her and then left us alone here.

"Do I . . . know you?" I ask.

"Um . . . ," she begins, looking like her head is swimming, like she might fall over. She glances at the chair Mom left behind and gestures to it, asking for permission to take it.

I nod. Like, *Of course,* and she sinks into it and breathes a sigh—whether of relief or a release of stress, I can't yet tell.

"No," she says, "you don't know me."

. . . Okay?

"But . . . you know me?" I ask.

That strikes a nerve somehow, and she looks away and swallows. When she looks back, her eyes are glistening, and she musters, "No, I guess I don't know you, either. Just your name. But I think after last night, all of Philly knows that."

"My name?" I ask. Oh God. Why does all of Philly know my name? What happened last night?

"Sorry," she says, dragging her wrist across her eyes and sniffing, "I probably should've written something down for this moment. I have . . . so many thoughts and feelings and fears and . . . I guess I should probably just start by explaining myself."

I sit up a little straighter in my hospital bed and cross my legs under me, getting comfortable, since it sounds like I'm in for something big.

"Seventeen years ago, I was your age," she begins, eyes focused intently on her own fingers as she taps the nails on her right hand against the knuckles of her left. "I was alone. And scared. And confused. And I had a choice to make."

She stops, takes a deep breath, and looks at me, her eyes traveling up to my forehead, where my birthmark is. Her eyes widen slightly, like she's just remembered something important. She lifts her purse into her lap, reaches inside, and pulls out a little notebook about the size of my hand. Her fingers tremble as she flips frantically through the purplish-gray pages with the edges faded to gray, until one page pops up in the middle with an edge torn clean off.

My heart skips as I realize what she's holding.

I reach to search my clothes before realizing I'm in a hospital gown.

"Can you, uh, hand me my bag?" I ask, pointing to the clear

plastic bag of my neatly folded clothes. She passes it to me, and I find my jeans pocket where I've left the torn-off page with my name. I pull it out and hold it up to her.

Her hands fly to her mouth.

"Your parents . . . They . . . kept it?"

I nod. Her eyes glisten with tears, and she swallows as one rolls down her cheek. She takes the paper as gently as if she's holding a precious gemstone and lowers it to the journal until the ripped edges match up.

Finally, after seventeen years, the pages are reunited.

And so are we.

"I didn't know you yet," she continues. "Hadn't even seen your face. All I knew about you was that you deserved better than me."

I sit frozen, staring at her, wondering if I'm still dreaming or if I'm really looking into the face of the woman who decided seventeen years ago that I should go home with a different family.

"I, um," she continues, "I don't expect anything from you. You didn't ask to exist. But . . . I'm glad you do. And I hope you're glad you do, and I hope you know that I would've given *anything* to put you on hold and have you when I could be the mom you deserved. . . ."

Her voice breaks now, and she buries her face in her hands. Cracks ripple through the silence, heavy in this room, as the beeping of the monitor cuts right through. Her shoulders tremble under her coat, her mouth pressed tightly shut as she holds it all back. Like a dam keeping a deadly flood of history from barreling down and killing me as I stand at the bottom, trying to figure out how to help.

But how can I when I don't even know her name? What does she go by? Surely not "Mom." I've called too many people that this week already. Not her first name, probably. Or maybe that's okay? "Ma'am" sounds too distant, and Miss X or Y sounds archaic and weirdly patriarchal, since it leaves the question of "Miss" or "Mrs." hanging in the balance. So I decide to skip the names. She knows mine. I know she gave it to me. So I jump to the important part. The part that I hope helps.

"I'm . . . not angry at you," I say.

She lowers her hands and looks up at me again, her whole face wet with tears, unreadable.

"You did what you had to," I continue. "I get it. And my parents are—"

I cut myself off. At the word "parents," I realize I've just confirmed that I won't be calling her Mom, and who knows how deeply that will cut. But I hope what I have to say next will make up for it.

"They're pretty great. Not perfect. But they try. And if it weren't for them, I don't know what kind of life I'd have."

I can only guess.

Whatever she was keeping me from, I won't ask about. It

THIS BOOK MIGHT BE ABOUT ZINNIA

must've been enough to warrant giving away her own child. Maybe it was drugs, or abuse, or poverty, or a combination. By the way she stares at me, she carries a lifetime of *something*.

And instead of dragging me through it with her, she got me as far away from the dam as she could.

She passed me off to someone who could carry me.

It took my parents, Kelly and Ben, raising me how they have, but before that it took this woman handing me over in the first place.

It took two moms to give me the life I have.

"Thank you," I say. That catches her attention, and she looks at me in shock. I don't know where we go from here, and I'm sure she doesn't either. The big lingering question between us now is *What do we look like?* Do we want to keep talking? Do we swap numbers?

I don't know. I don't know anything right now. And from the way she's looking at me, I can tell she doesn't either.

So I decide to start with something I hope isn't too far of an overstep. Something I've hoped Mom and I will have fun doing after I graduate, as adults. Something we could do together, or with friends.

Or with birth moms.

"Do you," I begin, easing into the idea myself, "want to get brunch sometime? With us?"

A smile plays in her eyes, and her mouth follows.

"As long as your mom's cool with it," she says. "Or . . . vibes with it."

Was . . . was that an attempt to sound like me? Yup, she's a mom, all right.

"Don't." I laugh, burying my face in my hands.

"Why, was that cringe?"

My God. There really are two of them.

"Zinnia?" she asks, her voice growing serious again.

I look up at her again, and she nods, her eyes still glistening.

"I'm really glad, after all these years, that you're safe. And happy. I think."

I think of Milo. I think of my parents. I think of my college prospects, and the possibility of submitting this essay to Harvard tonight in the regular pool of applicants and maybe getting in anyway. I think about how it felt to reach up and touch my face and feel nothing, alone, in the dark, in the cold, under somebody's house, and how lucky I am to be alive right now with all my limbs intact.

"Yeah," I say with a smile, "I am."

CHAPTER 33

Zinnia & Tuesday

2025

I SLIP ANOTHER BITE OF SALMON EGGS BENEDICT into my mouth and savor it.

Mom is smiling at me with the Mom face.

I roll my eyes.

"Let me enjoy these last few months with you," she says. "My baby's about to leave me forever."

"Nice try," I say. "You can't get rid of me that easily."

Mom purses her lips and glances at Tuesday, who stifles a laugh and takes another sip of mimosa.

"Thanks for coming to brunch with us," says Mom, resting her hand over Tuesday's. "We're so glad to know you."

Tuesday looks from my mom to me, probably for confirmation. I nod and smile.

"Mom's right," I say.

"I want that in writing," says Mom.

Tuesday smiles again and takes another sip of the bubbly sunflower-yellow drink.

"Ayo, can I try some of that?" I ask.

"No!" they say in unison, exchanging smiles.

"Oh God," I say, sipping my water, "there are *two* of them."

Tuesday takes a bite of her scrambled eggs. Mom takes a sip of her coffee. A light breeze rolls through, folding a corner of my lap napkin over my hand. The late-morning sun is at the perfect angle for our sun umbrella to cover all three of us perfectly. It's the perfect temperature out here, and my salmon eggs benedict are hitting the spot.

Is it a perfect morning?

If not, it's damn close.

"Hey, Zinnia?" begins Tuesday, setting her fork down and folding her hands in her lap. She lowers her gaze to her plate and continues, "Thanks for inviting me."

"Of course," I say.

She drags her fingers across her eyes and sniffs.

"I, um," she says, and her voice breaks, "I wasn't sure how you'd feel. You know. After all this time. I thought you'd think I didn't . . . want you. Love you. But I did. I do. I . . ."

Mom rests a supportive hand on her shoulder and sets her coffee down with the other hand, devoting her full attention.

"If I may," she says, "I owe you a thank-you that I couldn't give you seventeen years ago. Because of the sacrifice you

THIS BOOK MIGHT BE ABOUT ZINNIA

made, you gave Ben and me the greatest gift we could ask for. The gift of Zinnia."

Mom and I exchange a smile.

"We've loved having her in our lives. I haven't been the perfect mom either, and I'm just recently becoming okay with that. In fact, I think I put some of that on you, Zinnia, and . . . I'm sorry for that."

That shocks me. That she realizes this, is admitting it, and even apologizing.

"Thanks," I say. "It's, uh . . . it's weird to hear you admit you're not perfect. You don't have to be, you know. I don't want perfect. I just want Mom."

Her eyes brim with tears, and she reaches for her napkin to dab at them as Tuesday takes her free hand and squeezes it.

"And, uh," I continue, clasping my hands and preparing to confront my part in this, "I'm sorry for leaving for New York without telling you."

"I know why you did," she says. "Apology accepted." Then she levels her eyes at me. "Don't do it again."

All three of us crack smiles.

"I'll at least wait till I get to Harvard," I say, "assuming my application is accepted. My essay wasn't perfect, but . . . maybe they'll like how this story ended."

Tuesday reaches her other hand out to me, palm up, and I glance at it.

Her index finger is bent inward slightly, like mine, and I

wonder if she'll notice as I put my hand in hers.

She seems to, her eyes lingering before she smiles at me.

"I think," she says, "that's part of the magic of family. That nobody in it is perfect. In fact, I think the imperfections *make* the family."

Mom nods, sniffs, dabs again, and adds, "It's about trying to do the right thing. Moment by moment."

And I add, "No matter how hard it becomes."

A cozy silence settles in, and my phone buzzes with a text from Milo. Photo attached.

Milo: We're here!

I grin and look up between my two moms as a small black car pulls up to the curb.

"Oh, hey," I say, looking at each of them. "I have some news."

Mom's face grows serious. Tuesday looks confused.

"You're getting a tattoo, aren't you?" asks Mom.

"Not right now," I say, relishing the hint of horror that flashes in her eyes. Real answer? Who knows! "But this whole situation has had me thinking a lot lately about motherhood and what I want for my life."

They exchange a look of concern, obviously having *no* idea where I'm going with this.

I spot Milo stepping out of the car and racing around to the other side to open the passenger door.

"Mom, you know I've sworn up and down that I don't want

THIS BOOK MIGHT BE ABOUT ZINNIA

337

to be a mom, ever. Well, I've changed my mind."

Milo pulls the tiniest little ball of brown-and-white fluff from the passenger side of the car, shuts the door, and spots me.

I usher him over as Mom and Tuesday follow my gaze.

Nestled in the crook of his arm is our son.

"Meet Bonvoy!" I announce as Milo steps up and holds him out to me. "Milo and I will be trading off custody every semester."

He whimpers as I take him and cradle him against me.

"Oh my God, Zinnia, what?" exclaims Mom. "He's the cutest little guy I've ever seen!"

Tuesday leans forward, chin on hands, marveling at him. "What is he?" she asks.

"A corgi!" I announce as Milo joins us in the empty chair at our four-top.

"He's got a bad eye, a wonky leg that gives out sometimes, and, as far as we can tell, anxiety as bad as mine," he says, and shrugs.

I look down at Bonvoy as he returns my gaze, mouth hanging open, tongue flopped to one side.

"And," I add, "he's perfect."

ACKNOWLEDGMENTS

SHOUT-OUT TO MY THERAPIST, WITHOUT WHOM I wouldn't have survived 2024.

Thank you to my agent, Beth Phelan, who champions my work as I never could, and my editor, Deeba Zargarpur, who's helped this book sing.

Thank you to my entire publishing team for giving Zinnia the love she deserves.

Thank you to my friends who have stood by my side in love and support as I grow closer to becoming the woman I want to be.

To the folks I went no-contact with this year: I wish you love, peace, and happiness, even while away from me.

To those I dedicated this book to: everyone who's gone

no-contact with someone who didn't deserve you. I don't know your story. I don't know your circumstances. But whatever happened, whatever you're going through, whatever your journey with those people looks like, I'm proud of you. Good job protecting yourself and respecting your own boundaries. I admire your bravery.

And to my son, who lets me do the best job I've ever had: being your mommy. I love you, I respect you, and I want the world for you. Always.

AUTHOR BIO

BRITTNEY MORRIS IS THE AUTHOR OF *SLAY*, *THE COST of Knowing*, *The Jump*, and Marvel's *Spider-Man: Miles Morales – Wings of Fury*. She's a video game writer, a comic writer, a public speaker, a gamification consultant for teachers and educators, and a mom. She spends her spare time reading, playing video games, and not doing enough yoga. She lives in Philadelphia with her very curious four-year-old.